# The Fall.

George John Kingsnorth

Gullion Media Limited.

All rights reserved.
Published by Gullion Media Limited 2008

This paperback edition published in 2008 by
Gullion Media Limited, c/o 11 Slieve Crescent, Dromintee,
Newry, Co. Down. BT35 8UF. Northern Ireland.

Copyright © 2008 George John Kingsnorth

George John Kingsnorth has asserted his right under
Copyright, Design and Patents Act, 1988 to be identified
as the author of this work.

Gullion Media Limited

Editor: Lorraine Wylie
Proof Reader: Michelle McKeown

A CIP catalogue record for this book is
available from the British Library

ISBN 978-0-9560403-0-5

Scripture quotations taken from The Holy Bible,
New International Version Anglicised
Copyright 1979, 1984 by International Bible Society.
Used by permission of Hodder & Stoughton Publishers,
a division of Hachette Livre (UK) Ltd.
All rights reserved.
"NIV" is a registered trademark of International Bible Society.
UK trademark number 1448790.

Hymns taken from The Hymn Database © 2000 Andrew Clark.
Hymns include:
Scottish Psalter (1650) 'The Lord's My Shepherd, I'll Not Want'
& Charles Wesley (1707-88) 'Leader Of Faithful Souls, And Guide'.
Both hymns are out of copyright and in the public domain.

Printed and bound by Lightning Source

This paperback edition is sold subject to the condition that it shall not, by way
of trade or otherwise, be lent, resold, hired out, or otherwise circulated in any
form of binding or cover other than that in which it is published and without
similar condition including this condition imposed on the subsequent purchaser.

www.gullionmedia.co.uk

To Patricia.

## CHAPTER ONE

The strong light caused Michael to shade his eyes from the midday sun. A fly darted between his neck and collar, eager to drink the beads of sweat. Other than this brief irritation it was a good day. A memorable day in July 1987. No clouds. Thick blue sky peppered with black dots of highflying birds. Long dark shadows, which Michael realised would probably cause the photographer some worries. Can't have the bride and her maidens squinting or having dark shadows around their eyes. They would look like pandas. However, this was not Michael's concern. He felt relaxed. Confident he was making the right move.

"12:15, Michael. Do you think she's stood you up?" quipped Brendan.

"And do you think you're getting out of being my best man?" Michael laughed.

"It would be hard to escape. Just think of it, nothing will be yours ever again. You'll even have to ask permission to go out!" Brendan taunted.

"Ah up, here comes Danny. It's all up now. Better keep up with the boxing to give you an edge to fight back." Brendan threw a few mock punches.

Several crows landed on the telephone wires outside the graveyard.

"Mickey, Mickey, the car's here!" Danny raced up the cobbled pathway leading from the fifteenth century wooden Lych-gate to the church door.

He held onto Michael's shoulder whilst he caught his breath.

"He's like an old man at 20."

"He suffers from asthma, leave him be," warned Michael.

*George John Kingsnorth*

Brendan patted Danny on the back. "Sorry big fella, I didn't realise. Do you want me to get you some water?"

"There's no time," gasped Danny. "The bride's car is at the bottom of the street. You'd all better go inside."

The 1926 Rolls Royce Phantom pulled up outside, framed by the Lych-gate. Bleached out by sunlight, the driver popped open his door, stepped out and made his way round to the back passenger door. As he gripped the handle, a crow on the telephone wire bombarded his hat.

"Dirt bird," he complained. Several of the crows squawked at him as he pulled a handkerchief from his top pocket to clean his hat.

First out of the car were the teenage bridesmaids, three in all, who raced towards the church but were called back to help the bride as she was helped out of the Phantom by the driver. Danny squinted to see the bride but the strength of light made her a blur of white until she stood beneath the shade of the Lych-gate. She paused to give time for the maid of honour to organise the younger attendants. Suddenly a chill ran up Danny's spine making him shudder. The pleats of the bride's gown faded to a shade of blue revealing the face beneath the veil.

Though her entourage fussed with her dress, Melissa felt serene. The day was finally here. No more fighting with her sister, no more rows with mum and dad, no more stress of preparing for this moment. She was ready. Her father took her hand.

"Okay love, time to go."

"Thank dad, and sorry for all the tantrums."

"It's okay, we understand. Now enjoy yourself. It's your day."

The bridal group moved towards the church. Danny shielded his eyes once more as Melissa's dress shimmered in the reflected sunlight.

Danny raced inside, signaled to the organist, then in a more orderly manner, made his way up beside the groom and best man. Moments later the bridal party began to make their way down the aisle. Michael turned to see his bride. Melissa's hands began to shake and a tear rolled down her cheek.

*The Fall*

The explosion of glass sent a jolt of shock through the congregation as everyone was sprinkled with fragmented shards. A black form thudded onto the old stone floor and red blotches seeped into Melissa's white dress, before she could pull it away. Michael bounded to Melissa's side, cradling her in his arms.

"Are you okay?"

"A bit shaken but yeah, I'm okay."

"It's alright everybody," calmed the vicar, "we have a few problems with crows around here, they are always crashing into the windows. Is anybody hurt?"

Everyone checked themselves over but no-one reported any injuries. An alter boy rushed to cover the dead bird with a small cloth before taking it outside. A second boy took a small bucket from the side of the church and quickly sponged up the bloody stain. The organist notched up the volume and everyone began to settle back into their pews.

Forty-five minutes later, the six campanologists began to tug at the sallies on each bell rope. As the first hammers hit the bells, crows and pigeons scattered from the belfry. The gentle tugs increased the arc of bell from a downward position until they all come to rest upright. The conductor nodded to the treble ringer to pull the first round. All six sallies *shot* up into the church tower, the tail end of each rope pulling the ringer's arms taut. Another gentle tug on the rope brought the bell rotating back to the opposite upright position and the sallies all came down for the ringers to stay or pull once more. After the first of three rounds sounded out, the conductor called the first change. The treble bell was held back on the sally to allow the second and third bells to be pulled first. A method from a chart of numbers hanging on the wall showed the changes they had to make thereafter.

As the peal sounded out, the photographer finished her last shot and the wedding guests began to litter the air with confetti as the bride and groom raced towards the Rolls Royce Phantom.

Midnight loomed as the classic yellow 1967 Triumph Spitfire M3's pulled off the road. Its 75bph engine throbbed gently as the tyres crunched against the pebble drive leading to the Royalist's Arms, a spacious Tutor mansion-hotel surrounded by shrubberies and trees. The hotel was about five miles from Aylesbury along the A418 towards Leighton Buzzard in the sleepy county of Buckinghamshire. The ground floor was made up of red brick while the first floor was half black timber and white plaster, topped with a thatched roof. A few orange lights still burned from within the hotel as Michael turned off the engine and headlamps. The full moon allowed the surrounding gardens to remain visible under a bluish cast. A tawny owl took flight across the freshly cut lawn and vanished into the woods.

While Michael fetched their luggage, Melissa made her way to the entrance hall. She was attracted by the four large paintings by Gainsborough, Reynolds, Romney and Stubbs. The first three portraits of various gentry while Stubbs' piece concentrated on horses in a picturesque landscape.

"Shall we register?" suggested Michael as he lugged the two large cases into the hall. Melissa smiled and nodded and followed him through to the main desk.

A footman opened the door to the bridal suite and led the honeymooners inside. Michael tipped the man and then locked the door behind him. All walls and ceiling were paneled in mahogany. There was a large four-poster bed with hand carved linenfold panels, barley twist posts and a tester to support the tied back curtains. Melissa tested the springiness of the mattress.

"It looks old but the mattress is firm," she informed Michael.

"I would say the bed's not as old as you think," suggested Michael nervously. They were now together for the first time since that day. Both had promised to save themselves for this moment. At times they had struggled with temptation but Melissa had made it clear early in their relationship that she was not the kind of girl who slept with anyone before marriage. Based on her beliefs it was wrong to do so. Now, in almost an instance by saying 'I do' that all changed. Effectively, he had told a church full of people that this woman was his wife and he, as her husband was making it completely acceptable

*The Fall*

for them both to be in the same room together to do as they pleased.

His body shook as he took off his jacket and attempted to hang it over a chair. The coat fell off forcing him to pick it up. Melissa giggled. He returned her smile, then turned his back to undo his tie. Through a mirror he saw Melissa unzip her emerald coloured summer dress. She slipped the fabric over her shoulders to reveal her slightly bronzed body still with her bra and pants on. He pulled the tie through his shirt collar. Melissa bit her lower lip as she looked over at him and caught his gaze in the mirror. She giggled again and slid to the opposite side of the double bed to obscure his view. Michael unbuttoned his shirt, his heart pounding while his hands shook as he fumbled with each button. As he finally got to the last one he felt Melissa press herself against his back. Her breasts pressed against his shoulders and her hips touched his buttocks. Blood surged through his body making his trousers feel tight. He could smell her perfume filling his nostrils, adding to his arousal. Again his fumbling hands made a hard task of unbuckling his trousers. He felt Melissa's hand glide under his shirt across his rib cage, down his abdomen, and into his trousers.

"Relax, you're all tense," Melissa gently whispered. She began to kiss his neck. Michael closed his eyes as a great rush flowed over his body, every nerve ending, tingling and rippling across his skin. Melissa used her other hand to undo his button and pulled down the zip. Michael turned towards Melissa as she gently pulled both his underwear and trousers down to the ground, admiring him. He kicked the garments away from his feet and pulled Melissa towards him. He felt the firmness of her breasts, teasing his skin as they glided across his torso. Still shaking, Michael lifted her up so her lips were level with his. He closed his eyes and sensed the moisture of her mouth. Her tongue mapped out his teeth as he ventured forward with his own until the tips of each tongue danced around each other. As Michael glided his hand down her spine, she gasped and her head pulled back.

Michael was surprised when her lips left his, forcing him to open his eyes. Her body was covered in goose bumps. She sighed and opened her eyes. Blinking she realised he was looking at her. Briefly, she was embarrassed that she had let herself go so much. Michael smiled and his expression pleased her.

"I've wanted to do this so much for so long," she whispered and smiled. Her eyes were slightly moist with tears. "Let's get into bed."

Still in each other's arms they made their way to the side of the bed. Melissa lay down, still holding Michael's hand. For a few moments he soaked up the view of her slender body. Suddenly, she pulled him on top of her and again they began to enjoy each other's lips. He glided his right hand across her left breast, feeling her muscles rippling under her skin as she reacted to his touch. As his fingers gently traced Melissa's mound he noticed her shudder.

"Are you okay?" he asked.

"Don't stop, keep going," she pleaded.

Again Michael allowed his fingers to explore her. Suddenly, his arm was violently wrenched backwards, flinging his body away from Melissa's. He looked at her in disbelief. Her face expressed the same shock as his. An unseen force flung him across the room, dashing him against a set of mahogany drawers. A trickle of blood ran across his right eye from the deep gash in his forehead.

"Melissa, are you okay?"

The invisible hand slapped his face with such force he was nearly sent into unconsciousness. Michael struggled to raise his right arm but it was pinned to the floor. He attempted to raise his left but it too remained firmly fixed. He struggled to use his heels to drag himself towards the bed but instead he felt pain ripping through his lower limbs as though he had jumped into a bath of boiling water. He screamed, the room seemed to blur and darkness invaded the outer rim of his vision yet he knew he had to resist. To give in would mean he could not save Melissa.

The ceiling appeared as though vaporized. The blinding light burnt at Michael's eyelids as he tried to turn his face away as far as possible. When the intensity subsided, Michael ventured to look once more at the bed. Melissa, her body thrusting back and forth, lay suspended above the bed as a brilliant white humanoid figure

*The Fall*

mounted her. Melissa's eyes were closed.

"Michael, Michael, harder, harder," she cried.

"It's not me Melissa, it's not me!" he screamed but she did not respond. Tears streamed down Michael's face as he thrashed around trying frantically to release himself from the restraints of his invisible assailants. A mighty fist drove into his stomach like a mallet, winding him. He gasped for breath, his knees reflexively pulled into his body but his arms were still pinned down. The being of light climaxed. A voice of thunder roared out and Michael heard Melissa scream.

"Melissa," Michael cried out. Her eyes opened and she finally saw Michael. Tears streamed down her face. Something tugged under the skin of her stomach. Sharply she turned to see her own flesh being forced upward as a small hand reached up from within.

The figure of light faded and staggered backwards. Green slime fell onto Melissa and she screamed again. Once more the infant hand reached upwards, tearing at the flesh, eager to get out. Melissa shrieked in agony. Michael strained with all his might to break free. From the darkness of the room a hideous face slashed across the room like some ancient locomotive it bellowed soot as thick as smoke and came to rest just millimetres away from Michael's face. The fiend's breathe froze the air. Michael nearly choked as the lack of oxygen almost cast him into unconsciousness. The dark shape screeched.

Melissa's belly swelled. She was dropped to the mattress but prevented from touching her body as two more unseen beings pinned her arms to the bed. With the unbearable pain, Melissa lapsed into unconsciousness as a hurricane-like force spun through the room. Melissa's stomach ripped open and the child was sucked upwards. The debris spun round the room making it impossible for Michael to see. He felt the tension on his arms subside and, springing to his feet, leapt onto the bed. A gapping hole remained where Melissa's taut stomach once was. Blood had sprayed across the blanket onto the walls. Michael's body began to convulse in anguish, tears streamed down his face as he delicately lifted Melissa's lifeless body into his

*George John Kingsnorth*

arms. Melissa, his love, his life, his everything, was gone.

*The Fall*

CHAPTER TWO

Summer 2007, the unusual weather fronts meant week after week of torrential downpours. Many attributed this to climatic change and global warming. The ice caps were melting, sea levels were rising, rivers were not being dredged and river defences were not being maintained.

In the early part of June, Yorkshire was hit with flash floods due to the intense rain. People were even being airlifted from the rooftops of their work. As July arrived, southern England got their share as the Thames broke its banks, Oxford saw floods, then Gloucester was under water especially around Eversham.

Meanwhile, in Europe many countries were witnessing a soar in temperatures. 500 people died in Hungary from the unusual heat-waves followed by over 30 more deaths in Romania. Serbia lost more than 30 percent of its agricultural harvest while in Bulgaria temperatures rose to 45 degrees centigrade. Former Yugoslavia government bodies recommended that those who worked outdoors cease after 11.00 am to prevent sunstroke or heat exhaustion and in Macedonia, a fierce battle was being fought as a raging forest fire threatened Bitola, its second largest city.

Some considered this was a lead up to the end of the world. Christianity also seemed to have lost its way. Some priests, ministers and vicars were being arrested and shamefully found guilty of being pedophiles. No-one wanted to spend their lives as celibate or in the service of non-catholic denominations.

The news during July occasionally concerned protesters who had tried to prevent a sacred bullock from being slaughtered after the Welsh Assembly ordered the destruction of Shambo when he tested positive with bovine tuberculosis. A Hindu educationalist criticised the way the media had hyped a local story, making thousands feel their religious beliefs were under threat.

The war in Iraq was creating more problems associated with terrorism, thus fuelling the problem instead of swaying things. Muslims felt the American were giving them no other options, they saw their lifestyle as being threatened by the West's attempt to impose the *American way*.

But as Wednesday morning spun into being in the first week of August, those racing to work were more concerned with the illusions of materialism than the actuality of the world around them. Most were trying to keep up to date with technology to keep their jobs, regardless of whether they wanted to or not. Most occupations were no longer permanent, only temporary contracts. Homes were costing sometimes five or six times the average monthly incomes causing many to remain in the same houses for years. The young could not afford to buy, or even rent. Television programmes made them feel discontent, making everyone want to sell up and move on to better things. Most were over stretched and there was an increase in repossessions. Car insurance was so high teenagers resorted to breaking the law to get mobile. College fees restricted progression from school into higher education. Many young men turned to suicide, as they saw no future for themselves.

The rain, the constant rain, pummeled the crowded streets, further adding to their depression. They could not lift their heads to see what was around them, to get away from their inner thoughts, to see beyond their own small lives.

Yet, unnoticed, high above in the stratosphere another storm was brewing, not of metrological pressures of lows and highs but of something more sinister. Shafts of light splintered across the dark globe from the rising sun. Then came the speed. Falling, falling, falling. Whistling winds pierced ears. Falling, falling, falling. Puncturing clouds, descending towards the ground, still thousands of feet below. A dark shape, from a dot, grew closer. It too was in the same trajectory. More clouds. A jumbo jet was barely missed, as unaware, passengers ate their in-flight meal. Falling, falling, falling.

## The Fall

The dark shape now took on form, a demon. Dark wings folded back to increase its speed. It turned to see its pursuer. Panic. Nearly tumbling out of control then regaining composure, it darted away in another direction, heading towards the darkness of night.

As the demon streaked across the sky, a light punctured the clouds rapidly drawing closer. The demon, petrified by its inability to gain any more distance from its pursuer, sought refuge amongst the rain clouds of a nearby city.

At a large corporate building the concierge opened the double doors for a man in his forties. "Goodnight Mister Peterson."

"Goodnight Harold."

Peterson walked into the rain and began struggling to open his umbrella. He ran out to the side of the kerb.

"Taxi! Taxi!"

One came up close and straight through a puddle, drenching him in a cascade of water.

"Bastard!"

A second taxi did the same. Looking skyward through nail-like rain drops, Peterson cursed more profoundly. The words rose, reaching the demon's ears as it battled with the being of light. Each strike of the sword sent streaks of lighting in every direction. Anxious to escape the onslaught of the angel's blade, the demon desperately searched for the man who uttered the curse. Spotting him, the demon disengaged from battle and, free falling toward earth, plummeted straight into Peterson's body. He crumbled to the ground but no-one noticed. Nobody stepped aside from their own problems to give him aid. He may as well not have been there. No recognition was given to the businessman's existence. No one cared. Only when Peterson bounced onto his feet like a puppet, did anyone begin to take notice. There was something odd and those around the drenched businessman sensed a potential threat to their pointless lives.

"Get out of my way, drunk!" screamed a young female executive. A fat man poked Peterson with a brolly.

"Get away, go on. You can't stay there! Be off with you."

*George John Kingsnorth*

A young mother pushing a pram, nervously made her way over to a couple of police men. The two officers approached Peterson who seemed intoxicated.

"Come on, sir. This is no time to be walking around under the influence of alcohol. You can't stay here! Someone will get hurt!"

When the two policemen grabbed Peterson by his arms, one was suddenly flung across the street. The second was grabbed by the throat. Peterson's face took on the demonic form of his possessor.

"Too right! But I imagine you didn't expect it to be you, did you?"

Blood began to run down the side of Peterson's fingers as the policeman's eyes rolled upwards. Peterson looked up into the sky and laughed at the angel. The angel plummeted earthwards.

Peterson threw the policeman into the road. A taxi tried to avoid the body and steered into oncoming traffic. The crunch of metal and cars catapulting over one another sent the crowd screaming. Peterson looked about him and began violently to slaughter those in his way. More cars crashed into each other as they tried to avoid the mad man rampaging from one side of the street to the other.

The angel bounded across wrecked vehicles and plunged his sword into Peterson, piercing the demon within. The mortal looked at the angel in sheer surprise and terror, then dropped to the ground while the demon burnt and was vaporised leaving a pungent stench of sulphur in the air. Several people on the sidewalk vomited in the gutter. The angel sheathed his blade and folded away his wings. Unnoticed, his brilliance dimmed to a point where the angel was indistinguishable from any other human trudging through the rain. With his job done the angel strode into the shadows, while those around him raced to help those less fortunate.

*The Fall*

## CHAPTER THREE

Although overcast at the beginning of the day, by mid-morning the clouds had broken up to allow the grass time to dry. Michael was tending a rose bed when Nurse Bentley made his way across the freshly cut lawn, in front of the red brick Victorian building. The shadow of the clock tower gave Michael some protection from the blazing light as he pruned away the dead rose-heads.

"Michael, you're wanted inside," called Nurse Bentley. Michael was hesitant, he felt uncomfortable about the outcome.

"Do I have to?"

"They're waiting," replied Bentley. "Its your big chance!"

"I've still plenty of work to do here," Michael complained. "Most of the rose-beds need weeding and they all have greenfly. Who'll do this?"

"Michael, there's no getting out of this, let's go".

Bentley led Michael into a small waiting area. Pale yellow tiles covered the walls while the floor was checkered with black and white. All the doors and frames were vinyl black. A small coffee table, with an array of magazines, mainly women's periodicals, a few local and three national papers, stood in the middle of the room. Three black plastic chairs were placed against each of the walls. Michael sat on the opposite side to the door he was to go through. He could see Bentley through the frosted glass and hear the sound of his voice, yet he was unable to distinguish what was said.

Michael read a paper as he waited. The headlines were of the 'Heaven's Gate Cult' who had committed suicide believing their souls would be carried to a spacecraft piloted by Jesus, traveling behind the now visible comet Hale-Bopp. The heavenly body had been discovered two years earlier but had only become visible to the

*George John Kingsnorth*

naked eye in 1997.

The conference room door opened startling Michael briefly.

"Okay Michael," Bentley spoke gently. "You can come in now."

Placing the newspaper back on the table, Michael nervously pulled himself onto his feet. Bentley continued to coax him in. "Hey, Michael, it's not that bad. You'd think you were going to have a few teeth pulled!

Inside, the room was ablaze with the mid morning sunlight. Michael could see specks of dust floating through the haze. Five blue-silhouetted figures sat tidying their papers. Michael struggled to see their faces but knew that the sunlight streaming through the windows made his features clearly visible to the panel.

"Good morning Michael" came a voice from the centre of the group. By squinting Michael could barely make out the name board in front of the speaker. Dr. F. H. Baxter, Chief Consultant.

"Good morning Doctor Baxter."

"How are things today?"

"Good, I've just been working on the rose-beds," answered Michael, wanting to show the importance of his work outside. "They need a lot of care with all the greenfly and weeds."

"Good," replied Dr. Baxter, not really seeming to be that interested with the garden. Baxter looked down at his notes. "We're here to review your progress and to select the best way forward."

Michael's eyes fell to the ground, looking at the way Baxter's shadow touched the tips of his shoes. He inched his feet away, not wanting the darkness to fall on him. One shadow to the left of Baxter flicked their hair. Michael looked up to see a junior doctor sitting at the end of the group. Her features were soft, young, in her early twenties. Probably just out of medical school, Michael presumed. When her eyes met his, she became embarrassed and looked down at her notes. Michael glanced at her nameplate, *Doctor Judith Heskith*.

"Doctor Samuels, what are your recommendations?"

Movement came from the right of Dr. Baxter. Again Michael struggled to define the person's features. A woman's voice answered Dr. Baxter.

*The Fall*

"Well, as you can see from my report, Michael has shown no signs of psychotic behaviour for the past ten years or so." The nameplate in front of the voice read *Doctor Evelyn Samuels*. Michael put his hand over his eyes to block out the window. He could now see beyond the silhouette. Dr. Samuels was an older woman, in her late forties, also a consultant. She had seen Michael frequently over the years and he always felt unsettled around her. Everything was matter of fact, no emotion, no compassion, each patient just another functioning body requiring the brain to be fine tuned to conform to the social needs of the world outside.

"In fact there is a question mark to his previous episode," continued Dr. Samuels. "My team believes Michael is sufficiently stable enough to return to normal life within the community."

Panic struck Michael. He felt safe here and he had his plants to tend. They needed him.

"What are you saying?" stammered Michael.

Dr. Samuels looked across to Dr. Baxter and began to chew on her pen. Dr. Baxter nodded to her then turned to Michael.

"We think that your condition doesn't warrant further treatment within this institute," Dr. Baxter answered, "and that the resources could be more appropriately used elsewhere."

"So what happens next?" requested Michael anxiously.

"We'll find you suitable accommodation and employment," replied Dr. Baxter. "Doctor Fleming has informed us of how you have been trained in horticultural development and maintenance."

Dr. Fleming, a male registrar seated to the right of Dr. Samuels nodded.

"I've been looking after the gardens here for some time," replied Michael. "Is it possible to continue with that work?"

The young, inexperienced Dr. Heskith look startled for a moment then caught herself on. The rest of the panel, full of professionalism remained stony-faced.

"That will not be possible," stated Doctor Baxter. "These facilities are under review due to the government's restructuring policy."

"What does that mean?" Michael was apprehensive.

"As far as you are concerned, Michael, it means you'll be moving on. Thank you for your time. That's all for now. Good day!"

"Come on, Michael," Bentley gently tapped Michael's shoulder. "Time to go."

"But." Michael looked round to the panel, all were focused on flicking through the next set of files. Only Dr. Heskith looked concerned. Bentley helped Michael to his feet and led him out of the room.

Once in the waiting area, after Bentley had quietly closed the door behind them, Michael asked again what was happening.

"This place is being shut down, Michael. Everyone is moving on."

"What will you be doing, Bentley?"

"Oh, I'm bound to find another job somewhere. But you shouldn't be concerned with me. You're about to get a new life."

"I'm not sure I want to. I like the one I have."

"None of us have a choice in the matter."

"When do I go?"

"Tomorrow morning."

"That soon."

"Don't worry, there will be help from Social Services. You have support until you get settled in and they're not going to leave you unaided."

Michael was not reassured.

*The Fall*

CHAPTER FOUR

The headlines on most tabloid newspapers consisted of "LUNATIC EXECUTIVE SLAYER", "MASSACRE – EXEC GOES MAD", "STREET MAYHEM BY HARI KARI MADMAN". The broadsheets questioned whether the continuous storms had influenced the actions of the 'brolly' slayer but none came anywhere close to unraveling the truth behind the slaughter. Most assumed it just another random killing brought on by excessive game playing on the Internet.

Abd al-Hakiim was stacking the morning papers onto the various racks when two teenagers nearly fell through the door. He stepped behind the counter and eagle-eyed them to ensure nothing was slipped beneath their coats. He held his finger over the panic buzzer under the counter knowing that if there was any trouble Muusa and Ibrahiim would swiftly depart their beds above the shop and come to their father's aid.

The two youths sheepishly wandered round the shop searching. They made their way to the pharmaceuticals. Abd al-Hakiim's often felt uncomfortable with the white customers who frequented his corner shop. Often they would come in after a long night drinking. The girls wearing short shirts that revealed their bellies and skirts that rested high on their thighs. Had they no shame, Abd al-Hakiim wondered.

The young man hesitated as his hand hovered over a packet of Durex. There was a whole range to choose from. Twenty minutes of quivering pleasure, fruity flavours, vibrating rings and Intensify. What to choose?

"Hurry up, Gary," sighed his companion. "The mood'll be gone. It doesn't matter which one you go for as long as it works." Gary

*George John Kingsnorth*

lifted a packet at random then headed back towards Abd al-Hakiim.

"Two pound seventy-nine, please," Abd al-Hakiim stated. Gary rummaged around in his denim pockets and pulled out an assortment of coins, sweet wrappers, a bit of tissue and fluff. He counted out the correct change and slid the coins across the counter to Abd al-Hahiim.

"Want a receipt?"

"Yes, please," Gary laughed. "In case I need to return them."

Abd al-Hahiim was disgusted.

"Come on, Gary," insisted the girl.

"Okay, Mara. Keep your knickers on."

As the doorbell twanged, Abd al-Hahiim was relieved they were gone but as he turned, he found himself facing the barrel of a SIG-Sauer P-232. Abd al-Hahiim was stunned at not having noticed his assailant enter the shop.

Outside Gary had his arm back around Mara's shoulders trying to grope her right breast.

"Leave it out until we get into the flat," she complained. She unhooked his arm, grabbed his hand and begun to tug him towards the end of the street. The gunshot shook the two of them. They stopped in their tracks to look back. Gary came to his senses first and pulled Mara into a darkened alley. Hiding, they heard footsteps clatter along the pavement, heading away from them. A dog barked. A woman screamed and lights came on around the street.

"Come on, let's get out of here before we're involved," whispered Gary. He grabbed Mara's hand and tugged her towards the other end of the darkened alleyway. Mara stumbled into a black wheelie bin, scattering its content. They scurried along red brick walls unseen by the occupants of the Victorian terraced houses. Lights were coming on at various houses as folk were disturbed by the commotion. A series of police sirens could be heard in the distance. A few moments later they were out the other end.

"Gary, stop a second," pleaded Mara. "Do you think anyone saw us?"

"Not in the street, they didn't," Gary gasped, trying to catch his breath.

*The Fall*

"Did you see any security cameras in the shop," mumbled Mara in a state of panic.

"Calm down," Gary stressed. "There's no need to panic, we didn't do anything."

"But we were there," Mara freaked a little.

"And all they would see is us buying some condoms and leaving," Gary tried to reassure her. "We were out of the shop before anything happened. We didn't even see who it was that came into the shop. In fact, I thought we were alone."

"How far is it to your flat?" Mara asked him.

"A few more streets and we're there."

Gary put his arm around her shoulder once more and could feel her trembling. He tried to reassure her again and managed to bring a smile to her face. Some of her eyeliner had smudged onto her cheek. Her hazel green eyes were alert and anxious. She held her hands up to her mouth and was nervously gnawing at her knuckle.

A chill had crept into the air, and the sky was over cast. A thin drizzle began to fall and Gary could see a small haze of droplets clinging to Mara's spiky black hair. She began to shiver. The shock had sobered them both up. His selfish mind became concerned not so much with her well-being, but weather he could get her back into the mood and fulfil the task they had planned for the evening.

"You okay?" he asked.

She turned and smiled giving him a nod. She suddenly looked younger than he had thought. Instead of a confident 20 year old, she seemed more like a 16 year old school girl. He felt himself shudder briefly.

"Are you okay, more to the point?" Mara looked puzzled but tender.

"Yeah, I'm okay," Gary replied. "Lets get back to the flat."

Gary fumbled again when he tried to get the key into the door.

"Do you have any booze?"

"In the fridge."

Finally the key went in and the door opened.

19

*George John Kingsnorth*

"We should take these wet things off," Mara suggested.

"Yeah, we should." She was still keen, Gary thought. Mara looked about the room. It was not pleasant. Paper was peeling and damp patches were blackening the walls near the ceiling. An old dark brown sofa looked ready to collapse, injured by cigarette burns and torn fabric revealing the wooden frame. Dirty plates from several Chinese takeaways littered the floor. The sink in the kitchenette was cluttered with tea-stained cups. Hardened spaghetti in ketchup sauce clung to a variety of plates and mould was growing on the odd knife and fork.

"Good with the spring-cleaning, are we?" muttered Mara sarcastically.

"Cleaning lady's been off sick for a couple of weeks," Gary replied.

"So I see." Mara removed her black leather jacket and tried to find a place to hang it, opting for a wooden stall next to the fat-burnt cooker. Gary watched her catlike moves around the room, curious of her new surroundings. She sat on the stall and unbuckled the leather straps on her boots. From toe to the top of her thighs her goose-pimpled skin could be seen beneath the fishnet stockings. She unzipped her black skirt, allowing it to fall. Holding up her fishnets was a black laced garter belt over a thin g-string. Her confidence had returned and Gary felt excited. Mara opened a door on the other side of the kitchen and discovered a small cupboard. Spying a second door over by an old seventies looking television, she glided passed Gary, teasing him by gently glancing his front with her behind. This second door led to a small hallway.

"What's down here?" she inquired.

"Bedroom and loo."

"Oh." Mara smiled at Gary and coyly beckoned him to follow with her index finger. Gary let his soaking jacket fall to the floor and hastily made after Mara. She found the toilet at the end and again was shocked at how the opposite sex had such disgusting living quarters. As Gary approached from the living room, Mara twisted the handle on the second door, halfway along the short corridor. The room was

*The Fall*

dark and the curtains pulled shut, barely allowing any illumination from the street.

"Do you have a small lamp inside, so we can see?"

"Over by the bed," Gary replied. "But why not switch on the main light?"

"And spoil the mood?" Mara ran her hand down the side of his face, feeling the prickliness of facial stubble. She pulled him in close and brought his lips to hers. Gary could feel the warm sensation rising from his groin through his body. He was excited and eager but another sensation was also battling away coming from his head down. Fatigue. Oh no, he didn't want that. He fought it off and reached for the bedside lamp. As it came on, Mara regretted her request, wishing she had remained in the dark. The cluttered room, full of dirty magazines and soiled underwear was almost enough to make her vomit.

"Sorry," she puts her hand to her mouth. "I just…" She decided not to explain but closed her eyes and pulled Gary in close. He had unbuttoned his jeans and allowed them to fall to his knees, making him unstable and unable to remain balanced when Mara had pulled him. The two of them fell on to the unkempt bed.

"Ow," squawked Mara, as she felt something catch her in her ribs. She fumbled with the duvet to find a X-box controller. She threw it against the wall, frustrated with all the distractions. Rolling back on top of Gary she began to undo the buttons of his shirt. His chest was slightly hairy but this did not put her off using her tongue to lick his body. She heard a gentle groan and took it as a sign that Gary was enjoying the ecstatic moment. She began to divert her attention towards his lower regions, allowing her hands to trace out his hips and thighs. Gary moaned once more. She gently slid her fingers between his legs and up. Then came another surprise. He was flat, limp, soft and lifeless. Horrified she realised Gary was not enjoying her as much as she thought. She crawled up beside his face. His eyes closed.

"Wake up, damn you."

Gary's eyelids quivered as he attempted to open them. He could not even move his limbs the fatigue had gripped him that much. Mara used her tongue to part his lips and attempt to tease some fun out of him. She tried to rub the limpness out of him but all attempts were doomed to failure. She slapped him a few times. Dug her nails into his ribs. Pinched his droopy phallus. Zilch, nothing. Disgusted, Mara stood up and observed the limp form before her. There was a sudden snort and his mouth closed. She shook her head and flicked the light switch, closing the door behind her as she made her way back into the lounge to gather her things.

Pulling on her fishnets and attaching them to her garter belt, she stepped into the circle of her skirt, reached down and dragged it up her legs, clipped it and zipped up. Slipped her delicate feet into the biker's boots. Pulled each strap tightly into a buckle and reached for her jacket on the stall. As she straightened the coat over her shoulders, she heard a whimper from the hall.

"Hey, Mara, what happened to you?"

Fuming, she stormed down toward the bedroom to find Gary propping himself up in the doorway. She kneed him in the groin. Doubled in agony, he crashed to the floor. As an after thought as he tried to pull himself up again she slapped him across the face. Gary slumped to the ground once more, no fight left in him. Mara kicked him between his legs even more frustrated but this time there was not even a grunt. She grimaced and thrust her fist at his face then left, slamming each door she came across as loudly as she could causing the odd cry of *'keep it down'* from the wakened neighbours.

As Mara raced out of the building, two dark mists began to take shape in Gary's lounge. Within a heartbeat they had taken on almost human form. One rolled about in agony gripping between its legs. Their red eyes and the vapour trail they left behind them as they moved, forced a stray cat to hiss and dart away. Still translucent their flesh appeared dark and infected like rotting wood. The vapour was sulphur. Gary's nostrils flared with the pungency. He rolled over and threw up the Indian meal he had eaten earlier.

"I felt that," groaned the agonized demon. The other laughed at his companion's expense. "He will feel it tomorrow though."

*The Fall*

"All this to keep the girl's virginity," bemoaned the sore creature.

"Can't have tainted goods, that's what the boss said," replied the second.

Still soothing his pain, the injured demon made his way to the window to watch Mara scurry along the street. "Oh but I do fancy a bit of that," he drooled.

"Not if it provoked the boss you wouldn't," he was reminded. "Besides, there's plenty of young things to toy without there, willing to give themselves to you."

"But five times we prevented her from being with a mate and I'm always the one left in agony."

"And you'll do it again."

"It's okay for you," snarled the injured demon. "You had your bloody fun executing the shopkeeper. At least I thought I would have my chance with the boy here."

"Mustn't draw any more attention to ourselves. Leave the boy alone otherwise the girl could be apprehended and we can't have that, can we?"

"I suppose."

"Best get after the girl and keep her out of harm's way." The two demons sniggered as they dematerialised and, like willowing smoke cut through the night air to catch up with Mara.

## CHAPTER FIVE

"Three days after the brutal murder of Abd al-Hakiim, police arrested three black youths from the Smethwick area of Birmingham."

After reversing her ten year old Peugeot into a parking bay outside St Ann's Residential home, Phoebe switched off the radio. The car windows were still steamed up even though the blower had been on for most of her journey. She took a deep breath before brushing the fallen strands of hair out of her eyes. She checked her make up in the mirror then reached over and grabbed her umbrella from the back seat.

Phoebe jumped from the driver's side and then raced round to lock the passenger's doors. She had become used to this chore as she couldn't afford the garage bill to have the lock fixed. No-one wanted to bother with a decade old car and most of the small garages she had known only a few years ago had gone out of business.

Phoebe's overcoat did not offer much protection against the rain. Like the rest of her outfit, she had bought the coat from an Oxfam shop or from Primark. Under the navy blue mackintosh, she wore a light green cardigan, white blouse and gray pleated skirt. For comfort she had worn her favourite pair of trainers, even though they were tattered. Though in her early thirties, Phoebe had not a lot of time for buying fancy things; her mother had taken up much of her time. She wore only a small amount of make-up and felt fatigued, but Phoebe's rich blue eyes still held a girlish beauty and all the manual work she had been forced to perform at home had kept her trim.

She pressed the buzzer at the main entrance, noting the small surveillance camera stuck away up in the corner of the reception area. The door clicked open and Phoebe knew she had to sign the

*The Fall*

visitor's book before the next door would be opened. Her face was known so she was not required to announce herself over the intercom.

Once through the second set of doors, Phoebe made her way along a small corridor. On either side there were cubicles with beds and sitting areas illuminated by light from large double glazed windows. She passed a little old lady using a simmer frame who stopped for a moment to ask Phoebe for directions to the loos.

"Aggy, have you lost your way again?" came a voice from behind Phoebe. "Hello, Ms. Garrett. Are you here to see your mom?" Phoebe turned to see an assistant coming down the corridor, dressed in a pull-over and jeans. The woman was in her mid-forties, very skinny but with a slightly furrowed face.

"Hi Jean," replied Phoebe. "Is she in the usual place?"

Jean nodded but looked a bit apprehensive under her smile. "She's not quite herself today. You might want to stay for just a short time today."

Phoebe swallowed to prepare herself, closed her eyes briefly and took in a deep breath. "Okay, I'm ready."

"I'll see you up there shortly." Jean gave a reassuring squeeze on Phoebe's shoulder before helping Aggy to the toilets.

Through a door off the hallway, Phoebe made her way toward a set of narrow stairs. She felt her stomach churn, her heart felt heavy and her hands began to shake. She steadied herself on the handrail as the tears swelled up. But before the emotions could take a grip, she fanned her face and pulled out a hankie to dry her eyes and blow her nose.

"This'll not do," she said aloud.

Straightening herself, Phoebe made her way up two flights of stairs and through another door. The place was quiet, except for a television showing a morning magazine programme where the hosts were chatting to a doctor about anorexia. An old woman sat gaping at the TV monitor which hung from the ceiling and an old man stared across the room into nothingness while a second read the morning papers through his bi-focal specs. None took any notice of Phoebe passing by.

Swiftly, she marched on to the second sitting area and arrived just as two assistants were gently lowering Mrs. Garrett into a soft chair. One assistant made her way back to the nurse's bay and politely nodded to Phoebe, while the other sat down with Mrs. Garrett.

"Rachel, look who's here to see you."

Mrs. Garrett, gently rocking back and forth, slowly turned her head from the young woman to look at Phoebe. Though her eyes focused on her daughter there was no hint of recognition of the figure before her.

"Yes," replied Mrs. Garrett not certain of the question asked. Phoebe felt a lump rise in her throat and again her hand began to tremble. She felt a twitch just below her lower lip. "Hi, mom." Phoebe smiled at the assistant. "Thanks, Grace, for all your help."

"That's okay, Phoebe," smiled Grace's deep brown eyes. Phoebe found it hard to determine Grace's age, her skin was so youthful but her wisdom was that of a mature woman. She was a student, Phoebe had discovered recently, studying journalism but had been encouraged to work in the community by her parish priest.

Phoebe was a little envious of how beautiful Grace looked, even in threadbare jeans and tatty shirt. Her body was lean and athletic, almost like a child who had been stretched upwards. Her hazel-coloured skin revealed dark freckles on her cheerful face and her enthusiasm and bubbliness brought a smile to Phoebe's face.

"Your mother slept well last night."

"How aware is she?"

"Not very, I'm afraid, I'll leave the two of you together. If you need anything give me a call."

"Thanks."

Grace stood up and made her way to the nurse's station. Phoebe held her mother's hand.

"Hi, mom, how are you?"

There was no response. Rachel looked at nothing. She gazed somewhere across the room but at nothing in particular. Phoebe squeezed her hand. For a moment Rachel's hand squeezed back. She turned her head and her eyes seemed to converge on Phoebe. Briefly,

*The Fall*

the younger woman thought she detected a smile but it was gone as quickly as it had appeared.

Looking down at her mother's lap, Phoebe saw a damp patch gradually spreading.

"Grace!"

Grace darted back across the room.

"I think she wet herself," Phoebe informed her.

"That's okay, I'll take her to the wash room and clean her up."

Phoebe helped Grace lift her mother to her feet. They were joined by another carer and suddenly Phoebe felt surplus to requirements. Grace sensed her rejection and turned back.

"I'll be out with you in a few moments, Phoebe."

"Thanks, Grace."

Phoebe slumped back down into the soft chair. Tears were again rolling down her cheek. A few moments later Grace reappeared.

"Sally and Daisy are looking after your mom. So I thought I'd come back out and see how you were doing?"

"Thanks," replied Phoebe.

Grace held her hand.

"It must be tough?"

"It is," answered Phoebe. "I've had to look after mom for so long, I don't really know what to do with myself."

"Do you go out much?"

"Not really, I'm a bit old for all that."

"Don't be daft, you're a good looking woman and should be out."

Phoebe laughed. "I wouldn't know where to start."

"Do you like to sing?" asked Grace.

"I suppose. I haven't since school."

"I'm in a choir, do you fancy coming along? It's a good bit a fun and you can get to meet a few people."

"Oh, I don't know, I might be a bit silly."

"You never know until you try. Come on, give it a chance. We could go out to the pub after."

"Okay."

The two of them exchanged mobile numbers and Grace gave

*George John Kingsnorth*

Phoebe a hug. Sally came out from the washroom and advised Phoebe that her mother needed to rest.

"I'll come back tomorrow then."

"It'll be okay," replied Grace.

## CHAPTER SIX.

The sound of the door being unlocked and opened, echoed around the seat lecturer theatre. Professor Andrew Garrett stepped into the room full of apprehension. He laid his Masters Leather Business bag onto the front desk, full of students' first assignments. He had spent the previous few days marking and was depressed by what he had encountered. He found it odd that he always came across the good ones first and all the others went rapidly downhill. Sometimes he wondered if they had even been in the same rooms when he delivered the material, their assignments were so abysmal.

The blinds in the lecture theatre were pulled up allowing the Autumn sunlight to bleach into the room. The dust particles lit up like little ships on a vast voyage of discovery. As Garrett unwound the cord and lowered each set of blinds, the dust swirled like mini tornadoes. Garrett shuddered as he expected another form of tornado about to explode through the doors at any moment. He hoped he would have the laptop set up and projector warmed and ready before they arrived. Several of the more dedicated students had already begun to arrive and were taking their seats in the auditorium.

He asked one student to switch on the main lights as he had forgotten to do this when he arrived because of the external illumination. For a few more seconds Garrett fumbled around trying to locate the projector's remote control to switch it on. Then he began to unfold his laptop. As the computer booted up, he noted that the lecture theatre was nearly half full. It was almost nine-fifteen and he was reluctant to start the session on time as he could virtually guarantee about 20 more students would turn up late and disrupt his flow of thought. The downside of this inevitably meant that all the students would gradually come later and later and then begin to complain to the faculty head.

The title slide from Garrett's PowerPoint presentation lit the screen. Quickly, he checked the class attendance register. The system involved the students swiping their ID cards at the door which automatically signed them in as present. The information was then fed back to the lecturer's 'H' drive and to the Registrar so that she could monitor attendance levels. If tutorials or lectures were low in numbers, lecturers were required to provide an explanation. It seemed unfair that, while students spent their evenings drinking and clubbing instead of studying, their lecturers were held accountable.

There was a general hubbub of chit-chat in the theatre. Garrett tapped his whiteboard marker on the desktop to draw their attention to him.

"Good morning all," said Garrett. "I think we've left it long enough for the stragglers. As you will be aware, from this point onwards the register will show those arriving late and an e-mail will be sent to them as well as to the Registrar. If you receive three late attendance notices, you are required, under your student agreement, to attend a oral warning and explain the circumstances that brought about your lack of commitment."

"Please take notes. I know students like lecturers to provide handouts but I feel this is a lazy approach. By writing down in short form what you have gleaned from these sessions you will be able to use Google, an Internet search engine or browse the library for additional information to help you with the next assignment."

"Oh, by the way, you can pick up your last assignment at the end of this session."

The main door opened and another four students entered, apologizing for being late.

"Never mind, please just hurry to your seats."

Garrett paused for a moment to gather his thoughts.

"Okay, today's lecture looks at several texts that discuss the fall of angels."

The next slide revealed the content of the talk which Garrett skimmed over briefly. Click. A slide appeared of a nineteenth

*The Fall*

century drawing of angels watching women as they bathed.

"The beginning of Genesis Chapter Six states that, when man had multiplied, the sons of God, or divine beings, saw that the daughters of men were beautiful and took them as their wives."

"Randy lot were they," a male voice chirped up. Everyone laughed.

"No interruptions please!" Garrett's stern voice rang out. "There are two schools of thought on the interpretation of whom these beings might be. One school suggests that the sons of God were the descendants of Seth, Adam and Eve's third child. While the daughters were from the line of Cain and the cause of corruption."

Garrett slowly paced across the floor. Studious individuals scribbled in their notebooks. Others chewed gum or texted their mates seated either behind or in front of them. Garrett tapped the spacebar on his laptop and a second image appeared of a gathering of angels spying on the mortal women.

"The other school," Garrett continued, "suggests that the sons of God were in fact Angels who had chosen to disobey God." From the corner of his eye Garrett could see a paper dart launched across the room but he chose to ignore the intrusion and to carry on.

"In the book of Enoch, Semjâzâ led 200 angels to Mount Hermon, to plot their rebellion."

The next slide showed the majestic presence of Semjâzâ, though demanding respect seemed somewhat apprehensive.

"These angels knew that what they were plotting would send them to damnation but Semjâzâ wanted to ensure that he was not the only one who would be punished, so he made them all agree to a pact."

Garrett paused for a moment to see that he had caught the imagination of many in the auditorium.

"The rebellious angels, also known as Watchers, sent to look over humanity, began to take wives and defiled themselves by conceiving children. The children grew to some 300 cubits. A cubit is roughly the measurement from a man's elbow to his fingertips, about 18 inches. So the size of these giants were effectively 450 feet or just over one-hundred and 37 metres."

Garrett's next slide was an image of Noah's Ark as depicted in the movie *'Evan Almighty'*.

"Most of you have probably seen the film *Evan Almighty* at the cinema recently, where the filmmakers built a full size version of the Ark. Well, according to The Book of Enoch, the offspring of the Watchers and human woman grew to be this size."

"Oh, come on and you believe that?" squawked a freckled young ginger-haired male.

"It's not a case of whether I believe it or not, it's what is indicated in the text you are required to analyse."

"Bullshit," remarked the youth. "There's never been any fossils of such a creature."

"Don't forget, this unit is on Theology and Religious Text," commented Garrett. "What is important is the content of this text and the illustrations we are given by the writers of these passages."

"What ever you say, Prof."

Garrett selected the next slide. The image depicted angels teaching their human wives various arts and crafts.

"The angels corrupted their wives by teaching them how to use metals to create trinkets and jewellery. They taught them to mix pigments and create paints to use as make-up."

"What?" interrupted a young woman who looked as though she had just stepped out of a beautician's shop. "Are you trying to tell me that I've been corrupted because I wear make up?"

"You don't need much corrupting, Stephanie," hooted a male Goth. "From what we've heard you've just about been around everyone!"

Half the group began to laugh. Stephanie got out of her seat and stormed over to the goth and started to pummel him with her fists.

"Hey, cut it out," screamed Garrett from the front. "Behave yourselves, this is a lecture theatre not a fight hall. Go back to your seat Stephanie or I'll call security."

"You started it, sir," Stephanie barked. "This is your fault." She stormed out of the lecture theatre. Everyone laughed.

*The Fall*

"Settle down now," Garrett shouted. "R. H. Charles' English translation of 1917, indicates that the women learnt how to beautify their eyelids and used the metals to make bracelets. It then goes on to say that the godlessness led to fornication. They were also taught witchcraft and astrology. How to perform abortions..."

"Oh, come off it, sir," the ginger-haired lad interrupted again. "Next you'll be telling us that heavy metal is influenced by the devil and that we shouldn't be watching television. In fact virtually everything you say seems to be leading up to condemnation of the world and the society we live in today."

"All I'm trying to do is get you to analyse the text and see for yourself," explained Garrett.

"It doesn't seem like it to me. Your whole argument is totally biased."

From the back of the theatre, students were beginning to leave. Girls in short T-shirts revealing pink mid-riffs, others wore short mini-skirts and shirts with FCUK printed all over them. Heavy-metal fans with shirts that looked as though they had been splattered with blood. Girls and boys with tightly platted hair, some with black spikes, thick eye make-up and whitened faces. More with MP3 players blaring out urban music with every other word in the lyrics a profanity. Several Chinese students, confused by the exodus, looked about wondering what they should do. Several Muslim girls wearing Hijaabs, remained seated, alongside a few individuals whom Garrett knew belonged to the Christian Union at the University.

Garrett gave himself a few moments to regain his composure. He was about to begin speaking again when a buzzer sounded and the remaining students began to clear away their things. Garrett attempted to shout over the hustle and bustle of note-tables being folded away, bags crashing against the chairs as they folded up and the hubbub of student chit- chat.

"Look, I need you to read pages 11 to 13 from the new translation of the Torah and make comparison with the same verses in the New International version of the Old Testament. Then look at my notes on R. H. Charles' translation of The Book of Enoch, chapters six to 11

If you can't get the books from the library, Google them." Garrett's voice faded as he realised no-one was left.

"Another fucking waste of time." He looked toward the ceiling, his face wrinkled with trepidation. "Sorry Lord, my language gets worse." Shaking his head, he slid his arm along the desk at the front of the auditorium to gather his things and let them fall into his open bag, then left.

## CHAPTER SEVEN

The little Rover 114 van had seen better days. Around the back wheel arches rust had bitten deep and Michael knew that it would not be long before he had to think about replacing the vehicle. The front suspension needed pumped up as he could feel every bump on the M6 between the spaghetti junction and junction 3A, heading toward the airport along the M42. At the second junction he came off and headed down the A441 towards Redditch.

The weather had been reasonably dry for the past two days so he knew he should be able to make some head way with his new client's garden. He had been recommended and an hourly rate had been agreed. He was to clear out the rose beds of weeds and cut off the dead heads, spray them for black spot and leave them tidy over the autumn and winter months. Due to the extended summer rains, the grass was high but Michael hoped it would be dry enough to cut, if not that morning, by late afternoon.

Michael kept an eye on his speed as the A441 was littered with cameras. A car had overtaken him shortly after leaving the M42 and the flash had caught the speed king reaching eighty. Michael did not want any trouble so he always tried to keep to about five miles below the limit he was driving through.

He turned right into a small cul-du-sac of plush Tudor-styled houses, each with half an acre of ground around them. The side of the garden was framed by conifers but the front had low deciduous shrubs, mainly buxus sempervirens, a common box wood with small leaves.

Michael pulled into the gravel driveway leading up to the front door. To the left of the house was a double garage, so he parked there, leaving enough room for his client to come and go without

*George John Kingsnorth*

obstruction. Getting out of the car he counted about ten roses in a semi-circular bed directly behind the front shrubs. The weeds were rampant, nearly suffocating the roses. As the pebbles crunched under his boots he made his way to the back garden through a gateway to the right of the house. Down a short pathway, Michael found a paneled fence separating the garden from the neighbour's. The back garden, consisting mainly of lawn with shrubs running along the perimeter, stretched for over a hundred yards. A spinney lay at the bottom of the garden. As he drew closer he could hear the sound of running water. Through the spinney he could see a brook.

"Hey, you. What are you doing? What do you want?"

Michael spun round to see a teenage girl hanging out of an upstairs window of the neighbouring house. She was pulling on a black T-shirt, not afraid to reveal her form to strangers. Michael looked away.

"My name's Michael. I'm here to do some garden maintenance for Professor Garrett".

"What? I can't hear you," called the girl. "Hang on, I'm coming down".

As she disappeared inside, Michael made his way to the front of the house. He could hear the loud crunch of pebbles as they were trampled by running feet. Suddenly, the gate at the front of the garden, was swung open. The silhouette of the girl stood before him.

"Who did you say you were?"

"Michael, Professor Garrett's gardener."

"Oh."

There was a sudden awkwardness as the young woman realised the stranger's six foot stature dwarfed her five foot five petite frame.

"My name's Mara." She held out her hand.

"How do you do," Michael replied stepping out of the shade and into the light to shake her hand. Mara noted his grip was firm but gentle. As she ran her eyes along his arms she could see the roundness of his biceps and deltoid muscles which had been toned and strengthened through many years of heavy labour. His skin was coarse and weather beaten, dark from too many days in the sun. She

*The Fall*

imagined that under his sleeveless T-shirt his pecks were solid and his continual workouts in the garden would have removed any excessive fat to reveal a tightly formed *'six pack'* above his belly button.

Michael released her hand as her overt appreciation of his body began making him uncomfortable. He was nearly twice her age, old enough to be her father and in his eyes she was barely a child, so he did not take too kindly to such carnal scrutiny. "I must get on before the weather changes." In his haste to escape, Michael unwittingly brushed against Mara. It was obvious that the young woman savoured the sensation of his muscular body lightly touching the side of her breast. Hoping to detain him a while longer, Mara gave chase.

"Are you from around here?" she enquired as they reached the van. Michael swung open the rear doors and began to sort through his tools.

"No, the other side of Birmingham."

"Are you married?"

"Sorry?" Michael was surprised by her bluntness. "I've come to do some gardening and I feel as though I'm going through some kind of inquisition."

"Have to check out who's hanging around here." Mara jigged up and down coyly with her arms behind her back. "Have to check out all strangers if they're up to no good." She laughed. "Do I make you uncomfortable?"

"A little," Michael replied. "I just want to get on with my work."

"Do you like music?"

Michael lifted a petrol mower out of the van and placed it on the ground between the two of them.

"Yeah."

"I'll leave you alone if you promise to come to see my band playing."

Michael started to push the mower around towards the gate. "What type of music?"

"Heavy metal."

"I'm not really into heavy metal."

"I'll keep pestering you until you give in."

"I'll see. Look, I really have to get on now. It's been nice meeting you and hopefully you'll realise I'm not here to steal the crown jewels but just to cut some grass and pull up a few weeds."

Mara sensed the harshness of his tone and held back while Michael disappeared along the pathway toward the back garden. Relieved that Mara had not followed, Michael pushed the rubber cap over the spark plug and pulled the cord to start the engine. After several attempts and no joy he checked the petrol tank. It was dry. He wondered if the annoying girl from next door would still be there beside his van. He took a deep breath and began to make his way towards the pathway.

"Do you need some of this?" Mara held up a red plastic petrol container and a funnel as she appeared from the side of the house.

"Thanks, but I can do everything here."

"I know, just helping out," Mara smiled. She handed him the petrol.

"Thanks," Michael gave her a sarcastic smile. She curtsied. "My pleasure."

Michael was thankful that the petrol vapours smothered Mara's evocative perfume as he poured the liquid into the tank. He pumped the fuel through to the carburetor, set the choke and pulled the chord. The engine exploded into life and the racket was deafening. Mara watch as Michael cut the first stripe. As he turned to make a second stripe he hoped that Mara would have taken the hint and left but she was still there. Then his attention was drawn towards the roof where several crows now gathered. As he got closer to Mara he noticed how they seemed to watch her.

"Will you come?" Mara shouted.

He shrugged his shoulders and turned to cut a third strip. She began to follow him walking along the freshly cut grass. "I can be very persistent."

"I can see that," Michael replied.

As he turned the mower round to cut towards the house he noticed the crows had left the roof and were now collecting along the

*The Fall*

top of the fence directly behind Mara.

"Where did you say you were playing?"

The crows squawked at him in protest. Mara seemed oblivious to them as the birds were drowned out by the sound of the petrol engine.

"In a pub called 'Fiddler's Walk' near the centre of town. Will you come?"

"What time?"

"Eight."

"Yeah, okay. Now, will you let me get on with my work?"

"If I must?"

"You must."

Mara skipped back towards the house and down the pathway to the front. Most of the crows took flight and circled 70 or 80 feet above her while one stayed to continue its protest at Michael. Though she was out of sight, Michael could tell where Mara was by the location of the crows. He felt a sense of unease. The hair at the back of his neck prickled.

Several hours later, Michael began to load up his van. The sun was falling in the sky. Above Mara's house the crows settled on the roof. He could see Mara applying her make up as she prepared for a night out. Suddenly, Michael remembered Melissa in her wedding dress.

## CHAPTER EIGHT

The Summer nights had long since gone and the cool evenings of September had arrived. Phoebe was still unsure of what she was letting herself in for but had promised to meet Grace at the small Catholic Church just on the outskirts of central Birmingham. Late night shoppers continued to fill the city centre as she made her way from New Street Station passed the newly refurbished Rotunda, the cylindrical tower block, and through the Bullring to Moor Street. As she hurried across the traffic lights, a train bound for Coventry rumbled beneath her feet. The church was at the junction of Carr Lane where it joined Moor Street.

Once inside the building, Phoebe felt a little ill at ease. Brought up in the Anglican tradition of the Church of England, she had never been inside a Roman Catholic Church. However, since her mother's illness her attendance at any form of church had fallen away and her spiritual life had suffered. When Grace had suggested joining her for choir practice Phoebe had felt an inner call to find her way back to her faith. Now she was wondering if she had made the right decision.

For a few moments Phoebe stood near the main door watching several parishioners come in, bless themselves and make their way to the front of the church. Phoebe sat in a back pews, her heart pounding inside her chest with trepidation.

"Phoebe, hello! Oh I'm so glad you were able to make it," called Grace as she suddenly appeared from among the group at the front. "Come and meet the others."

"Are you sure it's okay? I'm not Roman Catholic, I'm C of E."

Grace smiled, "If it helps we all see ourselves as just Catholics, only those in Rome are Roman Catholics, we're Birmingham Catholics."

*The Fall*

Phoebe laughed as she got up and made her way with Grace towards the rest of the choir.

"We've had an influx of Polish Catholics in the past few years and our ranks have begun to swell, so we like to have a good singsong on at Mass. I'll introduce you to Father Thomas."

As they reached the front of the church Father Thomas was handing out hymn sheets and enjoying some chit-chat with a couple of the Polish ladies. Like Grace, Father Thomas was from a Jamaican-Irish background and had returned to Birmingham after spending several years in Uganda as a missionary. On his return, he had spent a further 12 years as school chaplain before accepting the position as Parish Priest almost four years ago. As many of his parishioners were Polish, he had made the effort to learn their language to say Mass in their mother tongue.

"Father Thomas," Grace called, "can I introduce you to a friend of mine, Phoebe Garrett. Her mother is staying in the home where I work."

"Hello, Phoebe," Father Thomas smiled and held out his hands to greet her. "What a lovely name, did you know that it means 'Bright or shining' and is a Greek name?"

Phoebe shook his hand and returned the smile. "I didn't know."

"She's come to help us with the choir," Grace informed.

"Ah, excellent, you're most welcome," Father Thomas beamed.

"Is it okay that I'm not a Roman Catholic," Phoebe began to explain. "I'm kinda out of the way of church. I grew up in the Church of England but since I've been looking after mother for the past 12 years it's not been so easy to go anywhere."

"Don't worry, my child, you are most welcome here. If you enjoy singing in the choir, perhaps, when you are ready, you might like to become part of our little flock but there's no pressure," Father Thomas reassured.

"I'll see how things go, thank you," replied Phoebe feeling a little less intimidated. "But then you haven't heard me sing yet, you might change your mind," she laughed.

The choir practice lasted nearly two hours and Phoebe's spirit felt revived and exhilarated. She may have started a little flat but quickly found her vocal tones as many of the hymns were recognisable and familiar.

At the end of the evening, the church warden set out a large pot of tea and biscuits in the parish pastoral centre, allowing about 20 minutes for the group to exchange news of births and deaths, marriages and breakups. Some gathered in threes or fours to pray for one of their number, while others introduced themselves to Phoebe. One, by the name of Krystyna Jazinski, was a friend of Grace's and was excited to be joining the two of them in the pub afterwards.

After the cups were washed and put away, Phoebe was led by the two younger women to Krystyna's car, parked a few streets away in Bartholomew Street. There was a full moon lurking behind the clouds occasionally casting its blue light into the shadows, contrasting with the glow of orange tungsten coming from the street lamps. Though nearly ten-thirty, the streets were still busy with people and taxis.

The three women climbed into the silver Skoda Octavia SDI, bubbling about the events of the evening and the anticipation of some alcoholic beverage along with some live music. Krystyna drove onto Albert Street round to the left to join the one way system, back towards Moor Street Ringway, and across Chapel Street onto Jennens Road passing by the rear of Millennium Point. Turning left at Woodcock Street into the University district, she parked outside a busy student filled pub. From across the road the music pounded into the night.

"Oh, it sounds a bit raunchy, doesn't it?" enquired Phoebe.

"It'll be fun, most of my Uni mates are here tonight," replied Grace. "Anyway, I promised you a good night out if you came to the choir."

Inside a smoke machine pumped out its swirls of haze, as a substitute for the nicotine sticks that had been banned earlier in the year. On stage the band jumped up and down with vocals that bellowed into a microphone. They were accompanied by the throbbing tones of a bass guitar, thumping drums, clashing cymbals

*The Fall*

and a strumming rhythm guitar, highlighted by the occasional lead guitar rifts. With the last chord echoing across the room, the raven-haired female singer dressed in torn fishnet stockings, black biker's boots, a mini-skirt that could not have been more than eight inches and a tartan jacket that covered her white cotton vest, screamed into her mike sending a high pitched squeal reverberating around the room.

"Hello, I'm Mara Spirit and the band is Dark Fantasies. Hope you enjoy the set!"

The crowd roared and the guitars and drums burst back into life. Phoebe followed Grace and Krystyna through the writhing bodies across the dance floor towards the bar. Jostled and pushed, Phoebe accidentally shouldered an older, less animated individual.

"Sorry," offered Phoebe as his drink spilt onto the floor, "I'll buy you another."

"It's okay, don't worry, it was just a coke," replied Michael.

"Look I'm terribly sorry, the least I can do is get you another one."

"Okay, if you must," he smiled. But as Phoebe struggled towards the bar, Michael made his way to the other side of the room where, concealed by the shadows, he continued to watch Mara and monitor much of the activities going on around him. After buying a replacement drink, Phoebe searched for Michael but he seemed to have disappeared. Occasionally, Michael glimpsed the slightly older woman who stood out among the freshers. He wondered if she was a lecturer. He gauged her age to be somewhere between 27 and 32. Unlike the teenage girls who looked more like children who had been stretched to gain some height, the mature woman had more curves and was more attractive to Michael. He tried to focus on Mara but his attention shifted to the two younger women who had joined the older one.

"Phoebe, are you okay?" asked Grace.

Michael noted her name. He liked it.

"Yeah, I'm fine," replied Phoebe. "I knocked someone's drink out of his hand and wanted to replace it but the guy's vanished."

"Don't worry about it," replied Krystyna.

Michael remained in the shadows. Again he found himself forcing himself to concentrate on the stage.

Mara's band played a set of seven songs before wrapping up for the night.

"Thanks everyone for your support," Mara sang out to the crowd. "We hope you'll come to our next gig at the Beater's Arms three weeks on Friday?"

The crowd roared and cheered as the band left the stage. Michael noted that the three women had settled in a booth that was furthest from the stage. As he was leaving he asked a waiter to get them a round, paid him and left.

*The Fall*

CHAPTER NINE

The vanity of Cassiopeia sparkled in the heavens. Michael traced out the constellation made up of five main stars, which formed the shape of a 'W'. Her spouse, Cepheus lay beside her, both placed in the heavens by the Greek god, Poseidon. Cassiopeia set in such a way that half the time she would have to sit on her thrown upside down as punishment for her arrogance and vanity.

The air was crisp. From the west the city lights reflected an orange tinge to the underside of the gloomy clouds. Rain looked destined to spoil the night, but for the moment Michael enjoyed the calm and peaceful surroundings. He was sitting on a park bench on the far side of the road from the pub and could hear a distant dog, a young couple several streets away clipper-clopped along the pavement, their leather soles and stiletto heels tapping out every footstep. The air carried sounds for miles.

Suddenly the double doors cracked open and the serenity was vapourised as revelers jostled each other, some looking for a fight, others in friendly banter, and a few with arms wrapped round their prize lusting to get home.

Dark shapes lingered in the night-time air, their wings out stretched they glided in to perch along a nearby roof top. There were five in all. Michael pulled his coat around his body and got to his feet. Down a dark alley another splinter of light cut through the blackness. Spindly silhouettes like spiders danced outside. Michael crossed the road through the dispersing crowd and made his way to the alley, observing both the small gathering of people and the crows hopping from tile to tile.

"Hey, you said you'd give me the full rate this time, not just 50 percent," Mara roared as a bouncer shoved her away from the manager. "Where's my other 80 pounds?"

The manager stepped out of the doorway, a heavy either side of him. Two others pushed the lead guitarist, Danny, and the drummer, Freddie further into the alley. On the floor, the rhythm guitarist, Gerard, nursed a swelling eye, as a fifth bouncer pulled him to his feet.

"Perhaps, if you're open to other duties, we could come to some kind of an arrangement?" suggested the manager as he straightened his mismatched tie into the waistcoat of a suit that looked as though it was a relic from the seventies.

"What kind of arrangement?" Mara enquired suspiciously. The manager smirked and stepped towards her. Mara backed into the wall as the stout man pressed her tight into the brickwork, using his left arm to position himself as his puckered lips descended to meet hers. Reviled, Mara jerked her knee up into his groin. The manager eyes almost popped out in agony, as he crumbled to his knees.

"I'm not your bitch. Go find someone else to play with!" Mara smarted.

With tears in his eyes, the manager squealed instructions to his subordinates to rough her up. Gerard was thrown against the other two band members and held in check by two bouncers while the remaining three flexed their muscles. Each appeared to have been past contenders for Mr. Universe but now, with the bulk drifting further South toward their stomachs, it seemed to Mara that a wall of beef had been erected around her. Suddenly, she heard the gathering pace of distant footsteps build momentum, as Michael raced towards them from the road. Drawing on all his energy and strength, Michael rushed as fast as possible toward the small group, hoping that the force of his speed would bowl the figures over. Danny, Freddie and Gerard, thrust forward were driven into the first two bouncers who landed on top of the manager. Michael found himself flying over them all into the three blocks of beef surrounding Mara. The force threw one into the wall knocking him unconscious as the weight of the other two impacted upon him. Mara drove her foot into the manager's face sending him into cuckoo-land. The three band

*The Fall*

members bounced the head of two of the thugs off the pavement then, taking to their heels, fled from of the alley. Michael found himself painfully winded as one bouncer threw him against a wall before driving his fist into Michael's jaw. Mara, lifting a loose brick, slammed it into the last bouncer's face, who then fell on his companion lying beside the wall. Mara brought the brick down onto the skull of the brute that was using Michael as a punch bag. Before the manager and his staff could gather their wits, Mara dragged the blood stained Michael to his feet and out of the alley, across the road and toward safety.

A few streets away the pair stopped. Michael slid to the ground, his face a bloodied mess. Mara listened to hear if anyone was following. With no sounds of anyone in pursuit, she leant against the wall to catch her breath, then turned and noticed Michael's rapidly swelling cheek and the bloody stains on his face.

"I should take you to the hospital."

"I'll be alright," replied Michael. "If you could just get me to my car, I'll get myself home."

"Where did you leave it."

"Near the pub, a couple of streets away."

Mara knelt beside Michael and gently brushed his hair from his wounds.

"You've got a couple of nasty cuts. You'll probably need some stitches."

"I have some friends who can help me," Michael replied, "I'll call by them on my way home."

"Are you sure?" Mara was concerned that he would not be fit to drive too far. Then anger gripped her. "Jeez, Michael, what the hell were you doing?"

"I thought you were in trouble?"

"I can look after myself."

"I just wanted to make sure you were okay?" Michael rolled his head to the side to try to see her with his good eye. "What about your gear and your friends?"

Mara turned to face him and smiled. "There were a couple of

bands on tonight and we used their kit. Once I get you to your car, I should be able to find the boys nearby."

"You sure you'll be okay?" Michael was more concerned with her well being than his.

"You've got enough problems to worry about without me adding to them," Mara chuckled. "You should stop trying to be my knight in shining armour. You're too old for that kind of stuff."

She got to her feet and pulled him up. "Let's get you back to your car."

"What about the guys that held you up?"

"That was the manager and his bouncers trying to pull a fast one," replied Mara. "Their probably licking their wounds, I don't think we'll have much to worry about from them, at least not tonight. Come on lets go."

Michael was still in pain and Mara noticed he was holding his side. She pulled his shirt up and saw there were some more bruises, then she checked his other side. Lifting his arm on the uninjured side over her shoulder and taking some of his weight, they began to make their way back to Michael's car. From there, Mara was able to see the pub. There was no sign of either the manager or his thugs, so she was able to relax and tend to Michael's cuts. She tore off part of her T-shirt and used some distilled water Michael kept in the boot for when the radiator went dry. With most of the blood wiped away his face didn't look as bad as she had thought.

"Are you sure you'll be okay to drive?"

Michael nodded.

"Do you want me to drive you to your friend's place and I can call for the band to pick me up?"

"No," Michael replied grimacing as he shifted position in the driver's seat. "I'll be fine, thanks."

"Okay, if you have to be a martyr?" Mara sneered. "When are you next at the professor's?"

"Early next week," said Michael.

"Look, call in and see me," she smiled. "And thanks, I did appreciate your help back there."

*The Fall*

She kissed him on his unscathed cheek. "See you soon."

Michael closed the car door, turned the ignition and the engine roared into life. With a couple of gear crunches the Rover 114 spluttered along the road for a few yards, while Michael tried to cope with the pain. After a few moments he felt settled and soon disappeared out of sight down Ashted Circus heading towards Dartmouth Middleway. Mara stepped back into the shadows so as not to be seen from the pub and pulled out her mobile to call Freddie, the drummer and get her lift back home.

"Where are you?" she whispered into the phone when it was answered. "Are you all okay?" Freddie confirmed they were. "Look, it's better that I make my way to you, you're only a couple of streets away. I'll see you in a few minutes." Mara rang off and put her mobile into the breast pocket of her jacket. She made her way through the University area unaware of the five airborne creatures gliding above her.

Through an alley she could see the band's transit and the three lads waiting inside. Mara began to run down the darkened alley, pleased to see her friends but mid way, a shadow cut across the light that spilled onto the path at the far end. Mara stopped in her tracks as she was unable to see the figure casting the shadow. She began to back up and run only to see a second shadow fall across her exit.

"Who's there," she screamed. "What do you want?" She turned back to see if she could make a dash for the transit and began to sprint. Only a few feet away from the entrance of the alley she was violently thrust to the side, crashing through the paneled fence. With the breath knocked out of her, she tried to get to her feet but was struck to the ground and rolled onto her front. A shadow crawled along her leg and under her skirt. Her pupils dilated and white foam dribbled from her lips. She began to convulse dislodging stripes of wooden panels from the alley fence. Then she was still. Motionless. Her mobile phone began to vibrate. One crow landed beside Mara and pecked at her breast pocket.

"Mara, where are you," Freddie asked urgently. "We're waiting to get home, hurry up."

"Nearly there," Mara's voice was mimicked by the bird. "Give me a couple of seconds."

## CHAPTER TEN

When the waiter brought over their drinks, Phoebe was eager to see if it had been the man she had bumped into whom had purchased them. But, despite his efforts, the waiter was unable to point him out and eventually gave up. Grace was keen to take photographs of each band with her digital SLR while Krystyna had ambitions of dancing and being chatted up. The flicking fluorescent lights froze each movement like a black and white photograph. Krystyna jumped to her feet and began to throw her arms into the air and wiggle her pelvis sending the long strands of her wavy hair flying in all directions. Grace snapped away then quickly looked at the last image on the LCD before it was saved to the compact flash card. Phoebe notice that both girls were full of smiles and energy, their perfume wafting on the air, unafraid of displaying their sumptuous bodies as they attracted suitors. But she could not determine whether the boys were wolves stalking lambs or if the girls were like spiders laying traps for their prey. The exchanges seemed fraught with tension as the sweat built up like beaded pearls flowing along bronzed backs, bellies and breasts.

Phoebe noted a sharp pang just behind her left eye and knew a migraine was imminent. "Are you okay, Phoebe?" Grace had placed her arm across Phoebe's shoulder to shout into her ear over the throbbing drum and bass.

"Thanks, Grace, I'm okay. I might need to step outside for a minute to get some air. Not used to this volume."

"Let me come with you." Grace stood up and began to lead Phoebe to the main door. As they approached the bouncers, Grace shouted something into his ear. He nodded and opened the door for them both.

*George John Kingsnorth*

Out of the stagnant air, Phoebe felt refreshed by the cool night. The sparkling dots in the black drew her attention upwards.

"Aren't the heavens wonderful?" Phoebe mused.

"Spectacular," replied Grace gazing into the clear sky. "My interest in photography came from watching the sky. When I was nine I wanted to photograph Hale-Bopp and my dad framed it and hung it in my bedroom. It's my favourite thing. It reminds me of when he was around."

"Oh, I'm sorry." Phoebe was distracted by Grace's tale. "What happened?"

"My mom left us a couple of years after Hale-Bopp and my dad had to look after me and my two brothers. We didn't know he was suffering from Leukaemia and he died the following year."

"That must have been hard for you?"

"We had to go and stay with my mom but we knew she didn't want us."

Phoebe did not know what to say but waited for Grace to continue.

"We ended up moving in with my dad's sister until we were old enough to take care of ourselves. David's now in Bournemouth studying Marketing and Management, while Peter is in Manchester training to be a doctor. I've just moved into digs close by so I can study photography and journalism."

"What led you to the nursing home?"

"I met Krystyna. She's from a Polish Catholic family and it reminded me of when I was small and we used to go to church. I loved the sense of community and belonging at a time when all my family seemed to be leaving. It made me feel good."

"I could do with a bit of that." Phoebe looked up once more towards the stars. "I can't remember when I've ever felt as though I belonged to my family. My mom has been ill for so long, I can't even remember what it was like before she was ill. Dad got so wrapped up in his work and studying that it kinda got taken for granted that I was spending all my time looking after mom. I was about your age when mom became ill and I had to give up Uni to take care of her so dad could continue bringing in the money to keep everything going.

*The Fall*

Before I knew where I was a month became a year and then five and now ten years have gone and I don't know where I am."

Grace smiled and rested her hand on Phoebe's shoulder. "That's why I wanted to help out at the home. I got a chance to meet so many new people and see that my own problems were not as big as I thought they were and I realised I needed to make the most out of every day I was given."

Phoebe smiled. "I appreciate you bringing me out tonight. The choir singing was great and I'm glad of your company now, though I'm not sure I'm into this kind of music," she laughed.

"I supposed it is an acquired taste," Grace grinned. "Perhaps we should take you to somewhere quieter next time to give you a chance to chat."

"That would be good," Phoebe smiled. "I'd like that."

"Do you mind if I go back in?" ask Grace. "I'd like to get some photos of the band before the night's out."

"Go ahead, I'll join you in a few minutes."

Grace ran back inside, switching on her camera ready for action. Phoebe looked once more into the heavens. A dark shape flew across her vision, drawing her attention to another dark figure sitting on a bench on the opposite side of the road. For a few moments she watched him and realised it was the man whose drink she had spilled. She wondered whether to go over and talk to him but then felt embarrassed.

"Phoebe, they're going to do the last set. Come in and see them their great," called Grace. As Phoebe stepped towards the pub entrance she took another look back but the man was gone.

About an hour later, Grace and Phoebe were being driven along the M6 in Krystyna's six year old Skoda Octavia SDI. Though none of them had been drinking they all felt a little dehydrated so when they reached the Garrett family residence, Phoebe invited the two younger women in for a mug of hot chocolate. Professor Garrett was still sitting in his study pondering over some theology books that looked as though they were ready to fall apart from intensive use. The room looked dusty and Phoebe was ashamed of visitors even passing the door never mind spending some time. Her father prohibited her from cleaning up in case something precious was lost. As Phoebe looked after most of the large detached house she had argued that he should at least make sure that the one room he dominated was kept tidy and clean.

"What does your dad do?" asked Krystyna.

"He's a lecturer at one local universities, teaching Theology."

For a while the three of them chatted. Krystyna talked about moving from Poland to Birmingham. Of how being a member of the local catholic church helped her to integrate into the community.

"It was so useful finding someone who spoke the same language, especially when I was having difficulties initially with English," Krystyna commented.

"I think I would find it hard moving away from home, especially to a country with a language I didn't know," Phoebe replied.

"Well, I knew a fair amount of English but it was text book so I used to get some odd looks from people when I put it into practice. Having people around me who could translate better was such a help as I could ask them things before attempting to say the same thing in English."

In his study Professor Garrett could hear the low tones of the three women. The table lamp formed a cone of light which did not spill off the table. All his books and the fireplace with an Edwardian striking clock could be seen only as dark shapes set against a dull gray mass. He tilted the lamp towards the clock and noted two hours had passed into the new day. He rubbed his eyes sensing the fatigue moving through his limbs and body.

From the kitchen, Phoebe heard her father make his way up the wooden stairs, the third step gave out a call of distress from his weight. "It must be late, father's retiring."

"We must go, also," remarked Grace gathering her things and rinsing her cup under the hot water in the kitchen sink.

Within moments, the two younger women were in the car and heading for the centre of Birmingham. Phoebe closed the front door after listening to the night sounds. An owl announced its presence

*The Fall*

and the odd bat darted around the cul-du-sac. Phoebe bolted the front door and ensured the key was taken from the lock. She noted that her father had left his table lamp on, as usual leaving her the nightly routine of switching everything off. As the study lamp was extinguished the light from the street lamps gave everything in the study an orange cast. The curtains needed drawn but as she pulled the first she observed some movement back and forth into her neighbour's home. For a few moments she stood behind the half draw curtains observing the goings on. From what she could discern, Mara was being helped into the house by the other members of the band she played with. Phoebe could not remember their names even though she had heard them only just this evening. As she tried to jog her memory, she saw Mara lifted by two figures and carried with her feet dragging up the two front steps into the house. All the actions were done in silence and the three lads quickly made their exit, jumped into the transit and wheel spun away from the gravel drive. On the opposite side of the street a light went on but after a few moments the sound of a toilet being flushed showed they were not aware of the strangers in the close. Upstairs in Mara's house a light erupted startling Phoebe. She stepped back from the curtains so as not to be seen. Some kind of rumpus was going on as the teenager could be heard screaming at her mother and a torrent of words thrown back at her. A door slammed and the light was extinguished.

Phoebe thought back to the band playing in the bar. Mara was not intoxicated and it was not long ago that they were all there in the pub. As she wondered why Mara was now unable to walk by herself her thoughts were suddenly scattered as a black object smashed into the windowpane. The bird died instantly, shaking Phoebe to her very soul.

## CHAPTER ELEVEN

Phoebe was suddenly aware of the bright orange strip that was gradually spreading across the ceiling of her bedroom. She could not remember the precise moment when she had woken but she was now conscious that the day was starting with brilliant sunlight pouring into her room. She felt positive within herself. The warm glow lifted her spirit and she felt encouraged. The previous night was put behind her and like a new beginning everything promised to be fresh.

After tidying away the clothes from the night before that she had carelessly let fall to the ground, Phoebe exchanged her pyjamas for a pair of sporting shorts, vest, tracksuit bottoms and trainers then picking up her MP3 player, she ran downstairs. Crossing the threshold, she pulled a hair-band from her pocket and tied her auburn shoulder length locks into a small pony tail. Still troubled by the previous night's experience with the crow, Phoebe set off for a two mile run.

Sunshine flickered through the leaves giving the impression of watching a ciné projector. The air was cool as summer was well passed and the autumn winds were beginning to build. The leaves were browning and collecting along the pathway. Phoebe had various genres of music on her MP3 player from Jazz, movie soundtracks to classical. It was the latter she liked to listen to as she paced the two miles from her home down the A441, up towards the M42 around the fly-over roundabout and back again, playing the strings of Edward William Elgar's Enigma Variations. The themes seemed to sparkle with the orange streaks breaking through the trees.

Since her mother's stay in hospital, Phoebe had seen four months to fill. Previously, her mother had been the centre of her life calling on Phoebe for this or that. She did not mind, it had given her a chance

*The Fall*

to talk and she remembered the wonderful conversations they had had about finance, politics, history, religion, faith and relationships. Her mother had often been concerned with Phoebe spending so much time looking after her but her daughter was quite contented. The hardest part for Phoebe came when her mother took a stroke. She had visited her in hospital in early April to find it was a different woman who inhabited her mother's body. The frame was the same but the agile mind was gone. She had sat down by her mother's bedside and held her hand, suddenly realizing how much weight her mother had lost. The change had been slow, unnoticed by Phoebe as her mother's wit and personality had always been so vibrant but the day after her stroke, Phoebe realised how much had been lost. After 30 minutes Phoebe had been asked to leave so her mother could rest. She had found her way to the ladies room, locked the door and sobbed her heart out.

Sometime later, she could not remember if it were days, weeks or even the next hour, she had suddenly found herself filled with rage towards her father for not spending more time with them both before the stroke. Even now he had not visited the hospital, lost in his books and research and, she did not know what. He had not even let his daughter in. There was next to no communication between them, he always sat in his study oblivious to all around him. Had he even been aware that his spouse had had a stroke and was now in hospital?

As she ran around the roundabout over the M42, she took care to watch the speeding traffic as some cars just came straight up the slipway and straight onto the junction without even looking to see what vehicles were there that had the right away. As she began to make her way back, Variation number IX Nimrod, Adagio was beginning. She remembered the name her father had once spoken when briefly he had engaged in conversation with her mother, many years ago. She tried to remember what he said the name meant. What was it? Yes, the mighty hunter who stood before the Lord. Her parents had discussed Biblical stories and loved to banter over what each thought of the significance of their individual favourites. Professor Garrett's had been the story of Babel and the first empire that had been established by Nimrod after the flood. Phoebe had sat on the stairs dressed in her girl guide's uniform, covered with various badges from First Aid to canoeing and camping, waiting to be taken to the village hall for a Saturday afternoon jumble sale the troop was holding to raise funds.

"Trust you to go for such an arrogant and pompous fool who thought he could build a structure to reach into heaven," Phoebe's mother had scolded her husband. "A bit like your science has done."

"Don't talk rubbish," scoffed Garrett, "science, Rachel, has revealed so much…"

"To the point where you all think you can do without God?" question Rachel.

"You always stick fast to your beliefs, even when the facts are as clear as day before you…"

"They are only as clear until some other theory is promoted," Rachel laughed. "How many times have I seen you spend nights going over something new doubting until the penny drops and you suddenly believe?"

"No, no, Rachel," Garrett began. "I only modify my views once I have examined all the evidence, cross referenced to other sources and…"

"All poppy cock, all someone's notion," interrupted Rachel. "But what do you feel within your heart? What does your spirit tell you?"

"Superstitious nonsense," Garrett remained defiant in building up his blocks, his own mini-tower around himself that would prevent his wife from reaching within.

As Phoebe had listened to this brief conversation, she wondered what it was that had come between her parents. What had created such a rift? Yet they were still living in the same house, like two strangers in a hotel. Phoebe had been about 13 at the time and her mother's illness had forced her at this point to walk around with a stick, hobbling from one side of the house to the other.

As the MP3 player began the 14 minute long Introduction and Allegro for strings at the end of her downloaded album a more terrifying memory seeped into her mind. Her parents' conversation

*The Fall*

had been held in the kitchen while her mother was peeling potatoes for the family dinner. During the heated debate, Phoebe could picture her mother losing control of her right hand, the knife slipping and cutting into her left wrist. He father had panicked, screamed for his teenage daughter who had raced from the stairs through the hall to the kitchen to find a pool of blood across the red tiled floor and her father clasping her mother's wrist to keep her blood from spilling any further. For all his knowledge gained through an endless library of books, Garrett was not a very practical man and struggled to apply any proper first aid. This had been left to Phoebe. She found herself calmly, giving her father precise instructions' concerning the items she needed to attend to her mother's wound, while he rushed to get the car ready to transport them all to the accident and emergency department at Birmingham's Heartlands NHS Hospital.

Phoebe was nearly at the end of her run. Spider webs covered in dew sparkled in the sunlight but Phoebe was too lost in her thoughts to notice. Even the heron taking flight from its fishing spot in the brook behind her house, failed to catch her attention. Equally, she was unaware of the van parked in the driveway. All she could think about was how, from the moment she had dressed her mother's arm, she had become her main carer. The shock of what happened had driven her father further into his books and study, a refuge he felt more comfortable with than facing reality. Though he cared nothing for the spiritual world, he became absorbed by theories and concepts of how theology had developed. Yet his motive was merely to prove it a superstitious nonsense. He mocked both spouse and daughter for their constant desire to attend Sunday communion and seemed to relish the moment when Rachel was unable to drive herself to church. Phoebe was too young to take over this role and by the time she had learnt to do so her faith had been so stifled that she could no longer find the energy to make the effort. Now 16 years later, she often felt a hunger within and her heavy heart longed to be filled. It was at these times that tears welled up and her emotions overwhelmed her. As her thoughts began to focus on her heart she could feel it pumping away, tapping out the beats of her life. Then her conscious was aware of the cyclical pattern of her feet pacing out her journey home. As she ran round the corner into the cul-du-sac she did not see the postman who was more focused on his bundle of letters. She brushed against his shoulder, sending the letters flying into the air but the stout form remained rigid and Phoebe, losing her balance, toppled over and slid across the tarmac pavement. She grazed the skin on shoulder, arm, thigh, knee and ankle. The pain was excruciating, doubling her up. The postman quickly gathered his letters scattered across the road. The sunlight blinded Phoebe's view of her home, but the tears in her eyes blurred it more. A silhouetted figure drew closer. Although, she could not discern features, she knew by the muscular build, that it was a man. The pain forced her to focus on her stinging limbs. She let out a cry.

"I'm sorry, miss. I didn't see you coming," the postman panicked.

"Is everything okay?" came the stranger's voice.

"The young lady crashed into me," answered the postman, "and she fell to the ground. I think she's cut all down her left side. It's Miss Garrett from number 11."

"That's okay," replied the voice still unrecognisable in silhouette. "If you could give me a hand, we can carry her to her house and I can sort her out. I'm doing some work for the Garretts at the moment."

The two men lifted Phoebe to her feet and helped her toward her home. Phoebe could hear the sound of a crow squawking and the odd black shape opening its wings and gliding from one roof top to another. She was unable to put weight on her left leg and relied on the two men being able to carry her. She felt embarrassed and wanted to take control but the pain forced her to hand over her will to these two strangers. She was a little fearful but was also aware that her mind was more alert than her body as shock took over and she felt faint.

Vague images of the front lawn, hallway and kitchen floated through Phoebe's vision as the stranger placed her on a wooden chair.

"Hold her there while I get her father," the stranger instructed the postman before disappearing from the kitchen.

*The Fall*

"Professor Garrett, sorry to disturb you." Phoebe heard a mumble of tones and from where she sat she could see through the kitchen door into the hallway to her father's study. Everything was blues, grays and blacks blocked out in hazy shapes with no real sense of what the patterns were. The stinging of her limbs kicked in again as she tried to shake away the faintness and take control of her senses. The stranger returned with her father and for the first time during the agonizing incident the exterior light revealed the man's face. It was the man she had bumped into at the pub the night before.

"Hello, we meet again. My name's Michael."

## CHAPTER TWELVE

Half a dozen crows landed on the roof of the house next door to the Garrett's. Their squawks sounded like a chorus of chuckling children, pleased with the prank they had just performed. Below their perch another project was well underway and being groomed.

Black and white photos of previous gigs showed Mara in mid flight, bellowing into a microphone. The audience arms waving above their heads were blurred, showing the camera's shutter was at a slow speed. Mara's eyes were also slightly blurred, half open and fully open. Her mike hand was static but her right hand and arm arced in a fan shape. At some point a flash had gone off during the exposure, illuminating Mara on stage. But with only enough power for the main performer, the image faded as it reached the drummer and bass player. The back of the stage was dark. A sidelight mapped out spiky features of Mara's black hair, almost punk-like and reminiscent of the mid-seventies styles, a good 35 years ago.

Beside this photograph a coloured square Polaroid snap had been pinned to the door, it's colours faded to tones of browns, oranges and reds as the sunlight from the window had taken its toll. The image was of Mara, aged about six, her ten year old sister, and their parents.

Underneath both images were several post cards of the opera house and bridge in Sydney, Australia and a similar one of the bridge in Newcastle, England. A letter scribbled in red pen, highlighted Alison's journey from the University of Cumbria to work down under in Canberra. Another image portrayed Mara's older sister in cap and gown on her graduation day.

Mara's black leather jacket, fishnet stockings, skirt and blouse now lay in a pile on the floor having missed their intended target, the clothes basket. Her underwear had thankfully landed where

*The Fall*

intended. Her bed was unkempt with pink sheets and a mismatch black duvet. Her dressing table was covered in an assortment of make-up with everything from lipsticks and nail polish, to deodorants and perfumes. In the mirror the face that looked back at Mara was of a girl she did not know. The reflection showed a girl with white-blonde hair, all dye had been removed, leaving it her natural colour. Make up had been scrubbed away and moisturizers added freshness to her skin.

She sat naked, grooming her hair. A tattoo that had been etched on her shoulder began to fade returning the skin to its natural pinkish tones. Slowly, all embellishments and blemishes were gradually removed. Her dandruff, spots, blackheads and earring punctures disappeared. Her tongue studs and belly button ring were pushed out of the skin and fell to the carpet at her feet. Mara was being cleansed. The cellulite around Mara's buttocks due to excessive consumption of fast foods could visibly be seen being broken down. The adipose cells were returning to their normal size. The localized fluid that had accumulated in the capillary walls was drained and the blood flow began to circulate unimpeded. The result, firmer skin tissue and more natural pigment colourisation.

Although, only in her late teens, Mara's breasts seemed rather flat and slightly droopy in shape but as the unseen surgeon remodeled her body her breasts began to fill out and become perky while her nipples protruded outwards and pointed upwards. However, unlike many expectations of the female breasts as perceived by the media, big is not necessarily beautiful as abnormally large breasts can start to sag. But in Mara's case her breasts had been remodeled to look natural for her height and size, as well as age. In other words, she had the perfect body for a 19 year old, fully grown woman, without assistance from any artificial means.

Mara stood and gazed at her new form. Unlike the anorexic images of female perfection that litter beauty magazines the world over, she was not skinny. On the other hand, neither was she overly voluptuous. Her well toned muscles did not hide the femininity of her five foot five frame that was wrapped in a sun kissed skin. The curves of her body were sensual, designed to attract more than just a mortal man. She had been crafted for a higher being. Even her fingers and toe nails looked unusually healthy. All trace of excessive nail-biting was gone. She ran her fingers across her breasts down toward her abdomen and over to her side. For a moment, she was startled that her finger tips had not detected the little gray scar that formed after her appendix had been removed. She scrutinized the mirror. It was gone.

She checked just above her hairline, when as a ten year old she had skateboarded into a wall, head on and gashed her scalp. This old scare had also vanished.

Just a few days ago, some nasty spots had erupted on her back. She looked over her shoulder, lifting her hair to allow a full view in the mirror. All the redness and soreness had disappeared. No blemishes remained. She smiled at herself in the mirror. But there was something about the smile that matched the difference that had transformed her body.

Behind her pupils, lurked a darkness that had not been there before. Through her optic nerve into her brain the sinews of darkness stretched into her brain and smothered her soul. An inner voice cried out to be released but was firmly restrained, although it was not yet choked out of existence. The darkness needed the minimum of Mara's own essence to remain in order to draw on her memories and personality and model itself into a human conscious. Mara's physical body was now the host to a sinister guest who was preparing her for a game that had been continually played out since the time of Adam and Eve.

A knock came on the bedroom door. "Mara, hurry up. Your breakfast will be cold and you'll be late."

The voice sent vibrating air to Mara's eardrum. The hammer, anvil and stirrup within her inner ear began to vibrate and various frequencies were transmitted through a watery substance within each of Mara's two cochleae to tens of thousands of hair-like nerves. At a certain frequency the hairs resonated sending an electrical impulse via the cranial nerve through the brain stem into Mara's cerebral

*The Fall*

cortex. Her soul interpreted the message of her mother's voice and attempted to cry out but was muffled. Instead the darkness compiled a collection of words. A signal was sent to the lungs to take in more air and a second to the vocal chords, all in a matter of milliseconds. Mara's mouth opened. "Okay."

"Look, Mara," continued her mother. "Are you sure you'll be okay over the next two weeks we're away?"

"Yes, Mum. I'll be okay, don't worry!" came the reply in Mara's voice.

"It's just with your dad not working for the next couple of weeks, we wanted to take advantage and get some time together. Your Uncle Tom has a place in New York we can stay at. I've never been to America, you know?"

"I said it's okay! You need the break."

"Good, we'll be gone by the time you get up tomorrow. I've left money for food and stuff on the sideboard."

"Okay, Mum. Just make sure you send me a postcard and bring me something good back?"

As the sound of feet descended the stairs, Mara's demon controlled face smiled once more at her reflection.

## CHAPTER THIRTEEN

A coccinellidae landed on a rose leaf, the black spotted red wing covers closed as it began to track down aphids. As a large green coloured glove manoeuvred through the thorns, several aphids could be seen clinging to it. The coccinellidae leapt onboard and caught its first prey. Toxins from the bug's legs were released poisoning the aphid.

As Michael clipped away another deadhead from the rose bush he noticed the brightly coloured ladybird on his glove and drew it closer to see it more clearly. A slight breeze ruffled his hair and the bug took flight once more.

The sun had risen to its apex and Michael found his limbs were beginning to burn. From within the house Phoebe came out, walking with a slight limp. Her legs were covered by a pair of baggy gray tracksuit trousers. She carried a tray of tea and biscuits.

"How's your leg and side," asked Michael.

"Still sore," smiled Phoebe, "but I'll survive. Thanks for helping me out earlier this morning. I'm just embarrassed that I nearly fainted. Dad's not too great when it comes to first aid. He's all fingers and thumbs."

"That's okay, I'm glad I could help."

"If there is anything else, just give me a shout," Phoebe offered.

"If you wouldn't mind, some sun block would be good," Michael requested. "I'm getting scorched out here."

"Okay, I'll see what I can find." Phoebe hobbled back inside pleased to be of some use to someone. Inside the hallway, she passed Professor Garrett's study to make her way up stairs to the bathroom. Garrett noticed her passing.

"Everything alright, dear?" he asked.

*The Fall*

"Everything's fine, dad. Just getting some sun block for Michael. We have some in the bathroom, don't we?

"Not sure," replied Garrett as he got up from his chair and made his way over to the window. He heard the stairs creak and Phoebe wince as the pain from her leg caught her breath. From his viewpoint he could see Michael continue to prune the roses. As he was about to return to his notes a second figure appeared from his neighbour's garden. It was only as he was beginning to look away that the mental image of whom the second person actually was clicked into place. It was Mara but she looked so different, not the punkish metaller with black raven hair but a blonde. He stepped to the window to take a better look. Yes, it was her but what a transformation! Everything from her toenails to her limbs, body, breasts, face, lips and hair. In fact, Garrett was taken aback by the sense of arousal he felt for a girl young enough to be his granddaughter. He stepped back and took his seat, shaken. Something was wrong. He had not felt this way since he and his wife, Rachel had had the fortunes of youth. Taking a moment he reminisced of his wife's body and how they had shared one another so many years ago until he had become lost within himself and his books, using them to drown out the changes he found occurring within himself so as not to notice the fragility of his wife and her illness that he could not face.

The thoughts began to bring him great pain as he felt his anxieties tug at the muscles in his chest. He tried to imprison his memories within the shadows of his mind and to blot them out with the words on the pages before him. His eyes were drawn to the Gospel of Luke, chapter eight verse 17:

'For there is nothing hidden that will not be disclosed, and nothing concealed that will not be known or brought out into the open.'

He slammed the book shut and then was startled. "What's wrong, dad?" came Phoebe's voice.

"Nothing, nothing, I was just lost within myself." A tear began to roll down his cheek inadvertently. He turned his chair to wipe it away hoping Phoebe would not notice.

"How was your last trip to see your mother?"

Phoebe was now the one to be taken aback, her father had never asked about his spouse in over 12 years.

Outside, Michael stood as Mara approached him. The scent of the roses was overwhelmed by the fragrance wafting from Mara, making him slightly dizzy, almost intoxicated. He shook his head in a vain attempt to clear his mind. Mara's movements allowed her to show off her curvaceous form as if tempting an audience from a catwalk. A tingling sensation erupted in Michael's groin sizzling through his nerves to the tips of his fingers and toes. The venomous perfume encompassed his nervous system. Michael's mind struggled with the effects Mara's presence was having on him. His involuntary actions drew him to a rose bush where he plucked one and held it up as a gift for the goddess before him. As Mara's fingers moved to take the rose their eyes were transfixed on each other. She did not notice the thorn protruding from the bottom of the stem and, as her hand grasped the flower, it punctured her finger. A bead of red bubbled up and Mara's smile faded. The flower fluttered to the ground as Mara screamed at Michael, snapping him out of his trance to feel the smart of her slap on his face. Rubbing his stinging cheek, Michael bent to retrieve the fallen rose. As he straightened, two crows swooped over him forcing him to duck once more. They hovered for a moment before attacking and clawing at his scalp. Michael managed to knock one to the ground as the other raced to Mara's side. The fallen bird quickly retaliated lunging at Michael with its razor sharp beak.

Both Garrett and Phoebe were distracted from their conversation as they moved towards the window to see the raucous. On seeing Michael assailed they rushed out to chase away the bird. With a great flapping commotion, the creature regained flight and darted back to its mistress just as Garrett and Phoebe dashed out of the front door.

"What was that all about?" Garrett quizzed Michael.

"Mara caught her finger on a thorn and the birds attacked me," Michael replied.

"Oh, come now, be serious," Garrett scoffed.

"Are you hurt?" Phoebe spotted some blood trickling passed

*The Fall*

Michael's right ear.

"I'm okay, it's just a scratch."

"Better see to it before you get an infection," insisted Phoebe.

"No, it's okay," Michael reassured her.

"Don't be daft, man," chirped Garrett, "if you don't put some pressure on it soon you'll carry on bleeding. Do as you're told, boy." Garrett took Michael's arm and guided him into the kitchen. Phoebe suppressed her own pain and raced in front to find some more bandages and gauze.

As Michael sat down in the chair he laughed.

"What?" asked Phoebe.

"Déjà vu," explained Michael, "we were here in reverse only a few hours ago."

Garrett allowed Phoebe to take control and quietly retired to his study once more. Michael jerked away from Phoebe as she applied some disinfectant to his wound.

"Sit still, don't be a baby," Phoebe taunted.

"It's sore," complained Michael.

"Shoe's on the other foot now, isn't it?" Phoebe commented. "That'll teach you to give pretty young things flowers."

"I wasn't," Michael reacted.

"You did, both dad and I saw you," Phoebe snapped back.

Michael looked puzzled. "I can't remember."

"What," Phoebe sneered, "you can't remember this gorgeous girl coming towards you, showing off everything she's got? Talk about temptation."

"I remember seeing Mara but then everything went fuzzy."

"That wasn't Mara, Mara's got black hair, that girl was blonde."

Garrett was puzzled too. He overheard the heated exchange from his study and returned to see what was going on but stopped just outside the kitchen. He too knew the girl was Mara and was embarrassed to admit the impact she had had on him. He also realised how she had affected Michael but what was even more curious was that Phoebe, who usually would have noticed even the slightest change in a person, had been totally deceived as to the girl's true identity. In the back of his mind he remembered a short quote from the first letter of Timothy. Quickly, he made his way back to his study and found a scruffy looking bible from one shelf. He flicked through it to find the passage he had in mind. There it was, *'And Adam was not the one deceived; it was the woman who was deceived and became a sinner.'* And the one who had deceived Eve was Satan. A cold chill traveled down Garrett's spine. He was suddenly aware again of his own sin at seeing Mara and it left a bitter taste in his mouth. He had felt lust for her and was aware that even to look at another woman with desire was considered the sin of adultery. He tried to lock these thoughts away with the others from earlier and hide them in the shadows of his mind.

His attention was sharply drawn back to the sounds from the kitchen. Michael's other cheek now smarted again, slapped by Phoebe.

"What did I do," pleaded Michael.

"It's what you haven't done," Phoebe barked.

"I'm lost."

"What would you know," Phoebe sneered and made her way out of the kitchen as Garrett came from his room. "You're just as bad," she scolded her father and stormed upstairs. Garrett made his way into the kitchen to find Michael rubbing his second red cheek of the day.

"What happened," Garrett enquired softly.

"I think there's a little bit of jealousy," Michael explained.

"Why," puzzled Garrett.

"I think Phoebe's got a crush and Mara's got her steamed up," Michael suggested.

"There could be something else going on," offered Garrett.

"What do you mean?"

"Something dark, that I can't quite figure," Garrett pondered.

"The only dark things I'm aware of are those bloody crows." Michael got to his feet and made his way to the front of the house and out to his van. From his tool box he pulled something out but Garrett could not see what it was. Garrett looked towards Mara's

*The Fall*

house as three crows squawked at Michael. Suddenly, one plummeted to the ground, its life extinguished. Garrett spun round to see Michael relaxing after firing a pebble from a catapult.

"Why did you do that?" Garrett demanded.

"Revenge."

## CHAPTER FOURTEEN

The humidity was oppressive. Even with the old air-conditioning unit chugging away, the unusual heat for early autumn was stifling. Sandra had left her desk a few times to take some water from the dispenser in the waiting room. Returning to her desk, she used one of the many brown card files with confidential letters, photographs, notes, faxes and bank account details to fan herself in an attempt to cool down.

Things had been quiet for the past few days and Sandra had been attempting to get through several piles of files that were stacked up on her desk. The floors and shelving were littered with similar stacks and she was beginning to wonder when the agency would start to expand. Although, she was fully aware that Stoneywell would not be investing in property. Some of the files had not been touched in a decade and were just collecting dust but when she had suggested burning the content, Stoneywell had been reluctant to let them go as he viewed them as prospective earners. Clients always come round again. So now he had her going through some old papers to give some of the older clients a ring to see if they needed any of their services and to inform them what Stoneywell Private Investigations Ltd could offer.

As a single mother with a 14 year old son she tried to keep out of trouble. Stoneywell had done some work for her husband but when he had not paid him, the P.I. took the opportunity to get his own back by helping Sandra take her husband for everything he had when they divorced. By giving her a job and demonstrating she was capable of sustaining herself, Sandra secured the custody of her son.

Ten years later her son was into the Xbox 360 games consul and had demanded an Intel Duo Core 2 processor computer with 160

*The Fall*

gigabytes of hard-drive space so he had the necessary power to play all the high definition three dimensional games and do his homework. When Sandra had been forced to go to buy him a computer, she was intrigued to find out how much could be done with it. With her son working towards his GCSEs and having to do Information Technology, she was finding herself picking up a few tips on how to use a word processor, spread sheets, presentations and databases. Her mind was ticking over how to transform the office and make things more efficient but when she had approached Stoneywell a week or so before he was still resistant to any form of change.

Sandra again tried to focus on the task at hand when the office door was knocked.

"Come on in, the door's open," Sandra called out. The dark shape behind the frosted glass moved and the door opened. Sandra dreaded the thought of whom was coming in. The last case involved Stoneywell having to carry out surveillance on a young woman married to an elderly gentleman. Sandra had to be brought in to go undercover as a barmaid to monitor the woman's activities with her younger lover. Unfortunately, for Sandra, this case led to her being assaulted by a few of the locals when the landlord had her investigated by another agency. From then on Sandra refused to be involved with anything other than what she did behind the desk.

As the door swung open, the light from a window behind her desk revealed a handsome man whom Sandra guessed to be in his early thirties. In reality, the stranger was none other than the angel who had vanquished the demon during the thunderstorm.

"Hello, how can I help you?"

"Mr. Stoneywell has asked me to come in and help out on an assignment," the stranger replied.

"Okay, I'll just see if he's available, if I could have your name?" Sandra enquired politely.

"Nimrod. My name is Nimrod."

"Thank you, Mr. Nimrod," Sandra smiled. "Please take a seat in the waiting area and I'll call you when Mr Stoneywell is available."

*George John Kingsnorth*

Sandra directed Nimrod through to the waiting room opposite her desk. Once Nimrod had closed the door, Sandra clasped her hands together and looked to the ceiling. "Oh thank you, Lord. Something lovely to break the monotony of the day."

She turned to an aging intercom and pressed a button. There was an initial squeal of electronic static and then Stoneywell's voice could be heard. "Yes."

"A Mr. Nimrod to see you, sir, about…"

"Oh, yes, send him in quickly."

The sound of his voice was chirpier than his normal gruffness. Sandra got up from her seat and went over to the waiting room door. When she opened it she found Nimrod reading one of the many female magazines spread across the 70's coffee table. "Mr. Stoneywell is ready to see you now, Mr. Nimrod."

Startled, Nimrod threw the magazine back onto the pile as though he had been caught reading something dirty. He smiled at Sandra. "I'll take you through to Mr. Stoneywell's office," she smiled back. "This way please."

Nimrod got to his feet and followed Sandra out of the waiting room, across the reception area to Stoneywell's door. She knocked and on hearing Stoneywell say 'come in' opened the door to announce Nimrod to her boss. Stoneywell got out of his chair and came round his desk to greet Nimrod. To Sandra's surprise, there was a new laptop sitting on Stoneywell's desk.

"When did you get that?"

"Not now Sandra, you can see I'm in a meeting."

Stoneywell gently moved Sandra back into her area and closed the door. As the door clunked shut, Sandra shouted through it. "When am I getting mine?"

The door opened sharply and Stoneywell snarled, "Not now Sandra, I'm busy." He promptly slammed the door.

Stoneywell motioned for Nimrod to take the seat in front of his desk and the two sat down. For a few moments Stoneywell played around with his new laptop. Some things he did not understand as he tried to save a document and failed.

*The Fall*

"Where did it go?" he called out bewildered.

"New toy?" asked Nimrod.

"Yeah, we're modernizing," Stoneywell answered. "Just have to get used to this little thing." Stoneywell turned to face Nimrod. "We've not had any reason to use computers until now. But with broadband being so cheap and new clients asking me to investigate chatrooms and search records for missing persons to determine if they are using internet accounts and that kind of stuff."

Nimrod nodded, "Sounds interesting. How can I be of help?"

"We have a new client, the parents of a teenage girl, Mara Sandford."

"And you are aware of my credentials?" enquired Nimrod.

"Yes, you've been highly recommended," replied Stoneywell. "Very highly."

"What's the problem with Mara?"

"She's a 19 year old college drop out who's in a heavy metal or punk band. Very much into the dark gothic look."

"A mixture of different genre's then," commented Nimrod.

"What?" puzzled Stoneywell.

"Doesn't matter," smiled Nimrod, realizing that Stoneywell was not well educated. On the wall hung a BTEC level three Advanced Diploma in Private Investigation gained through the Academy of Professional Investigators. There were a few other shorter courses but nothing that showed he had a degree or higher national diploma in any particular area.

"Well," Stoneywell continued. "It seems the Sandfords are going away for a two week holiday and they are concerned as Mara suddenly seems to have shed her heavy metal roots and become a good girl."

"That's a good thing, isn't it?" remarked Nimrod.

"Under normal circumstance you would think so," commented Stoneywell. "However, Mara is usually quite outspoken and to find their daughter conforming so readily is totally out of character. It's almost as though she's a different person, the Sandfords claim."

"So why don't they cancel their holidays if they are so worried?"

suggested Nimrod.

"It's an expensive holiday of which our fees would only be less than ten percent," remarked Stoneywell. "They can better afford us to baby-sit than cancel."

"Are you sure you're aware of what my credentials are?" quizzed Nimrod, a little puzzled that Stoneywell seemed to be continuing down the line that he was a hired hand.

"Yep, you come highly recommended. Right from the top."

"What do you want me to do then?" asked Nimrod.

"The usual. Stake out where she shops, where she goes for coffee, what she does at college, who her friends are. Any unusual activities."

"Okay," Nimrod replied, getting up from his chair. "And when do you want me to report back to you?"

"Whenever you have something interesting to tell me or every three or four days. Whatever suits."

Stoneywell's attention had returned to the laptop, so Nimrod let himself out of the room.

"Has the meeting finished, sir?" asked Sandra.

"I think so," muttered Nimrod. "I think he needs a hand with the laptop. You could show him how to save a text file."

Sandra leapt up from her seat and stormed into Stoneywell's office. As the door slammed behind her, Nimrod could hear a torrent of words being screamed at Stoneywell. Gently, Nimrod closed the main door behind him as he left.

## CHAPTER FIFTEEN

Heavy traffic cluttered the main arteries leading out of the dull and wet Birmingham city centre. Frustrated drivers hammered their horns as cars fidgeted from one lane to another in the vain hope that the motion was faster. Bus queues stretched around big store shop fronts while pedestrians danced their way in and out of the lines weaving a path through static bodies to make their way into the Bull Rink centre for the Friday late night shopping.

A doubledecker bus pulled up and a flood of eager bargain hunters launched themselves towards the best deals whilst trying to avoid puddles. Battle hardened office workers and telesales executives took the newly available seats on the bus ans released heavy sighs, thankful that the day was over bar the journey home.

As the bus pulled off a second took its place to deliver its load of discount jockeys. Among them was Mara, out to buy a new wardrobe for her new look. Clambering from the metal roof a black feathered fare dodger hopped on top of a bus shelter, keeping a keen eye on Mara. As she raced to reach some unknown deals through stationary home-goers, she mindlessly passed a Catholic church. An organ began playing followed by the voices of a choir singing out:

> "Leader of faithful souls, and guide
> of all that travel to the sky,
> Come and with us, ev'n us, abide,"

A sharp pain stabbed Mara in the temple and for a brief moment, fear was painted across her face. The tones of the choir reverberated around the brickwork of the street.

*George John Kingsnorth*

> "Who would on thee alone rely,
> On thee alone our spirits stay,
> While held in life's uneven way."

Mara attempted to steady herself. Her slight convulsion drew a passerby to her side to offer assistance. For a brief instant it seemed as though Mara was confused to find herself where she was.

> "We've no abiding city here,
> But see a city out of sight;
> Thither our steady course we steer,
> Aspiring to the plains of light,"

As a woman offered a steadying hand and reached for the cuff of Mara's sleeve, a torrent of feathers, squawks and stabbing beaks attacked sending the good Samaritan fleeing for her life.

> "Jerusalem, the saints' abode,
> Whose founder is the living God."

The birds landed on Mara's shoulders having fended off the danger and appeared to drag their ward away from the piercing words.

> "Through thee, who all our sins has borne,
> Freely and graciously forgiven,"

Tears streamed down Mara's cheeks as more crows gripped her other shoulder determined to pull her away. All the birds screamed out their dark calls attempting to drown out the weapon of words from the living saints.

> "With songs to Zion we return,
> Contending for our native heaven;
> That palace of our glorious King,
> We find it nearer while we sing."

*The Fall*

As Mara was drawn away, the demon within her regained its composure and managed to steer its host vessel unaided. From the other end of the street another lone figure made her way towards the church doors.

"Raised by the breath of love divine,
We urge our way with strength renewed;"

Phoebe gently closed the door behind her and for a moment gazed at the choir.

"The church of the first-born to join,
We travel to the mount of God,

Phoebe allowed herself a moment or two to soak up the splendour of the church, the side chapels; one dedicated to Our Lady, the Virgin Mary on the left and another to her spouse, St. Joseph on the right. As the choir drew close to the end of their hymn, Phoebe came across the 14 hand painted plaster relieves depicting Jesus' arrest, various stages of carrying the cross to Calvery, being nailed to the cross, his death through to his remains being placed in a tomb.

"With joy upon our heads arise,
And meet our Captain in the skies."

Phoebe wondered why the scene had not also included the resurrection but her presence was noticed and Father Thomas called her to join the rest of the group before they began the next hymn. As Phoebe made her way to a seat, she took off her overcoat. The choir was given a few kind words and gentle suggestions of how techniques could be improved. At one point the group laughed.

Gazing down on the humans gathered, was Nimrod. As new words were sang they shot upwards and out of the building like rays of sunlight.

*George John Kingsnorth*

> "The Lord's my shepherd, I'll not want
> he makes me down to lie
> in pastures green; he leadeth me
> the quiet waters by."

All around Nimrod, others of his kind also gathered. Many battle weary beings energized by each word of the psalm.

> "My soul he doth restore again,
> and me to walk doth make...
> within the paths of righteousness,
> e'en for his own name's sake."

A mighty presence stood beside Nimrod. In earthly form he would have been recognized as a warrior of Jamaican birth. It would have taken a man many hours using weights to attain even a fraction of his magnificent form.

"How are things with you, Nimrod?"

"I'm okay, Raphael. There are others less fortunate than me, here."

The dark skinned angel allowed his eyes to roam around the gathering. There were some here whose physical being caused him concern. Especially as they had all suffered some great punishment in recent times. He looked again at Nimrod and noted that he was less scared. He also sensed something less spiritually appropriate about this angel but before he could ponder further he was struck by another wave of prayer, revitalizing every molecule of his temporally corporal being.

> "Yea, though I walk through death's dark vale,
> yet will I fear none ill;
> for thou art with me; and thy rod
> and staff me comfort still."

"If only more people would pray," came a female voice. Both

*The Fall*

Raphael and Nimrod turned to find a more delicate form before them. It was Grace. Raphael opened his arms and she fell into them.

"Hello, brother," tears formed in Grace's eyes. "It's so good to see you. I thought you were lost?" She remained tight to her brother's chest, almost refusing to give him up.

"No, sis, you've held a strong fort here. It gave me all the strength I needed. And the Lord pulled me through."

"I'm so glad to see you again," Grace sobbed.

"I heard the Baptists lost their church," said Raphael with a heavy heart.

"Patience was beaten to the verge of losing her life," Grace reported. "The demons were in great force and the congregation fell apart with such despair after the minister was disgraced. The building had to be sold off to pay for the court case. It's been knocked down and a multistory car-park has been put in its place to cater for the increased Sunday shopping in the Mall."

Another wave coursed through them, with golden rays reflecting off the roof as though a pool of mead was rippling below them.

> "My table thou hast furnished
> in presence of my foes;
> my head thou dost with oil anoint,
> and my cup overflows."

"Materialism consumes the world and blinds them with technology," Raphael reflected.

"Without the prayer we are as vulnerable as humans," Grace anxiously warned. "We can as easily be deceived. Even the language is full of curses. It's like being tortured with pin pricks and makes me feel so irritable."

"Take heart, Grace," reassured Raphael. "You have come so far. Your work is going well." Below he could see the joy on Phoebe's face as she filled her lungs with air in preparation to release the next verse. The humans moved slowly, their perception of time different from the angels above them. Only when their song showered their

*George John Kingsnorth*

heavenly protectors did the two quite different species appear as kin.

> "Goodness and mercy all my life
> shall surely follow me;
> and in God's house for evermore
> my dwelling-place shall be."

Grace hugged her brother once more. "I must go."

"So must I," echoed Nimrod.

Raphael turned to Nimrod as Grace left them. "Take heed of what has been said."

"I will," shrugged Nimrod. "I can handle things. You'll see."

## CHAPTER SIXTEEN

The morning was dull. The sun struggling to break through the clouds, barely gave a glimmer of light. Heavy gray and black clouds were rapidly carried on the wind. Yet to the east, milky strands of yellow and orange highlighted the edges of the mass of swirling vapours, still not ready to burst their payload. Traveling from the west, the lower level clouds gradually began to thin out allowing the sun to bloom.

Mara had earlier felt the bite from the chilly air and once out of the warm doubledecker, hastily made her way to a favourite clothes shop. She avoided the route she had taken the previous night, anxious not to encounter... well, she could not remember but there was something she knew she had to avoid.

It was still early on Saturday morning, but a collection of late night revelers were attempting to sober up with a hearty fried breakfast while a few early birds were out, hoping to snap up some good bargains.

Mara made her way up the entry steps into the shop and fingered the various garments hanging on rails before taking the stairs to the second floor where the coats were located. Autumn and winter wear were on display. The colours reflected the oranges, browns and reds of the season and the sun, cast a similar palette as its arc remained low in the sky.

From one stand, Mara removed a long trench coat from its hanger, walked over to a full-length mirror and slipped the garment on. She twisted and turned to view all sides. She shook her head with disappointment; the coat was too thin and she knew the cold would penetrate it. Replacing the garment on the hanger, Mara rotated the circular coat stand and sifted through various other items before

*George John Kingsnorth*

locating a second she thought she might like. Again she made her way to the mirror and tried on the coat. As she did so, a shadow passed across the mirror, startling her. Spinning round, Mara nearly bumped into a second female customer who nearly jumped out of her skin.

"I'm sorry, miss," the woman in her mid-forties blurted out. "I didn't mean to surprise you."

"That's okay, I didn't realise anyone else was here."

The encounter somehow put Mara off the second coat and she returned it to the stand in search of another. Outside the window the sun made another brave attempt to cut through dreary clouds. The yellow rays managed to pierce the heavy blanket, forming a shaft of light within the clothes. As Mara looked into the reflection of the mirror, the pillar of illumination darkened the clothes and racks. A man stepped out from behind the column and as he did so, the light subsided as another cloud began to obscure the sun. Mara smiled, delighted that she now had an audience. The coat she hung against her shoulders seemed to have more vibrant colours and even Mara's face now shone, until the sun was completely blocked out.

"Do you often stand in women's stores and watch them trying on clothes?" enquired Mara.

The middle-aged woman turned from sorting through another stand, looked about and then stared at Mara.

"I'm sorry, are you talking to me?"

"No, your gentleman friend!" Mara nodded in the direction of Nimrod.

The woman looked puzzled. "Who? We're alone."

"No we're not, he's just there."

Mara pointed towards the man she saw but all the woman could do was give Mara a strange look and back away to another part of the floor.

"Don't you get some strange folk in here," commented Mara. Nimrod looked confused. Mara again began to check out the coat and tried it on. "What's your story?"

"You can see me?" Nimrod asked.

*The Fall*

"Of course I can," laughed Mara, "do you think you're supposed to be invisible?"

"Kinda."

"Did you forget your medication this morning?"

"What?"

Mara smiled at him. "I assume you're an escaped mental patient out to do a day's shopping to pamper your female side?"

"Excuse me?"

Embarrassed, Nimrod turned to a clothes rack and began to finger through a few coats trying to ignore Mara. Mara took off the coat and hung it up, then looked for another, while eyeing the stranger up, a coy smile on her lips. She lifted out her fourth selection and tried it on in front of the mirror.

"What do you think, mystery man?"

Nimrod looked over to Mara and smiled.

"Cute!"

For the next hour or so Nimrod found himself helping Mara to decide on various garments in numerous shops. She made him laugh, dancing around and pretending to be strutting a catwalk after trying on each item. Every so often other customers would look over in astonishment, muttering to shopping companions about the girl's odd behaviour, each unaware of the angel's presence. Nimrod began to notice how Mara was being perceived so when they moved on to pay for several dresses, tops, and skirts he felt it was more prudent to be visible to other mortals in order for Mara performance to become less noticeable. As soon as the sales girl had bagged Mara's clothes and handed them over to her, Mara passed them over to Nimrod.

"You don't mind do you?"

"No, that's okay," replied a startled Nimrod, now thankful he had taken his earlier decision.

"I'm thirsty, let's grab a coffee!" Mara headed out of the shop with Nimrod carrying the shopping. A few streets away Mara found a coffee shop she wanted to go into. They sat at a corner table nestling in a booth with a surrounding leather sofa beside the front

*George John Kingsnorth*

window.

"I love sitting near the window and watching all the people rushing by, totally focused on what they have to buy or where they are trying to get to but totally unaware of what's around them," commented Mara.

Nimrod turned to see what Mara was looking at as she gazed dreamily at the frantically marching shoppers who didn't seem to have enough time to draw breath. With deep furrows etched on their brows they zigzagged in and out, a massive flow of people traveling in both directions, weaving patterns more intricate than Celtic art.

"Can I take your order?" asked a thin young man, whose name tag informed Mara and Nimrod he was called Kong Ken nai. Though Chinese, he had a broad brummie accent.

"Chai Tea Latte, please," requested Mara.

"And sir?"

"I'm okay," answered Nimrod.

"No, no, you should try the Chai Tea Latte, they're lovely. Make that two, please," Mara instructed. Kong Ken Nai made a note and was gone.

"Don't worry if you don't have any money," reassured Mara. "I'll pay for both."

Nimrod noticed a little old Asian woman peek at them through a curtain behind the counter. She disappeared and he could her hear interrogating Kong Ken Nai about the two of them. Mara seemed to be oblivious to anything other than telling Nimrod about herself and how she wished to be a movie star or rock musician.

"But I thought you were a musician? Don't you sing for a local heavymetal band?" Nimrod was surprised by what Mara was saying as she appeared to be talking as though she wasn't in a band. In the back room came the sound of something crashing onto a tiled floor. The old woman screamed as scalding water splashed across her arms. Pandemonium erupted as all the staff came rushing to her assistance. Nimrod went to get up to see if he could help but was interrupted when Kong Ken Nai arrived with their order on a tray.

"Is everything alright back there," Nimrod asked.

*The Fall*

"Just a slight mishap but everything will be fine," replied Kong Ken Nai.

"What happened," asked Mara.

"I'm not too sure," puzzled Kong Ken Nai. "Mrs. Patel was sorting out some cutlery when the boiling kettle tipped over and scalded her hands. We've called for an ambulance."

"Do you want me to have a look?" suggested Nimrod.

"No, it's okay we have a first aider who is seeing to her," Kong Ken Nai informed them. "Please, enjoy your tea while it is still hot."

The waiter left them to serve some other costumers leaving Nimrod a little anxious.

"I'm sure everything's fine," commented Mara. "Anyway, it's not our concern."

"That's a little selfish isn't it," answered Nimrod a little surprised.

"Not really," Mara remarked as she sipped her Chai Tea. "Everything seems to be under control, there's a first aider there and we would only get in the way. Best if we just enjoy the reason we're here." Some froth hung to her upper lip as she smiled at Nimrod. He chuckled and leant across, wiping her lip with his finger. Mara blushed.

"What do you do," asked Nimrod. "Are you at college?"

"Not really," replied Mara as she wiped the remaining froth off her mouth with a serviette. "All I really wanted to do was play music and didn't really like the way you had to do all the theory, so I kinda dropped out." She leant across the table and whispered, "My folks don't know yet."

"So what do you do with your time? Do you have a job?"

"I do a few things which gives me a little bit of funds."

"Enough to buy all these clothes?"

"There are a lot of art students with rich parents who need models for their photography and artwork. I help them out and they give me a good hourly rate."

"Just for posing for photographs?"

"Yeah," Mara grinned. "And I do some nude stuff, which costs more."

"Any thing else?" enquired Nimrod.

"Hey, what are you implying? I'm a good girl." Mara was annoyed that he had implied something unsavoury.

"I'm sorry, I.." Nimrod began to apologise.

"You know, not all girls are sluts." Mara frowned. Then she blinked and her expression mellowed. "But when you've got a lovely body like mine, well, why not reap the benefits. How else could I afford these kind of clothes?"

Nimrod felt uncomfortable. He didn't want to chase her away as he was supposed to be her protector, her guardian. The coffee shop door burst open, sending the brass bell into spasms. Two paramedics dressed in green rushed through to the kitchen area, drawing the curtain behind them.

"What about your Chai Tea, are you not going to drink it?" Mara commented.

"No, it's okay! I'm enjoying the chat too much to drink," Nimrod smiled.

"Hasn't stopped me," Mara laughed.

"I'm curious," puzzled Nimrod. "Do you always pick up strange men in clothes shops?"

"Why, have I picked up a homicidal maniac?" she grinned.

"No, no, you're safe with me."

"Sure, I bet!" Mara replied sarcastically.

"Scouts Honour!"

"How do I know you were a scout? You were the one stalking women and hitting on me. You're the one who has to explain himself." Mara toyed with her spoon in the froth and delicately scooped some up to her tongue. She scooped up some more and touched his lips with the tip of her spoon. Nimrod wiped the foam away with the back of his hand, a little irritated by her action.

"You're a funny man, Mr. Lady stalker," mused Mara. "Where do you come from? Why are you here?"

Nimrod wasn't sure what to say but he was aware that Mara's persona had changed subtly. The old woman being taken out by the paramedics distracted his thoughts and he felt confused. He was

*The Fall*

unaware that a host of other, darker presences were veiled by shadows within the building. In his chest he felt the pangs of stress tugging at his heart, and a headache was needling its way across his scalp. Another sensation invaded his thoughts as he became aware of Mara's two hands clasping one of his. She was gently stroking his left hand, sending a tingling sensation across his skin and rippling through his entire being.

"You still haven't told me your name, stranger?" enquired Mara.
"My name is Nimrod."

## CHAPTER SEVENTEEN

The dean sat in his ornate office flicking through an assortment of papers. On one wall hung an array of certificates and photographs of him taken alongside ambassadors, ministers and academia as they had celebrated educational triumphs over the years. Another wall was hidden by bookshelves crammed full of leather bound encyclopedias, periodical educational journals and reports on various industries. Accompanying these books were copies of the dean's Master of Science dissertation on Electronic Engineering and his Doctorate of Philosophy in Digital Signal Processing.

In his early fifties, the dean had worked in academia for most of his adult life but had been keen to create links within industry. Such connections had allowed him to perform extensive research in his area of interest, computer imaging devices. First and foremost he was a scientist who loved solving problems through experimentation and analysis of raw data. To him, the marvels of the world were the inventions of man.

There was a knock at the door.

"Come in," the dean barked.

The doorknob turned and the door swung open to reveal Professor Garrett.

"Ah, Andrew, take a seat."

Garrett made his way to a leather chair in a part of the room where sunlight from the window had not yet managed to reach, knowing that the shade would be easier on his eyes. He noted how the dean was silhouetted by strong sunlight.

The dean continued to read through a document. Though irritated by the brief delay, Garret knew to be patient with the dean. He had witnessed the man's temper when annoyed and Garrett was in no

*The Fall*

mood for confrontation, the previous class had drained him of his energy.

Garrett noted the dean had recently purchased a high-resolution digital photo frame. The device was playing through a catalogue of digital stills from the dean's family album. In Garrett's mind such gimmicky gadgets were just postmodernist kitsch. Most of the dean's fishing practice came from playing with the WII. He knew nothing about wrapping up with layers of warm clothing and wellies before getting to grips with the crisp frosts of early autumn mornings beside some smelly river bank with only a flask of coffee for company and the prospect of becoming the blood supply of local midges. The comfort of a warm study with a high-resolution liquid-crystal display 42 inches in diameter was more the dean's scene. A more efficient use of time management.

The dean put down his pen.

"Thanks for stopping by, Andrew. I'm glad you could make it!"

"It seemed urgent," replied Garrett.

"Would you like some coffee or tea?"

"Uhmn, tea would be fine!"

The dean pressed a button on an intercom system.

"Janet, a pot of tea for two please."

"Yes, sir," crackled Janet's voice over the intercom. Garrett noticed the dean fidgeting with his pen, he seemed a little anxious.

"How are you coping?" enquired the dean.

"Doing grand," Garrett replied.

"I'm sorry I haven't had the chance to talk to you recently. How's Rachel?"

"Not so good."

"It must be quite a strain?"

"We cope."

"Is she still at home with you?"

"She's in a nursing home."

"I'm sorry to hear that. What about your daughter, she used to look after your wife I believe?" The dean shifted his position in his chair.

*George John Kingsnorth*

"Phoebe's having a lot more time to her self, I believe."

"Does she work?"

"Where's this leading to, Donald?" Garrett was becoming a little irritated by the questioning. "I've a lot to get done for tomorrow's class."

"Uhm…"

The door knocked. The dean seemed relieved.

"Come in."

Janet opened the door holding a tray of cups, saucers, jug and teapot. The dean jumped out of his seat to help her.

"Is that everything you need?"

"That's fine, Janet. Thank you!" The Dean smiled and Garrett could see a slight grimace on Janet's face as a reaction to an unseen gesture from the dean. She quickly exited the room, gently closing the door behind her. The dean took a deep breath.

Garrett was surprised as he had always seen a harsher side to the dean and was taken aback by the sudden apprehensive nature that was being displayed by him now.

"Milk?" erupted the dean.

"Just a spot. No sugar, thanks."

Milk was poured into both cups. The sound of the porcelain rattling against the silver tray seemed to emphasis the tension in the room. The dean handed Garrett a cup and saucer then made his way back round to his seat.

"You're nearly 63?" the dean continued.

"In a few months."

"Have you any plans about retiring?"

"Come on, Donald! Stop beating about the bush. We've been colleagues for years. You've always been quite sharp. Why all of a sudden this nervousness?"

"The board has instructed changes to the faculty," began the dean. "Major changes."

"And?"

"Okay," the dean found it hard to keep eye contact. "Student retention is a big thing these days. If the numbers aren't there, the

*The Fall*

funding dries up. It seems, Andrew, that in your classes there's a lot of absenteeism and retention problems. Last week registration informed me that five more of your students have withdrawn. What course of action are you taking to check your students?"

Garrett crossed his legs and folded his arms. "I get the office to check on a weekly basis, but I don't have time to chase them all the time."

The dean had detected a chink in Garrett's armour. "Mmm, what about the results you seem to be getting?"

It was Garrett's turn to break eye contact. "We're not quite making the Bell curve but we have a few high fliers."

The dean grew more confident. "Yes, but you are experiencing a 30 percent failure rate in the course and that's not including the 20 percent who seem to drop out by the end of the first semester."

"They just can't hack it! The standards seem to be very low in student intake."

"Perhaps your interviewing techniques need to be more stringent?"

"Come on, Donald. You know as well as I do we're nearly forced to take everyone that applies these days. Some of these kids can hardly put a sentence together yet they seem to have 'A' pluses coming out of their ears. It's all gone crazy."

"That's beside the point. If we don't get students attending classes and passing the course we don't get funding and at the end of the day this is a business whether we like it or not."

"It's becoming a joke," replied Garrett. "I had students plagiarising all their work off the Internet, of course I'm going to fail them. Surely you should be throwing the book at them and kicking them out?"

"We can't afford to do that!" snapped the dean. "Anyway the numbers for your units are dwindling and we have to consider what we're going to do about revalidation."

"Oh, this is ridiculous!" Garrett jumped out of his chair.

"Look, calm down, Andrew," the dean held out his hands in a stopping motion. "Sit down, let's take things a little easier."

*George John Kingsnorth*

Reluctantly Garrett sat once more. The dean placed his palms on the desk. "Perhaps it is time for you to consider taking things a little more slowly, letting younger blood take all the hassle? We've all seen so many changes in education and none of us are getting younger. Would you think about taking early retirement?"

"You mean you want an easier time with people who have no standards?"

"Now be careful, Andrew. I know I'm your friend but you can push things a little too far!"

Garrett shook his head. He slapped his hands against the arms of the chair and got to his feet once more.

"Look, Donald, thanks for the tea. I'll see myself out."

"Think it over, Andrew. It could be the best thing for you?"

Garrett turned his back on the dean, yanked open the door and slammed it behind him. The dean lifted his pen and threw it across the room. He took a deep breath before pressing the intercom.

"Janet, can you bring in Professor Garrett's file and a disciplinary form."

## CHAPTER EIGHTEEN

A week had past. The rain had gone and the sun had been given the charge to dry the land. An opportunity arose for Michael to attend to Professor Garrett's garden, probably for the last time before winter arrived. The temperature was unusually high, into the mid twenties centigrade. As he worked, the heat finally forced Michael to remove his shirt revealing his back glistening with sweat. He had spent an hour cutting the lawn and was now pulling deadheads from the roses and cutting away any dead branches.

All this time Phoebe had been in the utility room sorting the week's laundry for herself and Professor Garrett. Busily she washed; tumble dried, ironed and placed each garment onto a coat hanger. As she ironed and listened to her MP3 player, she could also see Michael's toil in the garden. For a man in his early forties he had kept himself fit. As the steam hissed from the iron, pressing down on some jeans, Phoebe explored Michael's torso with her eyes. Feeling thirsty she made her way into the kitchen to make a cup of tea and decided to pour a second for Michael.

Phoebe made her way into the front garden bringing a tray with both cups of tea and a plate of biscuits. As she approached Michael she noticed he was gazing into the sky and trying to shield his eyes from the sun's glare without much success.

"Hey, Michael, I've brought you some tea."

Michael turned and met her halfway across the graveled drive.

"What were you looking at?" enquired Phoebe.

"Watching angels in the sunbeams," he smiled.

Phoebe placed the tray on the ground and shielding her eyes, looked towards the sun. All she could see was the burning hot light surrounded by a gray disc of sky that eventually became the rich velvet blue of the sky's canopy. The diameter of the gray was about the length of Phoebe's hand if she placed it over the sun.

"That's funny," exclaimed Phoebe, "I didn't realise the sky around the sun was actually gray, I though it was always blue?"

"It just goes to show how much we really understand the world we see around us, doesn't it?" Michael commented.

"I suppose," Phoebe answered, "but I still can't see any angels."

"Oh but they're there," he assured her.

"You have a wonderful imagination," she smiled.

"I just see things in a different…" Michael shook his head.

"Are you okay?" asked Phoebe, puzzled by his expression.

"I…"

Michael looked as though he was about to sneeze but then it went. He could feel a vapour tingling inside his sinuses, then reaching into his head. His lungs felt heavy as he involuntarily took a deep breath. His mind seemed foggy and he found it hard to focus.

"Do you want some paracetamol?" Phoebe placed her hand on his shoulder to steady him. "Perhaps you should sit down while I go to get you some water."

Phoebe turned and with a sense of urgency, raced into the house. Michael was about to sit down, when he noticed a figure walk into the street. He could not focus on them but felt shaky and, yes, something else. A need, a want, a desire began to flood into his senses, cascading through every fibre of his being until it took control and became his sole purpose in life. It did not make any sense to him; nevertheless it was obvious that he was being driven. He pulled up one of the last remaining roses still in bloom and began to march towards the shape. The form, the texture, the tones and colours began to sharpen until he recognized the figure walking towards him. It was Mara.

Michael found words tumbling from his mouth.

"Hi Mara, I have a gift for you."

"Michael, isn't it about time you realised that I'm not interested?" Mara snapped.

Michael felt like a silly teenager, all dopey and awkward. He tried

*The Fall*

to shake off these feelings and emotions but the grip was firm.

"Leave me alone, Michael," Mara shouted. "There is someone else in my life now."

Michael was unable to stop himself from following her to her front door; like a poodle trotting after its mistress. Mara let herself into the house and slammed the door in Michael's face. The echo of laughter echoed in Michael's ears. He made his way back toward the Garrett's house confused. The rose had snagged his index finger and beads of blood fell to the ground. He looked up and saw Phoebe frozen in the spot where he had left her. Then she began to tremble.

"Are you okay?" Michael inquired.

Before he realised what was happening her glass of water was running down his face. He watched as Phoebe threw the glass to the ground, shattering it on the pebbles then storming back towards the house. Again peals of laughter reach his ears. Michael knelt slowly to the ground, his fingers searching the gravel for an appropriate tool. He whispered "in the name of Jesus Christ, Satan cease this tormenting of me."

Two misty forms became the solid shapes of black crows as each landed on Mara's front porch still chuckling with pleasure, their delight blinding them to Michael's activity. Suddenly, one stopped, fell to the ground, blood oozing from its body. The other looked over at Michael just as a second pebble catapulted through the air and was driven into the bird's skull.

Tears ran down Phoebe cheeks as she stood looking through her bedroom window. She was suddenly taken aback by the speed at which Michael had dispatched both birds and felt intimidated by the rage she had witnessed. Her legs felt weak. She sought the sanctuary of her bed, gnawing at the skin above the proximal phalanges bone on her index finger, her jaw shuddering with nervous energy. Her emotions were in turmoil as she reflected on her own actions and jealousies. She felt like a schoolgirl with a crush but was angry that a teenager could coax a man away from her. On the cusp of 30, Phoebe still felt young and was surprised to find she was becoming infatuated with Michael.

Deep down she knew her mother no longer needed her. Phoebe was not even sure if her mother knew who she was anymore and without the familiarity of their usual conversations, Phoebe felt lonely and, in a sense, lost. There was desperation to fill the aching sense of emptiness she felt inside.

"Silly nonsense, pull yourself together," she chided herself as she looked in the mirror. Bouncing up she dried her eyes and went over to the laundry basket and began to pull out the whites, determined to get on with the chore. But her aching heart remained. She coughed hoping it would shift the heaviness but no, there was no effect. She could feel the muscles across her shoulder tensing up and her back begin to hurt. She stood up and stretched. The sensations continued.

A noise drew her attention toward her bedroom door. The three knocks startled her and she felt her insides shudder.

"Dad, is that you?"

"Phoebe, can I come in?" Professor Garrett's voice was trembling.

"Yes," Phoebe replied, her voice suddenly very squeaky. She cleared her throat. "Is everything alright?"

The door opened. Garrett's face seemed greyer than usual. His hands were trembling and he seemed reluctant to let go of the door handle, almost as if he thought he would fall if he did.

"Dad, what's wrong?" Phoebe was growing impatient. The muscles knotted further in her shoulders and were becoming painful.

"I…I've…" he coughed, took in a deep breath then released a heavy sigh.

"What?" tears were welling up again in Phoebe's eyes, instinctively she knew all the pain she was suffering would not compare to the anguish and sorrow she sensed was about to follow.

"Your mother's dead!"

All the muscles in Phoebe's body suddenly gave way as she crumpled on the bedroom floor. Her shuddering breaths competed with her sobbing. Garrett looked helplessly at his daughter, not knowing how he should comfort her, not knowing how he should react. He felt as though he almost had no right to any emotions but actually felt so lost for not having had the courage to acknowledge

*The Fall*

that his wife was ill let alone existed. Yet somehow, he missed her more than he could ever imagine.

He left Phoebe to her own sorrow, closed her bedroom door, then made his way back downstairs to his study where the cordless phone still lay on the ground where he had dropped it in what seemed a century ago.

Several hours passed before Phoebe could get to the nursing home. As she passed through the doors to make her way up to where her mother's room had been, several nurses and assistants offered their condolences. When she reached the ward she had to steady herself before pushing through the double doors. Grace was standing at the nurse's station filling in some forms when she saw Phoebe.

Each step closer to Grace was torturous for Phoebe as she struggled to fight back her tears.

"Phoebe, I'm so sorry."

"What happened, Grace. Why did nobody phone me?"

"There was no time, Rachel just slipped away so quickly."

Grace led Phoebe into a small sitting room away from prying eyes. Phoebe fell against her and sobbed. Grace cradled her in her arms.

"Your mother's been released now. Her pain is gone," Grace spoke softly.

"But what am I going to do without her?"

"You have your own life to lead," replied Grace. "Your mother knew that."

Phoebe sat up and looked deep into Grace's eyes. "How do you know that? She hardly said a word that made any sense for nearly eight months."

"It was just little things," Grace smiled. "I would hold her hand and talk to her and on various nights depending on the subject, Rachel would squeeze my hand as though she was answering to things I was saying."

"What did you talk about?"

"Before her stroke, your mother always talked about how you had made so many sacrifices by staying at home to look after her."

"I thought it was the best thing to do," replied Phoebe. "Dad was so busy trying to bring in an income but mom had to be looked after."

"She was aware of the strain she had put on you and didn't want you to lose out," Grace told Phoebe. Phoebe thought for a few moments of all the times she had been frustrated with her mother for being ill but felt she had to be the dutiful daughter in taking care of her. Now her mother was gone, she was not sure how she would cope with her own life as an independent individual without ties.

"Can I see her?" she asked Grace.

Grace stood up and led Phoebe out into the ward, across the corridor to her mother's room. She was still lying in the bed but with a sheet across her face. "Is it okay to pull the sheet back?" Grace nodded. Apprehensively, Phoebe pulled the cover away from her mother's face, to be greeted by a woman with a gentle smile, at peace. Her eyes were closed.

"What happened?" asked Phoebe. "Did she go in her sleep?"

Again Grace nodded. Both women had tears in their eyes. Grace had been with Rachel for well over a year taking care of her needs when Phoebe was not around. It had been hard for Phoebe to let go of her duties. Her mother had not prepared her for any kind of life in the outside world and now she was gone, Phoebe realised she had to find her own way and discover who she really was.

"What do I need to do about a funeral?" she asked.

"We can find someone to help you with the preparations."

Phoebe held her mother's hand. It was cold to the touch, nothing like what she remembered even on her last visit. She wanted to hug her mother but knew that what remained was just a shell and the woman she knew was gone.

## CHAPTER NINETEEN

Heavy clouds drifted in front of the nearly full moon. Beneath them the darkness seemed impenetrable. Only a few street lamps fended off the oppressive nature of the night but even one of these flickered as the filament began to melt and the circuit was broken. The light outside Mara's home was extinguished.

Inside Mara stood in front of her wardrobe mirror checking to see how her new coat looked on her. She hummed a tune, slipped off the coat and sat down, taking a wire brush from the dressing table; she began to groom her hair.

Unknown to Mara other beings sat behind her, combing its fingers through her hair. Vanity whispered in Mara's ears, "imagine, imagine the movies and you're a beautiful actress."

Vanity's perfume began to seep into Mara's nostrils and the vapours intoxicated her mind. The images she saw were no longer the ones her eyes received but impressions etched in her mind.

A lavish movie set was being worked on as the set designers, carpenters, decorators and electricians independently applied their craft. In the rigging members of the lighting department adjusted a range of lights adding filters and trace to soften the glow. Fussing around Mara, were make up artists following Vanity's instructions. Vanity appeared as a striking brunette, of around 30 years of age in Earth time but her knowledge was that of someone who had seen several millenniums of history. Her complexion was pale and her eyes were a piercing blue capable of cutting right through to a human's soul.

A young woman accidentally snapped one of Mara's nails.

"Oh, I'm sorry, Miss Sanford," pleaded the girl.

Vanity scolded her. The girl cringed.

"Take her away, the silly bitch," screeched Vanity.

Mara nearly jumped but Vanity soothed her with more narcotic words as the young make up artist was dragged off the set screaming, "I didn't mean to, it was an accident, please."

"Surely, it's only a nail?" Mara dozily whispered.

"But you're to be perfect, in every way," murmured Vanity. "Don't trouble yourself with details. That's why you have all these assistants at your disposal. And if they do not reach such high standards?" Vanity snapped her fingers. "They're gone in an instance." She laughed as the director signaled for Mara to make her way onto the set.

Vanity screamed across the set. "She'll be ready when I tell you she's ready and not before. Don't you know who she is?"

The director shrugged his shoulders and apologised for disturbing them and retreated behind the camera.

"Darling," sighed Vanity in Mara's ear, "the director wishes the pleasure of your company on set. The camera is ready to roll."

Gracefully, Mara was helped to her feet. Her long gown flowing behind her as she appeared to float across the studio floor. A plush king size bed was the centre-piece of the set. All around, technicians waited for Mara to take her position, all eyes were on her. Mara climbed onto the bed and pretended to be asleep.

The assistant director barked across the set, "Quiet on set please. Going for a take. Run sound."

The sound recordist flicked the record button, on a compact flash card recorder. "Sound's running."

"Run camera," called the assistant director.

The camera operator pressed a button on the side of a large Sony high-definition digital movie camera, then waited a few seconds. "Camera's running."

"Clapperboard."

A young woman, with a digital clapperboard, called out a scene and take number, then slapped the two halves of the board together. The crack echoed around the set, all were poised.

The director called, "Action!"

*The Fall*

Smoke began to pour from the side of the set. Some double doors swung open and a young man stepped into the light. Mara sat up. It was Nimrod. She felt her heart pounding.

"And the winner is..." boomed a voice through the PA system. The large auditorium of guests in tuxedos and evening gowns waited with excitement as the actor on stage ripped open an envelope.

"Isn't this fabulous?" Vanity jigged up and down holding Mara's hand. Mara was still a little bewildered with the new surroundings. She squinted to try to see who was about to announce the winner's name.

"And the winner is, Mara Sanford!"

The audience erupted into applause and cheered. Mara was pulled to her feet, hands grabbing at her, lips kissing her, dead eyes in Botox masks transfixed in fake smiles with glistening teeth, filled her vision until a path was made clear for her to make her way to the stage. Her heart pounded, with a mixture of sheer panic and exaltation.

Ahead of her through the roaring crowd, stood Nimrod with his hand held out to her. She raced up towards him, eager to be with him again. As she climbed the steps her footing faltered and she began to fall but somehow, and Mara was unable to fathom it, Nimrod caught her in his arms. She looked up absorbed in his deep brown eyes. Her heart drumming hard, her lips parted expectantly as Nimrod's breast glanced hers, she felt his heart pumping. Her eyes closed and...

"When are his lips going to meet mine?" she thought. She dared not open her eyes but sensed no others. No-one. She felt an emptiness, a coldness of heart. There was no sound but a chill rippled along the skin of her arms, across her breasts, neck and ruffled her hair. Opening her eyes Mara saw a moonlit ceiling. Her fingers detected the silky fabric of sheets. Raising herself on her elbows, she realised there was no audience, no ceremony; she was in a darkened room only visible from the light reflected from the moon. Goosebumps covered her arms and body, which she now discovered were bare. Everything in the room was tinged in blue but Mara guessed in daylight everything in the room would be white.

*George John Kingsnorth*

A large set of French-windows allowed the luna illumination its presence. The chill Mara felt, was from the open French-doors. Wrapping a sheet around her body she tentatively stepped across the room to latch the doors. As she reached up to the catch, a man's hand grasped her arm.

She went to scream but his other hand covered her lips. Mara smelt the scent of the man she had been waiting to kiss earlier. She grabbed his dark coat and pulled him from the shadows into the moonlight to see the contours of his face. He smiled. The tension in her wrist went, as the sheet slipped to the carpet. Finally, their lips drew closer. A small blue click of static jumped from Nimrod's lower lip to hers but the sting only encouraged Mara on to make contact. She felt his hands glance across her back down towards her buttocks as she explored his mouth with her tongue. She hungered for him to fill her and in a frenzy began to rip away his clothing, following the directions of the words in her mind.

"Reach down and grab him," smiled Vanity. "Force him inside you."

Mara again was oblivious to her surroundings. Her new coats scattered on her bedroom floor, in front of the mirrored wardrobe, which reflected her posture as she squirmed and writhed around on her back. Scratching her thighs and body but completely unconscious of the fact no-one was there. No human, no man, no Nimrod, only her Vanity, a spectre squeezing Mara of her lustful nature, her longing to be full, her longing to be wanted, her longing to be complete.

## CHAPTER TWENTY

The full moon bathed the interior of the belfry with blue embers, occasionally succumbed to the rush of fiery rays that emanated from the voices of the congregation in prayer below. Raphael, Grace and most of the other angelic presence soaked up the energy but Nimrod found himself detached, snared in the moonlight. Mara's voice echoed in his mind, "Nimrod, Nimrod, come to me!"

"Something troubling you, Nimrod?" enquired Raphael. The heavy Irish-Jamaican stepped away from his brethren with concern for Nimrod.

"No... no I'm ... it's alright, I'm okay!" stuttered Nimrod.

"Sure?"

"Absolutely," confirmed Nimrod.

Raphael placed his sturdy hand on Nimrod's shoulder. "These are times of torment and danger. We have to be on guard. Focus on the here and now, Nimrod! Guard yourself and listen to the word."

Nimrod nodded but it took all his strength to concentrate on the Mass being conducted in the church. He still had not stepped into the rays of prayer but listened to the words spoken by the priest.

"One day he got into a boat with his disciples, and he said to them, 'Let us go across to the other side of the lake.' So they set out, and as they sailed he fell asleep. And a storm of wind came down on the lake, and they were filling with water, and were in danger. And they went and woke him, saying, 'Master, Master, we are perishing!' And he awoke and rebuked the wind and the raging waves; and they ceased, and there was calm. He said to them, 'Where is your faith?' And they were afraid, and they marveled, saying to one another, 'Who then is this, that he commands even wind and water, and they obey him?'"

*George John Kingsnorth*

Nimrod looked across the city at the lights and the night traffic. "Where is your faith, Nimrod? You know who he is, yet the world distracts you," cautioned Raphael.

"I'm okay!"

The priest continued to read the Gospel. "And as he stepped out on land, there met him a man from the city who had demons; for a long time he had worn no clothes, and he lived not in a house but among the tombs. When he saw Jesus, he cried out and fell down before him, and said with a loud voice, 'What have you to do with me, Jesus, Son of the Most High God? I beseech you, do not torment me.'"

In Nimrod's head he heard Mara's voice block out any other words from the priest. "Nimrod, come to me! I beg you!"

Nimrod closed his eyes to picture Mara but his thoughts were suddenly interrupted. "Our Lord saw Satan fall with a third of heaven to the earth for their sin," began Raphael. His words like a sword cutting through all else in Nimrod's mind. "Focus, Nimrod! Don't be tempted. There is no return if that path is taken."

"I'm okay," Nimrod replied with a warbled voice.

Raphael became sterner "For those who have known the Lord and still turned away there is no coming back. Even the Legion knew that!"

"And they begged him not to command them to depart into the Abyss," continued the Priest. As a tear rolled down Raphael's cheek Nimrod turned his face and was gone.

Mara seemed peaceful in her slumber, lying on her back with the sheets half covering one of her legs and her arms sprawled across the width of the bed as though crucified. Nimrod gazed upon her as the moonlight reflected her beauty but as a cloud began to pass across the full moon dark shadows fell into the room. Mara became restless and curled up into the fetus position. Her lips released a low moan and under closed lids her eyes darted from side to side. Suddenly, as the entire moon disappeared, Mara arched backwards as though stabbed in the back. She screamed. Nimrod was startled. Mara jerked into a sitting position, rapidly scanned the room and then leapt across

*The Fall*

to within inches of where he was beside the open curtains. Nimrod could not tell if she was aware of his presence.

Through the glass two black strands of vapour filtered into Mara's room like smog, each drew out their form into dark, misshaped figures, tormented by their transgressions. In her fearfulness, Mara grabbed Nimrod's hand and squeezed hard. The sensual contact sent sparks of pain through Nimrod's nerves as he realised his being was no longer spiritual but physical. He had no more time to consider the transformation as the two demons were tracking Mara and had finally located her beside him. Nimrod whispered into Mara's ear. "Do not be afraid." She smiled.

Nimrod released her hand, unsheathed his sword, decapitated the first spectre and thrust his weapon deep into the black heart of the second demon. Each dark spirit exploded into a million shards of dust.

As Mara watched on, an inky shape moved across the whites of her eyes as she smiled. Her countenance changed to fear as she raced over to Nimrod and wrapped her arms around him. "I knew you would save me, I did."

"You can see me?" puzzled Nimrod.

"Yes!"

Mara cupped her hands around his chin, drew him to her lips and kissed him with a passion that left him breathless. Nimrod pushed her away, weak with the intoxication of her fervour. He stumbled to regain his composure.

"We're not supposed to be seen by humans, we will to be unseen," Nimrod snapped at her.

"Deep inside you must have willed to be visible to me," replied Mara yearning to embrace him again. Nimrod drew further into the room, falling over the bed. As Mara launched herself upon him once more, he dematerialised, leaving her to fall on her bedclothes. Mara grabbed the sheets in each fist and pulled them in tight to her breasts, her face contorted with emotional pain.

"Why so sorrowful?" came a voice from the curtains.

Mara spun round to see Nimrod was still in the room.

"I thought you had gone?"

"I tried to but found myself here again," Nimrod explained. "I don't understand why?"

"Since we met, I've not been able to get you out of my mind," sobbed Mara. "You're in my dreams every night and my heart seems so heavy with yearning to be with you. There is something chasing me all the time and I feel you are the only one who can save me from this darkness."

"Why did you jump out of bed?" asked Nimrod wondering if she had seen the two demons in her room.

"I felt something dark and dangerous but I didn't know what it was," Mara tried to explain. "It doesn't make sense but when I found you in my room, I felt safe as though you were here to protect me not harm me. I should probably ring the police to tell them you're stalking me but I feel safe with you here know. The evilness has gone. Why is that?"

Nimrod sat on the bed. Mara put her hand on his as she slid beside him on the edge of the bed. Nimrod looked into her blue eyes, they seemed bright, the whites were clear of any protruding blood vessels, the usual with someone fatigued. "Do you believe there is a war going on and your soul is the prize?" he asked.

Mara gave a gentle laugh of disbelief. "Are you crazy?"

"No, I wish I was but there is."

"So what are you then, my guardian angel?" Mara mocked.

"Yes!"

Mara sat back slightly away from Nimrod. "You're serious, aren't you?"

"Yes."

She looked around the room almost in a daze then turned back to Nimrod and cuddled in tight, hugging his chest. Nimrod stretched his arm over her shoulder and gave her a reassuring squeeze.

*The Fall*

## CHAPTER TWENTY-ONE

The following morning the rain was constant. Michael knew it would not be possible to do any work but he needed to pick up his wages as bills were due to come out of his bank account the following week. So far he had managed to pick up a bit of work from other clients but the bulk of his income was earned from his time at Professor Garrett's garden. Jumping out of the van, he ran to the front door, rang the bell and waited. Across the way, crows sat on the peak of the roof, occasionally ruffling their wings to remove excess rainwater.

The opening of the door drew Michael's attention away from the birds and back to the Garrett's house. Phoebe stood in the doorway; her head hung low, not making eye contact.

"Hello, Phoebe, is your father in?"

"In his study."

As Michael shook rain droplets from his coat and wiped his shoes, Phoebe disappeared along the hallway into the kitchen and closed the door behind her. Michael, surprised to see she had gone, closed the door and hung his coat on the stand. The hallway was dark and the dampness outside added to the oppressive atmosphere Michael sensed in the house. The thought crossed his mind that it was a bad day to approach Professor Garrett for his wages but he had no choice, bills are bills and they have to be paid. Michael could not afford to go into overdraft so had to persist.

He slipped off his soggy shoes, pleased that he had remembered to find a pair of socks with no holes in them. They were odd but it was dark enough, he hoped, that no one would notice that one was black and the other navy.

Michael knocked on the Professor's study door. No reply. He

knocked again, then opened the door quietly to look inside. The books smelt musky. The room could easily be set in an old Victorian house. Professor Garrett sat in front of the fireplace in a soft chair. There was no fire and the room was chilly. On the professor's lap rested a collection of books. Michael could see gaps on the shelves from where he assumed they had been extracted.

Initially, Michael thought the professor was asleep but then as the older man flicked over a page, he realised he was reading.

"Hello, Professor," Michael began. "Sorry to trouble you but you said you'd pay me today."

Garrett looked up and stared out the window. Michael began to feel awkward as he thought he had not been heard.

"Professor?"

"Did you know, Michael," Garrett muttered, "after the two stories of the Creation and the Genealogy of Adam down to Noah there comes another fall?"

Michael smirked "no I didn't. A least I don't remember." Michael noticed the professor's books were the Torah, The Book of Enoch, another one from the Apocryphal books and The Book of Genesis. "Is that the subject you teach at the university?"

"On Mount Hermon nearly 200 angels made a pact to go against God", the Professor continued.

"Professor, its Michael. I'm here to pick up my pay."

"Don't you understand there is something wrong. Some great mischief is at play."

"Professor Garrett," Michael laughed, "I'm here because you said you could pay me today and I need to get some money into the bank."

Professor Garrett got up from his chair and went over to the window that overlooked the Sandford's house. Through the raindrops streaming down the glass he could see the half dozen crows huddled together on the roof trying to gain shelter from the rain and wind.

"The 200 angels lusted after the women on Earth, taught them secrets and fornicated with them," continued Garrett.

*The Fall*

Michael was confused by what the professor meant, then realised he was looking at Mara's house.

"Hey, professor," Michael stumbled to find some words. "I think you've got it wrong about me and the girl next door?"

"What?" Professor Garrett turned to look at Michael.

"Nothing," replied Michael, as he quickly thought of a way to get out of whatever it was he was getting into. All he wanted was his money. "I thought angels didn't have the right tackle to do that?"

"That's a more recent supposition." The professor stared out the window again at the crows. "Part of the conspiracy to disprove the Devil's existence."

"Oh, come on, Professor," argued Michael, "that's a bit far fetched. Nobody would take me seriously if I thought like that." Michael looked nervously out of the window to see the crows on the neighbour's roof. An image flashed into his mind of his wedding day 20 years early. Several crows landed on the telephone wires outside the graveyard of the church just as Melissa stepped out of the limousine. He blocked the memory, the pain of this vision was too much for Michael to take.

"I'm just here for my pay, professor. That's all."

"Oh, I'm sorry." The professor fumbled in his jacket pocket and pulled out his wallet. "It's been a hard few days, with Mrs. Garrett dying. You know."

Michael was stunned. "I'm sorry, what happened?"

"She passed away in the hospital." Garrett slumped down into his soft chair once more, wallet in hand. "I didn't realise how much I had missed her. I've been lost in my studies."

"I'm sorry, Professor Garrett," apologized Michael feeling awkward and insensitive. "Look, I probably shouldn't have called round."

"No, no, I'm the one who should be sorry, I've been blinded by my own problems." He opened his wallet and pulled out a bundle of 20 pound notes. "How much do I owe?"

"Look, don't worry about it. Another time," insisted Michael. "I can call back."

*George John Kingsnorth*

Outside several more crows joined the rest on the roof, catching Professor Garrett's attention once more. He grabbed Michael's sleeve. "Michael." The professor's eyes were wide, he seemed alarmed making Michael a little nervous.

"Are you okay, Professor?"

"There's something about those birds," Garrett pointed towards the Sandford's roof. "There seems to be more and more gathering each day. You'll think I'm mad but there is something unnatural about them."

"They're just birds," encouraged Michael. "I used to be scared of them too, but I was given treatment. They're just birds."

"Just be careful outside. I sense something uneasy about them."

"It's okay." Again Michael found himself trying to console the professor. Michael assumed the death of his wife had taken its toll on Garrett. Perhaps it had pushed him over the edge, psychologically.

In the garden, a crow landed on the handle of a spade Michael had left behind. With the rain he realised the metal blade would rust.

"Is dad okay?"

Michael spun round to sound of Phoebe's voice from the open door.

"He seems a little upset," Michael replied. "I'm sorry to hear about your mother."

"Thanks," answered Phoebe. "It's been quite a shock."

"Look, I'll leave now," said Michael apologetically.

"Thanks," smiled Phoebe.

Michael left the study and put on his shoes in the hallway.

Phoebe put an affectionate hand on her father's shoulder. He looked up at her with tears in his eyes.

"I'm sorry, love," he wept. "I didn't mean to burden you so."

"Water under the bridge, dad. Water under the bridge." Phoebe felt numb inside. She wanted to scream at her father but did not think that would do much except upset him further and he was already broken. She had heard him cursing the crows the night before and calling them demons. Now all she could do was attempt to remain calm and get through the days running up to her mother's funeral.

*The Fall*

Outside, Michael raced over to the spade and flapped at the crow to scare it off. As he opened the back doors of his van, the crow bounced onto his head and began stabbing him with its beak. Two more crows swooped down and joined in the assault.

Phoebe patted her father's shoulder. "Tea?"

"That would be good."

Phoebe moved to go out of the room but noticed a fluttering of feathers above the opened doors of Michael's van. She raced to the window and saw Michael shielding his face from the pecking birds. Phoebe swung open the window and screamed Michael's name.

Briefly, the crows were distracted, giving Michael the opportunity to smash the spade into one of them. The other two pulled back. Michael tugged a catapult from his toolbox, grabbed a pebble and fired a shot into the air, puncturing a second bird through the chest and sending its carcass plummeting to the ground.

Phoebe raced out of the front door armed with a broom. The third crow spied the oncoming threat and retreated to the rooftop with its remaining companions. Michael rummaged around the gravel to locate the bodies of the two birds he had just killed. To his surprise, there was no sign of them, they had completely vanished.

"Michael, are you okay?" Phoebe panted trying to catch her breath. The rain had soaked through her clothes and frizzed her hair.

"I'm okay, its alright," Michael smiled. Phoebe lunged forward and wrapped her arms around his neck. "God, I was so worried you were hurt," she exclaimed and began to kiss him.

From the window, Professor Garrett scanned the ground for the birds, then looked up at those gathered on the nearby roof. "I know what you are."

## CHAPTER TWENTY-TWO

The city was full of late night shoppers harassed by children searching for the next big things to be promoted by the big electronic or games corporations. Stocks were limited and no-one wanted to disappoint their offspring. For Mara it was a good time to use the local gymnasium and swimming pool to keep herself toned.

Inside the gym, Mara was wearing a tight crop-top vest, which not only revealed her abdomen, but helped keep her cool. A pair of three-quarter length jersey pants and a pair of training shoes, all colour coordinated with the same branded label, completed the outfit. Her hair was tied up in a ponytail.

As she worked through some training exercises she listened to music via a MP3 player. There were no other patrons in the building, as far as Mara could tell the only other person was the female attendant at the front desk two floors below. In the middle of her routine, Mara suddenly stopped and pulled out her earphones. Initially she was pensive, then a sense of calm flowed through her body and she smiled.

"Hello, Nimrod! I'm glad you're here."

Feeling relaxed once more she continued her routine but with deliberately provocative movements.

"Are you always with me, Nimrod?"

A voice came out of nowhere. "Most of the time."

Then Mara noticed a glass like form glide across the floor. Nimrod, whether by choice or not, was faintly materializing.

"Oh," replied Mara. "I see. Perhaps if you are not here all the time, you should train me so I can protect myself?"

"In what way," enquired Nimrod.

Mara smiled, "I always wanted to learn a martial art, perhaps you

*The Fall*

could teach me?"

"Why do you think I can teach you such an art?" puzzled Nimrod.

"Surely, you know everything?" Mara teased. "Don't you?"

Mara continued to dance but by now she was tracing out the area where she sensed Nimrod to be.

"Show me?" Mara insisted.

"I'm not sure that's the right thing to do!" warned Nimrod.

"Please, for my sake!" pleaded Mara. "Against my demons when you're not here."

She kissed the area she perceived his lips would be. A spark of static nipped her lower lip as Nimrod found himself fully materialized. Mara buried her head into his chest and hugged him.

"It'll take some time," Nimrod cautioned.

"I don't care," smiled Mara. "It can take all the time in the world if it keeps you with me."

For about an hour and a half Nimrod showed Mara various defensive moves and the two of them laughed and joked. Both seemed comfortable with each other's company. Their activities were only interrupted by a public announcement that the sports centre would be closing at around nine o'clock, giving them another 30 minutes to leave.

Mara skipped off to the women's changing rooms, leaving Nimrod in the gym. She peeled off all her clothes and placed them in her rucksack after taking out a bath towel and shampoo. One fluorescent lamp flickered while another gave out a continuous buzz. In the shower area, Mara pushed in the wall button and a jet of warm water gushed out. After about a minute the jet died as the button had automatically protruded to its off position again. Mara had only managed to lather up her hair with the shampoo before the water had stopped. She pushed the button flush with the wall again and leant on it with her back against the wall.

Some foam had seeped into her eyes and the sodium laureth sulfate began to sting. In a state of panic, Mara fumbled to find the shower button to start the jet up and rinse out her eye. As she finally got to the point where she could open her eyes again, she could see

Nimrod standing in the changing area watching. He turned away embarrassed.

Mara smiled. "It's okay! I don't mind you looking. Don't be shy."

Nimrod stood with his back to her. "It's not right, I shouldn't".

"But if I'm in grave danger, shouldn't you be really close to me? Even now?" The shower jet stopped, leaving droplets of water running trails down her goose-pimpled body, to form small puddles on the tiled floor.

"No other man has seen me this way before. You're the first," she lied. It was just that no other man had had the opportunity to touch her and she so much wanted Nimrod too.

"But I'm not a man!" replied Nimrod.

"You look like one to me."

Mara coyly walked up beside him, rubbing her skin against his coat, knocking off pearls of water. Gently she turned towards him and raised herself on her toes to kiss him but before their lips could touch, the cream brickwork of the shower walls exploded knocking them both to the ground. Three demons materialized and entered the changing rooms. Two went for Nimrod while the third grappled with Mara. She managed to escape and raced to the other end of the cubicles. The demon gave chase but slipped on the wet floor, crashing through wood and metal compartments.

Nimrod threw the other two demons off him and scrambled to his feet. Swiftly he unsheathed his sword, previously hidden under his long coat, and swiped it through one demon cutting it in two. Moments later the creature erupted into a gaseous spray of sulphur. The second demon raced into the shower, accidentally pushing the button. A jet of water drenched it blurring its vision. Nimrod plunged his sword through its heart. The gaseous spray merged with the water from the shower and was flushed away down the drain.

With no time to spare, Nimrod twisted and turned searching for Mara and the third demon. Down the corridor he heard her screams and sprinted away after her.

Mara burst through a door into an empty pool area. She raced down the side of the pool, slipped, lost her balance and plunged into

*The Fall*

the deep end. The snarling beast pursuing her took to the air and pounced on top of her, using its talons to hold her below the water, while it remained in mid air. Frantically, Mara splashed at the surface with her hands, unable to get her head above water. A golden ray bounced off the far wall distracting the demon. Following the beam, it discovered the origin was a metal blade protruding from it's own stomach. The light grew with intensity and the creature roared with pain until it burst into a million black particles. Almost instantly, Mara broke the surface of the water gasping for air. Nimrod pulled her up out of the pool, lifting them both on his own wings, touching down by the edge of the pool. Nimrod wrapped his wings around Mara. The heat from his wings vapourised the moisture on Mara's skin. She snuggled into his chest, feeling the security of his arms.

"Don't leave me, Nimrod," Mara pleaded. "I need you here always. I can't protect myself against those monsters."

Nimrod escorted Mara back to the changing rooms where they found a female attendant surveying the damage to the changing rooms. "Are you hurt, miss?" asked the stunned attendant. "You must have been blown right through to the swimming pool? Is anything broken?"

Mara realised that although she could see Nimrod, the attendant could not. "I just need to get my things and go home."

"Are you sure you don't want me to call an ambulance?" The attendant checked Mara out for any broken bones. All her injuries were a few bruises.

"I'll be okay," protested Mara "but I could have been killed by that gas leak in here."

The attendant looked worried, she was beginning to panic about insurance claims and losing her job. "I'm so sorry about what has happened. I'll get the manager to call you in the morning."

Mara began to sob. "I just want my clothes and to go home." She grabbed her things, quickly pulled on some pants and trousers over her legs and pulled on her jumper and coat, leaving everything else in her rucksack. As she went to leave the attendant called out to her. "You should probably wait until the police get here to take a statement?"

"I'll have my parents' solicitors contact you tomorrow with my details," Mara shouted back in a hurry to escape the nightmare she had just witnessed.

Outside the building, Nimrod was visible to her again. He wrapped his coat around her as she sobbed in his arms and he dematerialised both of them, transporting them back to Mara's house.

## CHAPTER TWENTY-THREE

The first frost glazed the surface of the road. Several cars also had a coating of ice across their roofs. In the headlights of Michael's van the glittering array of reflections looked like a sea of sparkling diamonds. Michael had wrapped up in three layers of clothing to keep the cold out but still felt the chill. His van was about ten years old and the heater was not always reliable. Tonight was one of those nights when the heater had gone on strike.

Though the radio cautioned drivers about the hazardous roads, Michael was intent on driving to Professor Garrett's to get his wage. He knew that if he was fruitless this time, the oil bill would not get paid and the end of November would be too chilly at home.

The pebbles crunched under the pressure of the van's tyres, snapping the ice that bound them together as Michael entered the Garrett's drive way. He was a little nervous, he always hated having to put pressure on his customers to pay up but he had to do it otherwise he would be further out of pocket. Besides, he was not gardening for the fun of it, he had to make a living.

Michael pulled up outside the front door and switched off the engine. As he opened the car door the cool air bit into his cheeks. He played through his mind what he was going to say and prayed that the professor would be obliging. Michael stepped up to the front door and prepared to knock. From the corner of his eye he detected movement and instinctively turned his head towards the Sandford's property. There was a flurry of black wings as the crows scattered from the front porch to high viewpoints on the roof.

Michael stepped back curious of the sudden activity. Then before his eyes Mara and Nimrod materialized out of thin air. Michael also noticed that the crows momentarily stepped back from the rays of the streetlights into the darkness of the shadows, unwilling to be seen.

In his mind, Michael was flooded with images from the past, his wedding day and the crows leaping off the Lych-gate to hassle the driver of the limousine. The image of some demon draining him of energy and his bride, Melissa being raped by…

By what? There was light and a being. There was darkness and other creatures. There had been crows. 'Oh my God,' thought Michael, 'the crows were part of it.' He felt a jolt to his heart as all his emotions burst inside him. He had blocked out the memories for so long, yet here, where he now worked, the same thing was happening again. Only this time Mara was the victim, Michael realised.

Through the windows of the Garrett's porch, Michael was unaware that all his expressions had been noted. Phoebe stood at the door waiting for the doorbell to ring when the headlights had arched round into the driveway five minutes or so previously. When she had seen the figure moving towards the door she had instantly gone to open the door but had seen Michael standing there. She was reluctant to answer having decided to wait and see if Michael would go away but before he had reached for the bell, he had been distracted by some activity to the left of the house.

Phoebe's curiosity was getting the better of her but she was also interested to find out why Michael had reacted the way he had. She could see his pain and wanted to run to him and mother him. Her instincts were so strong but she still felt embarrassed about kissing him the last time they were together. She was niggled with fear that perhaps Michael would not be interested in her, perhaps she had only made a fool of herself. These worries were now stopping her from opening the door but something deep inside was reassuring her, telling her to fight her fears. There was also a sense of danger.

Through the window, Phoebe could see Michael was about to move away. Quickly she undid the latch and swung the door open, startling Michael.

"Hello," Phoebe greeted him, "I was wondering if you were ever going to ring the bell?"

*The Fall*

"Oh, I'm sorry," Michael stuttered. "I was distracted."

Phoebe came out onto the drive to see what Michael had been looking at but found only the Sandford's empty garden and a few pesky crows on the roof.

"I see those birds are still there," remarked Phoebe. "Were you concerned they might attack again?"

"No." Michael was uncertain how to explain the inner turmoil he had just experienced. He did not know how Phoebe would react. He was now concerned that Mara's life was threatened and that the birds were somehow involved. Phoebe moved towards the fence away from the cone of light from the porch. Above her the crows were becoming restless.

"Phoebe, look, I should come away from there if I were you," cautioned Michael. "I wouldn't want a repeat of before."

On hearing the birds becoming livelier, Phoebe decided to retreat to the safety of her own home.

"What do you think is wrong with those birds?" she asked.

"There's something evil about them. I've seen it before," Michael confessed.

Phoebe turned back to Michael intrigued. "When?"

"It was a long time ago, I'd rather not say."

"Why not?" Phoebe pushed. "You surely can't spike my interest and leave me wondering?"

"It was hard then, I'm not sure if I can face it again," insisted Michael.

The crows squawked and began to flap their wings aggressively. "We had better get inside," insisted Michael. The two of then stepped into the house away from any harm. The crows were eager to make an assault but were hesitant and Michael was aware of this. What was holding them back he wondered but instinct told him to get Phoebe somewhere safe. As he closed the door behind him a figure stepped out of the shadows. The crows staggered back into the darkness and cackled, "They know, they know." The birds were scared.

"Stand firm, cowards!" bellowed a grating voice from the depths of the blackest shadow. "She can do no harm, she is not here for

121

Mara but has another care to protect. That battle will be soon but not now, so stand your ground and do not be intimidated."

The crows squawked louder being encouraged by the hidden creature there to support them in minding their ward.

Grace stood in the light not flinching and the birds knew she could not be budged. But if her task was to defend Mara's neighbour then she posed no threat to the schemes that were being played out in the Sandford's household that night.

As Grace watched, the black winged beasts multiplied on the Sandford's roof. An army of squawking crows threw a shield over the house blocking out all external influences. Instinctively Grace wanted to rush in and cut a path to Nimrod but a firm hand clasped her shoulder.

"No, Grace," whispered Raphael. "Nimrod has made his choice and there is no going back. To pursue any course of action other than the task set for you, would put you in peril too."

*The Fall*

# CHAPTER TWENTY- FOUR

Droplets of water splashed against the tiled walls, racing down towards the shower tray base. Curled up in the corner was Mara, her make-up streaming across her face like inky lines, dropping to her shoulder, down her arm, onto her thighs before being chased by the spray, into the drain. Her mind was confused by images of demons crashing through walls and exploding into a cascade of particles. Across her shoulders her muscles were screwed taut. A pain stabbed at her heart. Cramp wretched at her limbs and her head throbbed with a migraine. Vanity dug her long nails into Mara's ribs, dragging her to her feet. Shampoo oozed from its container and was scratched roughly into her hair. Her favourite body lotion lathered up and then scrubbed into her skin the length and breadth of her body, stinging her like poison until all the pain and agony forced Mara to surrender and hide within the depths of her mind, relinquishing control of her body, she fell once more into the tray base of the shower in a catatonic state, her eyes staring into space. Vanity laughed, pleased with her work. There was a knock at the door.

"Mara, are you okay," inquired Nimrod.

Vanity knelt down close to Mara's motionless body, placed her hand on Mara's head and turned towards the voice.

"I'm okay," spoke Vanity with Mara's voice. "I'm just finishing off in the shower and dropped the soap. Give me a few more moments."

Vanity could hear Nimrod walk back across the hall to Mara's bedroom. She knew the house was secure and her sentries would keep out all physical and spiritual invasions. She was in control and the prize was near at hand. Vanity began to turn into a mist starting with the tips of her fingers and gradually progressing up her limbs to her body. The blue vapour seeped through Mara's nostrils, into her ears and through her mouth. Mara's heartbeat began to flutter and for a brief moment there seemed to be two competing beats and Mara's limbs jolted as though given an electric shock. The shower door was kicked open and a leg fell onto the linoleum floor cover. Mara's eyes blinked, her head twitched and her right arm flipped itself out from under her torso. There was awkwardness to her movements as Vanity attempted to co-ordinate this fleshy lump that was now her host. It took a few more moments to align the shape and form with how she perceived her own shape. Vanity coaxed Mara's body toward the full-length mirror and observed how the creature worked when sent various messages through the brain to each limb.

To aid her she called two other demons, the ones who had been Mara's minders for most of her life. Under their consultation, Vanity was able to master Mara's precise movements within seconds.

"Is Mara still there?" enquired one demon.

"Of course," snapped Vanity. "If she wasn't there would be no way to control her body. She's no good to us dead. Her spirit and soul still need to be connected to her body for her to conceive."

"That's good," pondered the demon. "I kinda liked her."

Vanity spun round and her stare melted into the demon's skull. The second demon began to panic as it watched its partner disintegrate.

"So do you think we can convince Nimrod I'm Mara, body and soul?"

The demon frantically nodded at Vanity's comment.

"Good," she smiled. "It's time."

Each of Mara's skin paws began to excrete a vanilla smelling pheromone, which lingered about eight inches away from her body. No other perfumes were added by Vanity. She opened the shower-room door and stepped into the hallway completely naked. Her hair remained wet and stuck to the skin on her back. A thin trail of moisture ran down her spine as she strolled towards Mara's room.

Nimrod sat in a small soft chair beside Mara's computer scanning through various browser pages. As Vanity entered Mara's bedroom,

*The Fall*

he was stunned to see her without any clothes. Before he was able to say a word, Vanity knelt in front of him. The pheromones were drawn into his nostrils and began to intoxicate him.

Gently, Vanity unbuttoned Nimrod's shirt.

"Are you nervous?" came the words formed by Mara's lips.

Nimrod felt a wave of fatigue wash through him. He was unable to focus, unable to shake off his physical form. Spiritually, he had been locked into a body like an ordinary human and the corporeal world imprisoned him. There was no escape.

Mara's fingers slipped beneath the buckle of Nimrod's belt but as her wrist became restricted she pulled loose the leather strap, unfastened the trouser button and pulled down the zip. Her hand was given more freedom to reach down between his legs. Internally, blood flushed into the region and Nimrod was surprised by his physical reaction yet he was not given time to collect his senses before Mara's tongue separated his lips and began to play with his own tongue.

The bodily sensations exploded throughout Nimrod as his eyes closed and he found his own hands exploring Mara's body. His fingertips felt on fire with darts of electricity shooting through them down his arms. As he stood, his muscles flexed lifting Mara and he threw her onto the bed. Mara, lay on her back, watching with excitement as Nimrod removed his boots, socks and jeans. His jacket and shirt fell to the ground. Vanity used Mara's eyes to soak up the vision, as Nimrod took each step towards her. She leant forward and glided her fingers across his protrusion, sending a shudder of ecstasy throughout Nimrod's every nerve. His mighty hands clasped Mara's shoulders pushing her deeper into the mattress. With his knees, he forced apart her legs. Mara interlocked her fingers around his neck, pulled Nimrod's head towards her own so their lips could engage but her actions were postponed with the sensation of him thrusting himself deep inside her. Mara's fingernails dug furrows into his shoulders as she gritted her teeth. So overcome by the alien sensations he was experiencing, Nimrod was unable to control himself from exploding within Mara.

Instantly Nimrod's seed penetrated one of Mara's fertile eggs, unholy life erupted within her womb sending a visible shockwave rippling through her body with such force that the framework of the bed shattered. Nimrod was propelled across the room slamming into a wall and Vanity was expelled from Mara's body.

Outside, all the crows took flight as a shaft of lightning shattered a chimney sending a cascade of bricks and ceramic across the garden below. A skull-crunching clap of thunder punched out windows in every neighbouring house. The clock in Michael's van exploded at 11.15 p.m. Various car alarms sounded and lights sprung on as sleep was wrenched away and curiosity ruled the night.

A burning sensation emanated from Nimrod's crotch. Stabbing pains shot into his limbs. His stomach felt knotted. His lungs laboured to suck air as his chest became increasingly tight. Patches of pain skittered across his temples and ran down the back of his neck. Any attempt to raise himself failed.

Across on the bed he could see Mara was motionless. Her naked body lay amongst the ruin of the bed, her limbs hung over the edges of the timber frame. There came a murmur and her head rolled from one side to the other. A hand moved up to her forehead and brushed away loose hair that had fallen across her eyes.

After a moment, Nimrod could see Mara rise onto her elbows and look around the room surveying the damage. Her eyes then fixed on Nimrod. Briefly she jolted backwards with revulsion before leaning over the edge of the bed to throw up.

Nimrod's chest grew tighter and he found his breathing laboured. He no longer had the energy to lift any limb off the ground and even moving his head was too painful but he needed to see what had caused Mara's reaction. As he rolled his eyes downwards he could see his legs were a festering green with dark blue patches. Green gunge had begun to seep out of tears in his skin. His toes showed bone where the skin had peeled off in flakes as the flesh had rotted away. His chest began to sag inwards as he snatched in breaths every second. Breaths that became ever increasingly shallow. He could hear his heart beat briefly match that of a ticking watch on Mara's

*The Fall*

dressing table but as every moment passed each heart beat slowly coincided with two ticks, then three then...

Nimrod's heart stopped and the last vapours of air seeped back in to the room as his life was extinguished. His pupils dilated. The oozing gunge foamed up briefly but with the heart stopped no more came out, the moisture rapidly evaporated leaving a crusty residue.

## CHAPTER TWENTY-FIVE

The kettle boiled, popping the switch. Phoebe lifted it from its cradle and poured water into the two coffee mugs. At the table she could see Michael looked unsettled. His head hung low. Then he would shift his position in the seat and look across to the window at the Sandford's house.

Phoebe placed a mug of coffee in front of Michael and sat down opposite him. The clock on the wall read eleven-o-five.

"What brings you round here so late?" enquired Phoebe as she sipped her coffee.

"Huh." Michael seemed to be surprised that someone else was in the room, sparking some annoyance in Phoebe. Perhaps he wasn't here to see her after all?

"Your dad owes me some pay and I needed to get some bills paid."

"Oh!"

Michael's mind was preoccupied with the events he imagined were unfolding next door but his thoughts drifted back as he noticed the look of hurt on Phoebe's face. Her hair was tied up in a ponytail, with the odd strand falling down beside her ears. Without makeup, Phoebe still had a fresh complexion. She wore cotton flower printed pyjamas and a pink toweling dressing gown.

"Were you going to bed?"

Phoebe's looked towards him and her eyes brightened. She smiled, "no, I was going to settle into a DVD up in my room."

"What kind of films do you like?"

Phoebe blushed. "Oh, you know, the girly ones, *Pride and Prejudice*, *Emma*... I've been collecting the BBC Classic Drama set. So far 20 discs. There's about 40 or so."

"Do you prefer the DVDs to the books?"

*The Fall*

"I like both. I've started listening to the director's commentary. You know, where they explain about why they chose certain shots and how they interpret certain parts of the book. I like jumping in and out of the books and then watching the films to see if they have done what I imagined the scenes to be. What do you like?"

"Oh, I dunno. I like a lot of things. When I was younger I loved the late films on BBC 2. Things like One *Flew Over the Cuckoos Nest*, *Electro Glide in Blue*, *Deliverance* but I also liked Russian films by Tarkovsky. My favourite was *Mirror*. I don't really like modern stuff. It all seems to glitzy, not much story, you know?"

Phoebe tucked her feet up onto her chair and rested her chin on her knees. Her whole face was lit up with a smile.

"Surely you like something more recent?"

"Well, I suppose, stuff like *Eternal Sunshine of the Spotless Mind*. I liked the way they could erase memories."

"Yeah, but wasn't the whole idea wrong, that you shouldn't play around with people's minds. That you can't just rub out memories of people you don't love anymore?"

Michael put his head down, clasping his hands together. "Oh, but I wish you could, it would be so much easier than the pain I feel at times."

"I'm sorry, I didn't mean…" Phoebe put her feet back on the ground and reached across to Michael. She squeezed his upper arm. "I care, you know?"

Michael looked up to see Phoebe now kneeling beside him. Her hands found his and he felt their warmth. Tears welled up, threatening to fall down his cheek.

"What's wrong, Michael. Why are you in such pain?"

"It's all coming back!"

"What is, I don't understand?"

"They killed her."

Phoebe was suddenly shocked.

"What, who did?"

Michael wiped his face with his sleeve and let slip a little laugh.

"They told me I was mad. No-one believed me so I tried to block

*George John Kingsnorth*

it all out. I thought it was just some crazy dream but each morning I still wake up to find she's gone."

"Who?" Phoebe was beginning to get a little frustrated. "Who are you talking about?"

"Melissa, my wife."

Phoebe stood up and let go of Michael's hand.

"You're married?"

"No, not anymore."

"When?"

"About 20 years ago."

"Twenty years ago. Why is it so important now?"

"Because, I think the same thing that happened then is going to happen tonight."

A sense of fear gripped Phoebe as she played through her mind what she had just heard. Michael was married and his wife was murdered and it was going to happen again. Her heart pounded. Who to? Me? She thought. Was Michael going to kill her.

Phoebe was slowly edging her way towards the door when Michael stood up.

"It was the birds that triggered it all," Michael continued, tears blinding his vision. Phoebe's mind was flooded by images of the crows, Michael being attacked and killing them.

"What are you saying, Michael. The birds killed Melissa?"

"I don't know. We had only got married. Crows had threatened the driver of the bridesmaids. Melissa and I had gone on to stay at this hotel and something dark pinned me to the floor while they raped and butchered her."

"What happened to you afterwards?" Phoebe was beginning to shake. She could feel her bladder about to burst with fear.

"It doesn't matter what happened to me," his words slapped her. "It's going to happen tonight, again."

Phoebe looked around to see if she could find something to protect herself with. Michael turned round to look out of the window. Phoebe rushed to the cutlery draw and slid it open. The blades seem to sparkle.

*The Fall*

"I think Mara's life is in danger."

The words cut through the mist in Phoebe's mind. Mara. Phoebe took a deep breath and her whole body relaxed involuntarily. She looked over to Michael to see him still observing the Sandford's house. She slipped a small sharp knife up her sleeve and carefully walked over behind Michael. Her eye glanced toward the clock. It was 11.15 p.m.

Michael suddenly swung round and before she could refocus on him he jumped across the room knocking her to the ground covering her with his long trench coat. As they hit the floor the wind was blown out of her. Timber splintered, glass shattered and a wind tore through the kitchen. All kind of emotions erupted from within Phoebe compelling her to scream and shake and panic. She didn't know where the energy came from but without too much effort she had thrown Michael's unconscious body over onto its back, scanned the debris all around the kitchen, screamed and released her urine.

## CHAPTER TWENTY–SIX

Mara pulled herself to her feet still dazed by what had just happened. A bead of blood ran down the inside of her leg as she felt a cramp in her groin. Her body felt wrecked by fatigue. Her memories seemed jumbled. Her big toe stumped into something hard on the floor. There was a stone-like form against the wall. Hopping toward the switch, she turned on the light and discovered the dark carcass of a man's body. Before her eyes the crusty shape was disintegrating, turning to dust.

A stabbing sensation tore through her womb. Mara screamed then doubled up on the floor. The intensity of the pain became so unbearable that she passed out. Deep inside her womb the zygote cell combining the ovum and sperm had begun the meiotic cell division but instead of this process taking a day, minutes had just passed. The second cleavage stage occurred then split from four cells into six, eight, 12, 16, all in a matter of minutes. Within a quarter of an hour a solid ball of cells had formed. The cluster of cells had rapidly moved down from the oviduct into Mara's uterus and formed an interior hollow secreting oestrogen and progesterone. A further ten minutes passed and inside Mara's body, what would normally have taken seven to eight days to occur, the blastoyst had begun to implant itself into the uterus wall. Cells had begun to reorganize themselves to form skin, a nervous system, gut lining, interior organs, muscles, bones and a heart.

The sense of nausea awoke Mara and she scrambled for the bathroom but as she flushed the toilet another bout of pain sent her crashing to the floor. A yolk sac formed followed by an embryo within the disc shape of the blastoyst. The amniotic cavity filled with fluid. A placenta began to form.

*The Fall*

Sweat dripped from Mara's body as her temperature rose. She began to shiver in her unconscious state. A second wave of nausea swept over Mara, returning her to consciousness.

The embryonic disc had begun to mould itself a neural groove along its length. Down this channel somites, that would soon become skeletal structures, muscles and vertebrae, were formed. A brain was shaped between the two enclosing flaps at one end of the embryo. Though Mara had lost all sense of time, the spirit of this rapidly gestating organism knew its identity and was aware of the short span of time that had passed. It was eager to harness the temple that was being built within Mara's uterus and was impatient to take control but, being built at such a speed, the physical body still required time to be structured properly in order to prevent its own premature destruction.

A sense of panic gripped Mara. Something inside her body was trying to take her over and she was scared. A sound outside drew her attention to another human and she focused her mind on trying to draw their attention. She forced herself to her feet and pulled herself along the wall out into the landing. So as not to risk further injury, Mara sat down and slid down each step of the stairs.

Once at the base she pulled herself to her feet but stumbled when the pain in her groin suddenly intensified. She grabbed the handle of the front door and with all the strength she could muster, yanked it open. Ignoring the cold air of night, Mara stepped out onto the gravel of the drive. Goose pimples rose all over her naked body. Across the fence she saw a light was on at the Garrett's and sluggishly she dragged her feet in that direction. There were no street lights, only the glow of tungsten bulbs from within the depths of the house Mara was steadily progressing towards. She ignored the pain tearing into the soles of her feet. As she drew closer the front door burst open. Phoebe raced to a car parked in front of the garage doors, unlocked it, then raced back towards the front door. She stopped in her tracks on seeing Mara.

"Oh my God, where you caught in the explosion too?"

"Please help me, I've been raped."

"You've been what?" The pitch of Phoebe's voice had risen.

At the door, Professor Garrett was holding Michael up under his arms. Phoebe realised her father needed help and raced over to help him struggle to get Michael to the car.

"Didn't you hear me, I've been raped!" screamed Mara.

A car pulled up outside the drive and a young woman raced across the gravel.

"Phoebe, are you alright?"

"Grace, what are you doing here?"

"I was on the M42 when I saw the explosion and wanted to see if you were okay. It seemed to come from this direction. I was worried." She ran over to Mara and took off her coat to cover Mara up.

"Phoebe, will you hurry I can't hold him up much longer. He's losing blood. He needs to get to a hospital."

"What happened?" asked Grace.

"Michael got hit by glass and wood from the window when it came in. We have to get him to a hospital. And Mara's claiming someone has attacked her." As she said the words, it dawned on Phoebe what Michael had said. He wasn't trying to kill her he was worried about Mara. Professor Garret strapped Michael into a back seat. There was no time to think this all through, Phoebe knew her priority was to get Michael to the hospital.

"And Mara?"

"We don't know. Look Dad and Grace, can you take care of Mara, while I get Michael to the hospital."

"Should you check Mara out first?" ask Garrett.

"She's walking and talking, Michael's not. Could you take her to the hospital if she needs to go, Grace?"

"Yeah, sure, I suppose."

Phoebe thrust the gear into first and a cascade of pebbles struck the garage doors as the car tore down the drive, out into the road and was away towards the M42.

Mara had collapsed to her knees as Professor Garrett and Grace came over to her.

*The Fall*

"Didn't you call for an ambulance," Grace quizzed Professor Garrett.

"All the phone lines are out."

"We had better get her inside and clean her up," instructed Grace. As they lifted her, Mara threw up. Her stomach began to grow taut.

"Argh, it's agony," screamed Mara.

"Perhaps we should just take her straight to hospital?" suggested Professor Garrett.

"No, she's not badly hurt," stressed Grace.

"How do you know?"

"I think she's pregnant."

"What?"

"Look at her belly."

Mara's stomach was becoming more rounded than when she had first left her house.

"What's happening to me? This isn't right."

"How long have you been pregnant, Mara?" asked Garrett.

"I'm not."

He placed his hand on her belly, then sharply withdrew it.

"What's wrong?" asked Grace.

"The baby…"

"What?"

"It just kicked me."

"They do when they reach four or five months."

"No, I know what that's like but this one seemed to attack my hand. It hurt."

"I'm not five months pregnant. Why don't you believe me?" pleaded Mara. "I've only just been raped, how can I be five months pregnant?"

"Let's just get her to the hospital," suggested Garrett.

"No, I know some people who can deal with this," insisted Grace. "We'll take her there."

"Is everyone all right," came a voice from outside the garden. Both Grace and Garrett spun round.

"Yes, everything's fine," shouted Grace to the man.

"What about you?"

"Yeah, we're alright. The gas explosion just put in the windows but no-ones hurt."

"Good, you should try a few houses down and see if everyone's okay. Our neighbour is a bit shaken but she'll be okay. We'll take care of her."

"What's going on, Grace. Who *are* you?" asked the professor.

"I'm a friend of Phoebe's, Professor Garrett. I'm here to help, trust me!"

*The Fall*

## CHAPTER TWENTY-SEVEN

Grace pushed across the large double doors that hung on gliders. The sound echoed around the warehouse interior.

"Bring her inside, Professor."

Professor Garrett struggled to hold Mara in his arms. Although her frame was light, Garrett estimated that she weighed about eight stone, he realised he was not fit enough even to carry this load. Grace smiled at his efforts then decided she should give him a hand. Together they placed Mara into a small wooden chair stationed inside the industrial lift.

Earlier, Grace had raced into Mara's house to gather some clothes and brought them back to the Garrett's. She had dressed Mara while the professor had hidden in his study. When Grace had Mara ready to go, there was some persuasion to extradite the Professor once more. Now at the warehouse he was beginning to show the mental and physical stress of all that had gone on. Grace only hoped he would to keep on going.

"Wait there, while I lock the doors." Grace hastened back to the double doors, pulled them closed, swung the swivel bar 90 degrees from vertical to its locking horizontal position, wrapped several chains around the bar and metal strips on the door and turned a large key in the nineteenth century lock.

"So nothing's going to come through there tonight?" commented the Professor on Grace's return to the lift.

"You'd better hope they won't," replied Grace as she hit the button for the fifth floor. The professor's smile changed to that of concern as he puzzled over her comment.

As the lift passed through the lower four floors, the professor could see vast halls of empty spaces once occupied by immense spinning machines as part of a linen industry. Only dust and scraps of paper littered this old mill now. This building may have seen many industries pass through its walls but now all of that had gone.

"What's going to happen to this place?"

"Oh, it's due to be torn down sometime this year and redeveloped into a new cultural and creative arts economic centre of excellence," Grace laughed.

"Why do you laugh?"

"Oh, no reason."

"Come on tell me?"

"Oh, it just seems to be another one of those schemes the government conjures up in its attempt to keep this country economically sound but there are other forces at work plotting to ruin everything."

"You're very cynical for someone so young?"

"Looks can be deceiving, Professor. Nothing is as it seems, believe me. Nothing."

Finally, the lift jolted to a halt. Grace pulled across the inner mess of metal strip that formed the doors and tugged open the outer grid. Together, Grace and the professor lifted Mara from the wooden chair and carried her across the floor to what looked like stage walls. Through a paneled door, the professor was surprised to find the interior was that of a small urban bungalow.

"What is this place?"

"Oh, I use it as a place to escape to," sighed Grace. "I couldn't afford a proper place but friends of mine helped me put together the panels from an old set we found below. Someone must have dumped the material from a film set. We just borrowed them for a bit. Makes me feel as though I've got a home. Put Mara on the bed through that door." She pointed to a door to the professor's right. On opening it, he found himself in a large bedroom with a double bed, built in wardrobes, dressing table and a couple of chairs. One of the walls had a window with heavy net curtains and glazed glass so that nothing could be seen of the warehouse interior beyond. Gently, the professor laid Mara onto the bed. She was still drowsy and her

*The Fall*

stomach was quite large. The professor left her on her own and made his way back to Grace who was in a kitchen area.

"Grace, do you think she'll be alright? Whatever it is inside her is growing so rapidly. I've never seen anything like it."

"I don't know Professor Garrett. This is unusual and I have to get some people I know here to help her through delivery."

"When do you think that will be?"

"Well, guessing on her current condition it could be anytime in the next two to three days. Look, I need you to stay with her until I get back. Will you do that?

"But I've got to… Phoebe won't know where.."

"Professor, this is important, more important than anything else that has happened in your life. You must help!"

"Look, Grace, I don't know who you think you are but I have a life and responsibilities."

"Professor, you'll have nothing unless you help here." Grace's voice was like thunder. Inside Professor Garrett felt a resonance through out his body, warning him not to challenge this young woman. A sense of fear gripped him.

"I don't mean to frighten you professor but I need your help. Mara needs your help more than anyone else in the world. Will you stay?"

The professor suddenly felt like a seven year old being chastised by his mother. "Okay, I'll stay but please don't be too long, Phoebe will be wondering where I am."

"I'll try not to be."

Grace left through the mock front door. The professor started to look around the set in more detail and began to notice things, the shape of the hall way, the shape of the kitchen, lounge and, yes, he found the stairs and realised what he thought was the front door was actually the back door. He was standing in a replica of his own house. Yet all the décor was wrong, the colour scheme was wrong. In fact, when he thought about it the set was a mirror image of his house but the details were all wrong.

"Oh, professor, what are you doing in my house?"

*George John Kingsnorth*

The professor spun round to see Mara standing before him.

"Do you know where you are, Mara?"

"Are you joking me?"

"No," the professor was surprised by her response.

"I'm at home. Did you want something?"

"Are you alright?"

Mara gave a nervous and confused laugh. "Yeah, are you?"

"Can you remember what has happened?"

"What? You mean being stuck here for nearly seven months waiting for the brat to come along." She laid her hands across the top of her swollen belly. "I need to go to the loo. Are you here to see mum and dad? Give me a second, I really need to go."

Mara rushed into the downstairs toilet. The professor took the opportunity to run up stairs to see what the rest of the house was like. It was laid out in the same manner. A lot of detail had gone into the replication. When he heard the toilet flush, the professor raced downstairs to the kitchen only just making it back in time before Mara opened the toilet door.

"Oh, hello professor. You here to see mum and dad?" Mara's voice was a lot softer than it had been previously.

"Yeah, I just called over to see how you were doing?"

"Oh, I'm doing just fine. Still having the strange nightmares but the doctor said that was usual for a young woman in my condition."

"When were you at the doctors?"

"Oh, three or four times since I last saw you." Mara frowned. "Yeah, what happened to you a few weeks ago. I was talking to you in the house about here and you just disappeared. Didn't even say goodbye. That's very rude."

"I'm sorry, Mara. I apologise. So that was when?"

"You remember, three weeks ago. I caught you in the house and you surprised me. Don't you remember? It was just here, right where you are standing now."

"Three weeks ago?" the professor was puzzled, Mara was talking about an event that had just happened literally three or four minutes ago. Not only was her baby growing at such a rapid speed but her

*The Fall*

mind saw the event as though it was happening in its natural time. Mara's experience was that of a young woman going through a pregnancy of nearly eight months to date. Yet the sense of time was not constant. Mara seemed to be going through spurts of accelerated time then drifts of normal time. The professor assumed this must coincide with growth spurts the baby underwent.

"What did the doctors say, Mara? What did they tell you?"

Mara went to the fridge and pulled out a bowl of fruit, sat down and began to eat. "I was having these terrible nightmares about a monster growing inside me and I wanted to rip the thing out but the doctors gave me some drugs to calm me down. They told me many young women get these dreams because they see their bodies being invaded by another being. You have to remember," Mara sat up in her chair, "this is another person, who thinks and wonders who it is, with a spirit and everything. It's amazing when you think about it, isn't it. Another human being inside my belly." Mara's face lit up with her amazement and awe.

Professor Garrett was deeply concerned. This poor child seemed totally unaware of what had happened over the past twenty-four hours. Something was influencing her and if he could dare to imagine it, Mara was experiencing what he knew to be the real world and, at the same time, the unseen world of spirits. What he wasn't sure about was if they were demons or angels? And if they were the former, did that make Grace something from another world? Was she real or just a figment of his wildest dreams? Now he just had to trust. But was it Grace or his instincts that he put his faith in? Now even more than before, he wished he could walk away but he felt helpless to do so.

## CHAPTER TWENTY-EIGHT

There was the rattling sound of a trolley accompanied by chattering teacups and saucers. Crockery added to the occasional ching or chang with the beat being tapped out by heavy plastic soles. Mumbled whispers came, too low to distinguish words but enough to bring Michael back to consciousness.

A warm tingling sensation occurred in his fingers and he realised someone was holding his hand. It took some effort but he managed to raise his eyelids. The scene was out of focus and it took Michael's eyes a few moments to see things sharply.

"Phoebe?"

There were tears in her eyes.

"What's wrong, Phoebe?"

"I'm sorry." She wiped her eyes dry with her free hand.

"What's happened?"

"I thought." She stopped for a moments trying to compose herself. "I got it all wrong."

Michael smiled, "You're not making much sense. Where am I?"

"Do you remember the explosion?"

Michael's mind snapped back to the last thoughts he could remember. "Mara's in danger. I was trying to tell you when the window came in."

He attempted to pull back the sheets and suddenly froze as the stitches in the numerous cuts on his back grew taut.

"Take it easy, Michael," demanded Phoebe. "I don't want you getting more hurt."

Michael eased himself back down into the bed.

"I thought you were going to kill me. You got all spooky. I was scared. I got a knife to protect myself and then you went and saved

*The Fall*

my life."

A nurse pulled back the curtains. "Ah, Mr. Davies, you're back with us I see." She strapped a pressure pad around his right arm and pumped it up. A needle went up so far on a dial and then dropped down.

"Blood pressure's fine."

She wrote the details into his chart.

"Are you hungry?"

"Yeah."

"I'll go and see what I can get for you. Back shortly."

As she left she drew the curtains revealing four beds opposite Michael's and two to his left and one to his right beside the windows.

"Is there anyone you want me to call for you?" asked Phoebe. "We didn't know who to contact."

"No, there's no-one. No-one I can remember. All the people I knew thought I…"

"Thought you killed your wife, like I did?"

"Yes. I don't blame them now. I know what it looks like but it wasn't me. They even had me believing it but last night I remembered. Just before the explosion."

"That wasn't last night."

"What?"

"That was two nights ago. You've been unconscious since then. I kinda lied and told them I was your fiancée."

Michael smiled to see how embarrassed she felt. Though it caused him some pain as the stitches were pulled tight, he leant across and kissed her on the cheek.

"Thanks, I'm glad you're here Phoebe. It means a lot."

"I'm sorry I doubted you. The whole thing just seems crazy to me. And to think it happened again right next door."

"What happened?" Michael insisted. "What happened to Mara, is she okay?"

"Everyone thought it was a gas explosion. Grace saw it from the motorway and came over to see if we were okay. Mara had run out of the house naked, screaming she had been raped. It was all very confusing. When the police came with the gas board's people there was no sign of a leakage but inside Mara's house they found the remains of a man, they think he was scorched in the wall of a bedroom. His shape was outlined but they couldn't work out what the substance was. It looked like some kind of resin."

Michael could see Phoebe was becoming a little emotional.

"Where's Mara now?"

"No-one knows. I thought Grace and dad were going to look after her but when I got back from here two nights ago they had all vanished. Dad's mobile's dead, so's Grace's. And the police took me down to the station to make a statement. It was quite intimidating."

Michael could see the tears welling up around her lower eyelids. He reached out and squeezed her hand.

"We'll find them, don't worry."

Phoebe leant across and hugged him. He felt the stitches catch on his back once more but didn't want her to pull away so held the pain in. Phoebe kissed him.

"Thanks, Michael."

Their foreheads touched.

"Sorry, Miss. Visitors are not supposed to sit on the patient's bed," scolded the staff nurse as she suddenly returned. Phoebe released Michael and sat back onto the soft chair bedside the bed. The nurse put a tray of food down in front of Michael.

"How long do you think I'll have to been in here for?" he asked the nurse.

"You've only just woken up after being out for two days. I'm sure you'll be here for a few more just so we can monitor you. Your body has taken quite a beating from the force of the explosion and you have multiple lacerations on your back."

Michael looked across to Phoebe who looked helpless with the realization that nothing could be done for a few more days. The nurse left Michael to eat his food.

"Look, where are my clothes?" he whispered to Phoebe.

"What, you heard the nurse, you have to stay for a few more days."

"There may not be a few more days. We have to find Mara before

*The Fall*

it's too late."

"I don't know that you should."

Michael could read her face, what she was saying was not the picture he got from her expression. She wanted him to help find her dad, she did not know who else could help her but he knew the way she was disciplined and following the rules were important and something one should not go against. Now for the first time she was being forced to break her own principles and Michael could detect a little sense of excitement in her, that he was giving her permission to do so.

"Are you sure?" she hesitated.

"Certain."

A smile stretched across her face as she fumbled with his clothes in the side cupboard.

"Quick, I'll close the curtains." Phoebe got up and checked to see the other patients were still asleep and drew the curtains around Michael's bed as he struggled to pull his shirt over his back. Phoebe slipped behind the barrier of cloth and helped Michael zip up his trousers. For a moment their eyes met. Phoebe grinned, arched her head and landed a lingering kiss on his lips. Michael did not want to pull away but the urgency of their mission required instant action if they had any hope of finding Mara, Grace and Phoebe's father.

"We had better go before the nurse returns," Michael sighed. Phoebe slipped his jacket over his shoulders, then checked outside the curtains to see who was around. Each of the patients opposite were asleep or too busy talking to their own visitors. Phoebe held Michael's hand as he led them out into the main corridor. As they turned the corner Michael saw the nurse talking to a doctor with her back to them. As she was about to turn Michael spotted a patient's toilet facility, ushered Phoebe inside and held the door until he heard the nurse's footsteps pass. Holding the door open slightly, he checked to see where the nurse had gone.

"Okay, let's go before she comes back." Michael pulled Phoebe out with him and hurried down the corridor passed the nurses' station.

"Mr. Davies, what are you doing out of bed?" The voice was that of the Ward Sister.

"Quick, let's run for it," urged Michael. The two of them sprinted out of the corridor into the lift area but took the stairwell as their means of escape. As they reached the third flight below, Michael began to feel the pain of the cuts. Blood was beginning to seep through his clothes.

"You're bleeding." Phoebe was concerned they may not make it out of the building.

"I'll be okay, just get me to your car."

"What about security. Won't they come after us?"

"Don't worry, it'll be fine," Michael reassured her.

In the reception area of the hospital there were no unusual activities, no one coming after them, no one seemed to care. Michael and Phoebe made their way out of the front doors and on to the visitors' car park. On a small monitor in the security office the sister from the medical ward watched the two of them get into Phoebe's car.

"Should I call the police?"

"No, don't bother, he's effectively signed himself out. All we have to do is deal with extra paper work and some flak from above. Take a note of the car registration and if there's any come back we can get the address of his fiancée".

"Do you think they'll call the police?" worried Phoebe.

"They'll see me as someone who signed out. It'll be too much hassle to spend time on us."

"Are you sure? What about going home? There were police still there this morning."

"Well, if you don't mind my place? It's nothing much but I call it home."

"Okay, tell me which way?"

"Head towards Erdington, I have a flat there."

*The Fall*

## CHAPTER TWENTY-NINE

The professor checked the fridge. Both he and Mara had enough food for another day or so. Although, the milk was beginning to go off and they needed a fresh supply. He poured a little into a cup of tea and then put the carton back into the fridge door and closed it. He was growing anxious with boredom. There were no books to console him and he was finding it hard that Mara was getting cross with him for no apparent reason, as she experienced the equivalent of 38 weeks of a pregnancy in just over three days. He could only hope that Grace would turn up over the next few hours, in time for the birth. The professor really did not want to have to tackle something as messy as delivering a baby into this world. Where would he start? He had not even been about at Phoebe's birth so had no experience and did not know what to expect.

"Professor, have you gone mad?" shouted Mara. "Who invited you into this house to just do as you please?"

"Sorry, Mara. We were just talking and you said I could make my…"

"Don't be ridiculous," scolded Mara. "You've not been here for a week and then you just turn up out of the blue, for no reason."

The professor could see the baby had grown further and Mara was becoming impatient with the whole inconvenience of pregnancy.

"Shouldn't you be resting, Mara?"

"Don't tell me what to do. You've no right coming into my house and lecturing me. I think you should leave." She pointed towards the door.

"I think someone should look after you?"

"Get out."

"Mara, please. I'm trying to help."

"GET OUT."

The professor put his cup down and like a naughty boy with his head bowed slowly paced to the door. He turned to say something, but she again insisted with her finger and there was no reasoning with her.

As the door clicked shut, the professor wondered how he could keep this pretence up. Mara was obviously psychologically traumatized by the events that were unfolding but he was not equipped to know how best to tackle the situation. He desperately needed help but from where. He sat on the cold concrete floor of the warehouse and held his head in his hands.

"Dear Lord, what am I going to do," he thought to himself. "I feel totally helpless."

The sound of the heavy metal lift doors sliding open on the lower levels snapped him back to his senses. He could hear several sets of shoes or boots clatter across the lift floor. He stood up. The door clanked shut and the electric motors began to whirl. Inside, his chest the professor felt a sharp stabbing sensation as his muscles tightened with anxiety. He could sense his heart pumping faster, thudding away and his blood zipping through his veins and arteries. Was this danger approaching?

The lift clunked to a halt, the electric motor stopped and the heavy metal inner doors were slid open. The professor felt as though his head was going to explode with the stress of it all. Then the outer doors rolled apart. Tungsten light invaded the bluish night glow of the interior of the fifth floor and three silhouetted figures stepped out.

"Is she alright, professor?"

It was Grace. The professor felt himself slump but he was still standing, though a little wobbly. He took a deep breath and felt his heart simmer down.

"Yes, yes she is but things are happening fast."

A second voice sounded out. "Have her waters broken?"

"I don't know, she's just ordered me out of the house. She doesn't know where she is. Something to do with the pregnancy has made her perception of time go haywire."

*The Fall*

"Sister Teresa, prepare an area we can safely deliver the baby."

"Yes, Sister Philomena."

The younger of the two walked into the light from the windows of the house and for the first time the Professor could see she was a nun dressed in a short dark navy blue skirt, light coloured blouse and a navy blue cardigan. Unusual for this day and age, he thought, the young nun also wore a white veil covering only her hair. When the older nun walked through the shaft of light the professor noticed that she wore a second darker veil over the white one.

"Professor," Grace called, "I'm sorry I took so long. There were problems trying to locate Sister Philomena."

"I was beginning to think you had abandoned us."

"I'm sorry."

"Phoebe will be worried sick about us. Look, I need to get back to see if she is okay."

"It's not safe for you out there at the moment, Professor. You already know too much. I'll look after Phoebe, you stay here and help the nuns."

"But I have other commitments. My students, the dean will be…"

"Professor, you have to stay here. I have to go. Look after the nuns."

The professor wanted to say more but Grace had made her way to the lift, closed the outer and inner doors and pushed the button for the ground floor.

"How long will I have to be here?" he called down the shaft.

"I don't know, Professor. I really don't know."

He slammed his hands against the metal mesh of the outer lift doors. The clatter echoed around the warehouse. Frustrated he made his way back into the mock up of Mara's home but once he entered through the door everything had changed.

"What's going on?"

"Hurry, Professor, we're in the bedroom," called Sister Philomena.

Now the place looked like a dingy flat with one large sitting or lounge area with a door leading to the kitchen and a small hallway leading to a bedroom and a bathroom. There were newspapers and magazines scattered all over the place and the place smelt of damp, spilt beer and body odour. The professor was repulsed.

Confused he made his way to the bedroom and was surprised to find a small room with a double bed squeezed into it with a single door wardrobe and a three draw chest.

"This place is disgusting," chastised Sister Philomena. "Why did you bring her to a place like this?"

"It wasn't me. Grace brought us."

"Who?"

"The girl you came with just a few moments ago."

"What, are you mad. You called us on your mobile and gave us directions to this apartment."

"But you're not in an apartment. This is a warehouse with a set built in it. This isn't real."

Sister Philomena got up from the bed, leaving Mara lying with Sister Teresa holding her hand.

"Pull yourself together man," scolded Sister Philomena. "You're obviously denying the fact that this is some kind of love-nest you have and you've brought this poor girl here to hide your deeds?"

"What?"

"Why didn't you take her to the hospital?"

"Grace brought us here because of what happened?"

Sister Philomena was becoming impatient. "Have you not even registered the girl with a midwife?"

"There hasn't been time."

"Don't be ridiculous. You've had nine months or so."

"No, we haven't. You don't understand, this isn't a normal baby."

"You'd better explain yourself," insisted the nun but before the professor could say another word Mara was on her feet again pacing up and down the hallway becoming more irritated. Sister Teresa stood beside her holding her hand.

"Sister Philomena, Mara's contractions are more regular lasting just over a minute. Her back's quite sore."

"What should I do?" ask the professor. Sister Philomena looked

*The Fall*

up at him from her small five foot two frame.

"Go and boil a kettle of water, that should keep you out of mischief."

The professor reluctantly made his way back to the kitchen to carry out his chore. Sister Philomena took the opportunity to use the professor's absence to quiz Mara.

"Hello, Mara. Professor Garrett has explained the situation as best he could. I'm a midwife and can help you. Have you been concealing this all this time?"

"No, I've seen many doctors and had loads of visits to the hospital. This hasn't just happened all of a sudden."

"Do you know where you are?"

"I'm at ......" Mara looked puzzled. "I was at home. How did I get here?"

"The professor must have brought you here?"

"Why would he do that?"

"Isn't he the father?"

"What," Mara laughed. "Are you kidding me? Do you think I'd go with an old man like him?"

"So who's the father?"

Mara's expression changed, she was upset by the question as a flood of memories invaded her mind of the night she conceived.

"An angel."

Sister Teresa looked astonished and tugged at Sister Philomena but as the older nun was about to speak, Mara gripped her arm and squeezed tightly. Mara's breathing grew deeper as she went through another contraction.

"Their getting closer together, Sister," commented Sister Teresa. Down Mara's left leg a fluid trickled, then there was a sudden flood of water, leaving a puddle on the carpet.

"We need to get you back onto the bed, dear," Sister Philomena indicated to Mara.

"I'm scared."

"It's okay, we're here to help you."

"I need something for the pain. It hurts!"

"Just breathe."

Before the two sisters could get Mara to the bed, she began a low extended wail that ended in a grunt. She began to bear down.

"Don't push yet, dear. Let's get you on the bed. Just pant."

They eased Mara onto her back and pulled away her underwear to facilitate the birth. Professor Garrett came into the doorway with the hot water but was instantly chased out by the two nuns.

"Stay in the lounge until we call you," insisted Sister Philomena.

"There's a heavy show," announced Sister Teresa. Mara began to grunt again and push down.

"I can see the head being eased out," Sister Teresa informed the others.

"Just pant, dear," Sister Philomena instructed Mara. Sister Teresa gently supported the baby's head as it was eased out, covered in a bloody mucous. Then the shoulders began to emerge. Within a moment or two the whole of the baby suddenly slid out. The umbilical cord still trailed back inside Mara. Sister Philomena looked at the strange expression formed on the younger nun's face. There was horror and disgust. The young woman seemed so repulsed by what she held in her hands that she swiftly gave her superior the child and rushed out of the room. Sister Teresa had no time to reach the bathroom and threw up in the hallway.

"I'm sorry, Sister Philomena," sobbed Sister Teresa. "I wasn't expecting to see..."

"It's okay. Neither was I but we must do our best for the child and his mother." Sister Philomena clamped the umbilical cord in two places and snipped between the clamps.

"But it is an abomination."

"It's still a child," cautioned Sister Philomena as she wrapped the child in a blanket and handed him to Mara.

"Here's you baby, dear."

"What's wrong with him?"

"I don't know, but he's still your son."

With the child resting on Mara's stomach, the afterbirth was soon delivered.

*The Fall*

"Stay with Mara for a moment while I talk to the professor," ordered Sister Philomena to Sister Teresa. She then stepped out of the bedroom and made her way to the sitting room to find the professor.

"You'd better start telling me what's going on or help me God!"

The professor stood up from the sofa.

"Where to start? Well, there have been strange activities at Mara's house for a few days I suppose."

"Yes, yes but are you the father?"

"No, he's dead."

"What?"

"He's dead. He died at the moment of conception, according to Mara."

"What nine months ago?"

"No, three days ago. This has all happened in just three days. The whole gestation has spanned three days but Mara thinks she's gone through a full term in the normal 39 weeks. She's not even experiencing time in the way I have. She goes out of a room and when she comes back a few moments later thinks she has experienced three or four weeks. She thinks I've vanished and come back weeks later. It's totally bizarre."

"And you're crazy," snapped Sister Philomena.

"But I wish I was. Look I came into this set and it was a replication of Mara's house."

"What are you talking about, we're in a flat five floors up."

"No we are not. We're in a warehouse with what looks like a film set of what is now a room in an apartment block but before you came in here with Grace it was a replica of Mara's house."

"You're definitely out of you head."

"But you don't even remember coming here with Grace."

"Who's Grace?"

"Grace is a friend of my daughter, Phoebe. Three nights ago there was an explosion at Mara's house. Our gardener saved Phoebe's life and Mara came over totally naked, claiming she had been raped by an angel. Now I've been looking at scripture and I think this is something to do with an angel taking a human wife. That's why the baby is like it is."

"When did you see the baby?"

"After Sister Teresa vomited in the hall. Look, Mara told me over the last three days, actually she didn't mean to but she spoke in her sleep. She said an angel, called Nimrod had been chosen to be with her but that their union had destroyed him. It was an act of abomination, not sanctioned by God."

"Are you serious?"

"Remember that story in Genesis where the Sons of God came to take women and their offspring were the Nephilim?" quizzed the professor. "This is what we have just witnessed here tonight. Mara's child is a Nephilim. The product of an union between an angel and a female human."

"Nonsense," argued Sister Philomena. "The church centuries ago believed the sons of God referred to the sons of Seth, Adam's third son. That it was them cohabiting with the daughters of Cain. Angels are purely spiritual, not physical."

"But what if they were wrong?"

"You're talking heresy!" Sister Philomena stressed.

"You've seen it with your own eyes, woman. The girl's condition is not normal. You've seen the child."

"I wish I hadn't. It's too much to even imagine."

"Should we kill the child?"

"Heaven forbid, no!"

"What do we do?"

"This is beyond belief."

"According to my research, if the child dies it's spirit becomes a demon to walk the earth. Its soul is forbidden to enter heaven. It is damned like the angel that fathered him."

"So killing the child could be worse, so why did you suggest it?"

"I don't know what else to do."

"We need a priest. Who or what do you think Grace is?"

"I'm not sure but she seems to know a lot more than we do. Is she a demon or an angel? Everything that is happening here is all about

*The Fall*

deception so it makes it hard to imagine she is an angel if she has anything to do with this."

"Professor, there are no female angels," scoffed Sister Philomena.

## CHAPTER THIRTY

Both Phoebe and Michael ran up two flights of stairs to get to his landing. Michael had to stop a couple of times to catch his breath. He could still feel the burning sensation from all the cuts in his back. Most of the other apartments had their lights on. Those that didn't were usually boarded up or had had a brick thrown through the glass. Michael opened the door to his flat.

"You keep this place tidy," commented Phoebe. The room was well maintained, everything in its proper place. Nothing like the chaos Phoebe had seen outside.

"I lead a simple life. It doesn't take much to keep this place in order," replied Michael.

"Have you been here long?"

"About ten years, I think."

Michael rummaged through a bookshelf looking for the yellow pages. He pulled the volume out and pulled it open near the middle. The first page was loans, so he flicked through the pages towards the 'P's, got to *printers* then *promotions*.

"What are you looking for?"

"A private investigator."

"Look up detectives!"

Michael pulled the book open again a quarter of the way through finding *chiropractors*. Again he flicked towards the middle until he came across *detective agencies*.

"Do you want me to make some tea?"

"Yes, please."

Michael traces his finger down the two-page listing for detectives. The one that seems to stand out was Peter Stoneywell, P.I. Michael took a note of the number and the address.

*The Fall*

"Do you think they can help us find dad and Mara?" called Phoebe from the kitchen. Michael heard the sound of water gushing from the tap into his metal kettle.

"It's a start."

"Do you have enough money to pay for someone like that?"

Michael had not thought about that. The professor had not paid him and things were tight.

"I had called round to pick up my pay from your dad but I wasn't able to get it because of the explosion. Could you pay me and I'll use that?"

"How much is it?"

"About £600."

The kettle hit the linoleum floor, water cascaded all over the place.

"Is everything okay?" Michael dropped the yellow pages and made his way to the kitchen. Phoebe was already pulling off kitchen roll to soak up the spillage.

"Sorry, Michael. I didn't realise dad hadn't paid you for sometime. I've been so pre-occupied with mum I didn't think."

Michael knelt down beside her and put his hand on her shoulder. She looked straight into his eyes. His copper-brown iridis decreased as the pupils enlarged. His focal point scanned from one of Phoebe's eyes to the other. She felt a tear run down her cheek. Michael's eyes seemed to light up as he smiled. Phoebe leant forward, her eyes shutting out the kitchen as her lips moved to engaged Michael's. A light sting zipped across from her lower lip to his from a charge of static but it was not enough to stop her. Her lip-gloss clung to his lips.

A wave passed over her and she was willing to give into to her passion, ready to pull his clothes off and allow him to explore her wherever he dared BUT a voice whispered and a niggling thought seeped into her mind.

"Don't trust him, he's dangerous," she heard the whisper again. Her mind became anxious.

"Leave me alone, I don't believe you," her mind responded but the thoughts continued.

*George John Kingsnorth*

"He did kill his wife, you know he did. He can't be trusted. Remember you're a Christian. You must remain pure. He'll dirty you and defile you, he'll kill you. You need to escape."

"No, leave me alone!"

Michael pulled away confused.

"I thought you wanted me to kiss you?"

"I did, I do, I do."

"So what's wrong, why do you want me to leave you alone."

"I didn't mean to say that."

"But you did."

Phoebe got to her feet and braced herself against the sink.

"I'm sorry," Michael said.

"No, no, you don't have to be… Look, I'm confused, a lot has happened and I don't know where I am with anything. I don't understand."

"What?"

Phoebe turned once more to face Michael.

"You came to the house before the explosion and started to say things. I got scared, I have feelings for you but.."

"But what?"

"You were saying things the night of the explosion, about something that had happened before, to Melissa, your wife. About her murder?"

Michael took a deep breath and did not know where to look. He turned his back on Phoebe.

"Did you kill her?"

Phoebe wanted to see his eyes to see how he was reacting. She spun him back round to face her.

"Did you?"

"No, I didn't."

"I want to believe you Michael but I'm scared."

Michael looked once more into her eyes. She sensed gentleness within him, caring and loving. She could not believe he could have done something so terrible to someone he loved.

"When I try to explain what happened, it's as though no-one can

*The Fall*

comprehend the possibility."

"The possibility of what?" Phoebe was growing more impatient. "What?"

Michael's body tensed up. He could feel the anger rise inside him at being forced to face the past and prove his innocence. He resented having to justify himself time and again.

"I believe, though I've tried to forget, that demons attacked me."

Phoebe was dumbfounded. She stepped away from Michael. What was he saying? He believed demons were responsible for killing his wife.

"He killed her, he's making up a story to hide the truth," came the whisper in her mind.

Michael shook his head, he didn't know what he could say to convince her. He wanted the past to be forgotten and he wanted to love again. He wanted to love Phoebe and the last thing he wanted to do was force her away.

"It's the truth."

"He's a liar. You need to escape! Run! Run! Run for your life."

"I want to believe you. You saved my life. I'm confused," Phoebe sobbed.

"Look, for the time being we should concentrate on finding your father and Mara. They're still in danger and time is running out."

"Run! Run! Escape or die," sang the voice in her head.

"I have to go. I need time to think. You do what you think is best."

Phoebe pushed passed Michael and made her way to the door. Michael felt helpless. He did not want to stop her in case she misunderstood his actions. He knew he had to refocus and find a way to save the Professor and Mara.

"Can I have some money, anything to pay for the detective?" asked Michael in a soft voice.

As Phoebe turned he could see her mascara beginning to bleed down her face.

"How much? I don't have a lot."

"Fifty pounds, say, for a deposit?"

"Okay." Phoebe pulled out her purse and found a few tens and a twenty. "I got this out to do a little grocery shopping. I can stop by the ATM and get more on my way home." She threw the money on the dressing table and hastily walked out the door.

Deflated, Michael mustered his energy and picked up the money. From the corner of his eye he noticed a dark vapour seep out as the door clicked shut. He raced over, yanked the door open and ran to the balcony rail. Phoebe was walking down the last set of stairs. By the time she had reached the path leading to her car, Michael had reached the first landing. As he caught sight of her again he leant across the rail.

"Phoebe! Phoebe!"

Phoebe turned to see Michael.

"Keep praying."

"What?"

"I said, keep praying. Ask Jesus to protect you."

"I am, I will. Don't worry, I'll be okay. Just give me time."

"Just keep praying," Michael insisted.

"I will."

Phoebe jumped into the driver's seat and within moments pulled out of the estate. Michael turned to make his way back to the apartment. As he looked up, a dark figure stood before him. He found it hard to look the stranger in the face and there was a strong repugnant smell that almost made him vomit.

"She's not yours. You can never have her. Leave her alone."

Michael felt his cheek smart as a dark hand slapped across his face. The force sent him crashing into the door and dropping to the floor. As he attempted to gather himself together, he looked about to see if his assailant was going to strike again but there was no-one there. He had gone. More than ever, Michael knew he had to find the professor and Mara but also Phoebe's life was now in danger and no-one believed what he was trying to tell them. He was alone.

## CHAPTER THIRTY-ONE

The golden light of early morning seemed to lift Michael's spirit. The troubles of the world appeared to be hidden in silhouette as the sun pulled itself up from the horizon. Michael sipped at a cup of coffee watching the city outside his window gradually come to life. His face still felt sore from the previous night's attack and there was a bruise just under his eye on his right cheek.

As he thought back to the dark figure who had struck him, a picture of the night Melissa died also came to mind. Briefly his memory took him back to the moment when he had been thrown against the bedroom wall of the hotel. A dark apparition had prevented him from saving Melissa. Mixed with anger, Michael had also experienced a deep dread that seemed to penetrate right through his soul. He had felt helpless, even hopeless. Now it seemed the demons of his past had returned to torment him but he was determined not to let them succeed and resolved to find Mara and the professor. He needed help, so his first port of call that morning would be to Peter Stoneywell, the local private investigator he and Phoebe had found in the Yellow Pages.

Having finished his coffee, Michael quickly showered, then cooked himself a fried breakfast of egg, bacon, sausages and a small can of baked beans. He dressed quickly and put on an US M65 regiment field jacket, that he had bought from an army surplus store. The coats double layers offered good protection against the bitter cold that he knew waited outside. For a moment he experienced a tremor of trepidation and felt the need to take the same advice he had given Phoebe, to pray. He recited a prayer he had learnt in primary school but stumbled over a few of the lines and hoped that Jesus would forgive him for his bad memory.

*George John Kingsnorth*

Most of the prayer had been said in his head but he found himself vocalising the last line. "Deliver us from evil." Instinctively he traced his finger along a bookshelf in his bedroom. Most books were just collecting dust and at first he could not find what he was looking for. The four shelves were so packed with books that they were stacked in layers. He found himself having to remove nearly a dozen books before he could locate the volume he wanted. Eventually he came across a small white leather bound bible. He flicked through the pages and stopped. The words leapt off the page.

'The great dragon was hurled down – that ancient serpent called the devil, or Satan, who leads the whole world astray. He was hurled to the earth, and his angels with him.' He read through the next paragraph about the coming of God's salvation and the authority of Christ had hurled down the accuser out of heaven. How the martyrs had overcome the devil through the blood of the Lamb even in the sacrifice of their own lives but their reward was heaven. The scripture then indicated sorrow for the earth and the sea as the devil wreaked his fury knowing his time was short.

Michael read further about the dragon pursuing the woman who had given birth to a male child and how she was given eagle wings to escape to the desert where a place was prepared for her to keep her safe and out of the serpent's reach for 'a time, times and half of a time'. When the dragon was unable to do harm to the woman because the earth protected her, he turned his attention on the rest of humanity and waged a war against those who were followers of Jesus.

Michael sat back against his bed and wondered what this revelation meant. Was it connected to what he was experiencing? Was there a connection with Mara and her pregnancy? Was this what had been the cause of Melissa's death?

He flicked back a page and read through the notes commentating on some of the passages in that part of the book of Revelations. The notes referred to a view of Christmas with the birth of Jesus discussing simultaneous events that were happening both in the seen and unseen worlds, where a mighty battle between the forces of

*The Fall*

heaven raged with those in league with Satan who was making a counter-claim for every aspect of this planet. The writer showed that visible violence was a result of the heavenly battle tearing through the fabric of the visible world.

But from Michael's discussions with the hospital chaplain during the time he was recovering from the trauma of Melissa's death, he had learnt there was only one Saviour and that his crucifixion had saved the world. So was all the evil Michael saw around him the result of Satan attacking humanity for believing in Jesus and how much more time was left before the woman with eagle's wings would return? Why were young women being raped to conceive children from beings of darkness? Then Michael had a thought. As he remembered his wedding night he pictured not only the darkness that had held him away from Melissa but a presence of light that had hung over Melissa. Were there demons and angels present?

Then a rush of images flooded Michael's mind. Memories of the day he had first gone to ask the professor for his pay. The professor had been ranting on about Satan and 200 angels rebelling against God by taking women as their wives and having children by them. Michael recalled the professor had mentioned the Book of Enoch. He flicked through his bible but could find no such book. This puzzled him so he went to the end of his bible and found an index. Tracing his finger down to 'E' he found Enoch the man who did not die. The page number took him right back to Genesis to a commentary relating to Enoch walking with God and being taken away and not dying. The note referred to Chapter Five but was directly above the beginning of Chapter Six. Michael's eyes ran through the first few lines to find himself reading about the sons of God on seeing the daughters of men were beautiful had taken them to be their wives. Their offspring were the Nephilim, known as the heroes of old but God was aggrieved by the wickedness of man and resolved to wipe out every living creature with the flood.

Michael felt a shiver run up his spine. He looked back at the bookshelf and wondered if there was an entry about Enoch in the set of encyclopedias he had. He pulled out the volume that ranged from

'Delusion to Frenssen' and found entries about two books by Enoch. There was no reference to what the first book was about but the second showed Enoch walking with God and receiving secret wisdoms and journeying through seven levels of heaven. Michael replaced the encyclopedia, frustrated that his little bit of research still left much to be answered. Yet, he felt that he had begun a journey and was eager to pursue things further.

There was now an urgency to find the professor. He would be able to answer Michael's questions but how much was the professor's life in danger or even his own. Michael zipped up the army jacket and pulled on a woolly thermal hat and stepped into the cold air outside his flat.

*The Fall*

## CHAPTER THIRTY-TWO

Across the city, Phoebe drove into a small car park close to St. Michael's Church. Buses were ferrying passengers from the suburbs to do their weekend shopping. Most were streaming into the Bullring for the latest bargains. As Phoebe reversed the car into a space she felt the wheels slip a little over an icy patch. There had been a hard frost the previous night and the sun was still too low in the sky to reach over the inner city buildings to have much affect.

Phoebe left the car in gear and locked it with her infrared key before making her way to the pedestrian crossing. She pulled her coat around her body to keep the heat in but to scant avail. A middle-aged woman bumped into her.

"Hey, why don't you look where you're going? Little madam."

Before Phoebe could say anything the woman was lost in the crowd muttering under her breath. Phoebe was quite stunned but had more important things on her mind. Her father had still not returned home and a deep dread hung heavy on her heart and she didn't know how to lift it. Her feelings for Michael had also grown but she did not know whether to go with her heart which was telling her to trust him or listen to her head which warned that he was dangerous. Her anxiety tensed the muscles in her chest and across her shoulders. At times she felt as though she could not breathe the pain was so sharp. There was so much stress in her life and she did not have the time to run and release the energy that was building up inside her.

Through the double doors away from the hustle of shoppers there came a sudden calm. She dipped her right hand into the holy water font and blessed herself. The thought struck her how unusual this was as she was not a Catholic but instinctively she had known what to do. A second notion came into her head. The pains in her chest and

*George John Kingsnorth*

across her shoulders also subsided as though a foreign body had been thrown aside. She felt less heavy. The sensation was so weird she found herself looking about where she stood to try and see what had just left her. There was nothing visible there, whatever it was, she just knew it was gone.

Moments later she sat in a pew. The church was dark with light streaming through the stain-glass windows adding bright reds, blues, greens and yellows to the mahogany wall panels and benches. A great exhaustion flowed over her and she felt her energy ebb towards her feet. Her body felt so relaxed that she found it hard to keep her eyes open. It was as if she no longer had to be on guard, no longer had to be in a state of alert, ready to take on some kind of assailant.

Father Thomas was saying a prayer in front of a small congregation in a side chapel. He was sprinkling holy water over people and they were blessing themselves. In a low tone Phoebe could hear the priest's words.

"Have mercy on me, O God, according to your unfailing love. Wash away all my iniquity and cleanse me from my sin. Cleanse me with hyssop, and I shall be clean; wash me, and I shall be whiter than snow."

Phoebe lost all sense of time and was unaware of whether it had been seconds or hours that she had been sitting in the pew with her eyes half closed. She could see hazy images of Michael and her father, memories of events from just a few hours ago and of decades past. She felt guilty about some of the things she had said to her father, her mother and to Michael.

A tear ran down Phoebe's cheek. In her mind her mother held her hand.

"I'm sorry, Phoebe. I'm sorry you had to stay to look after me."

She could feel her mother's fingers slide across her own, until a fleeting glance of fingertips signaled their detachment and her mother was gone. Involuntarily, Phoebe gasped air into her lungs and a curtain of tears fell blurring her view of the church.

"Are you okay, Miss?" came a man's voice. Phoebe looked through the tears towards the origin of the sound. A dark figure stood

*The Fall*

over her. A pang of fear jolted her as she rubbed her eyes. The man came into focus and she could see he was in his early fifties with graying hair and glasses smiling at her. He was a priest.

"Sorry, Father. I'm being silly."

"I'm sure you're not. There must be every good reason why you feel the way you do. My name is Father Declan." He sat down beside her. "Why don't you tell me about what's troubling you?"

"Where to start?" Phoebe sighed. Father Declan smiled causing Phoebe to echo his gesture.

"Okay, my mum died recently. My dad's lost in his work so he doesn't have to face it all but now I've met this guy and… …well, I'm jumping ahead of myself. The thing is this guy, I've just discovered was accused of murdering his wife, years ago mind, and…" Her eyes filled once more with tears. "He saved my life. There was this explosion and before it I thought he was going to kill me but he saved me. I'm so confused, Father."

"I'm sure you are. That's a lot to contend with."

"You might think! But it goes on," Phoebe laughed trying to wipe away fresh tears. "You see after the explosion, and we don't know what it was, the girl from next door came round naked, screaming she had been raped by an angel."

Father Declan's eye widened. Phoebe continued, "I know, it seems all crazy. I took Michael to the hospital and a friend, you must know her, Grace, she comes here?"

Father Declan seemed uncertain. "Grace?"

"That's right, Grace. She sings in the choir. Father Thomas knows her."

Father Declan still seemed unsure.

"Okay, well, Grace and dad were going to look after Mara, the girl from next door but none of them have been seen since. When I got back home from the hospital, there were police all over the place. They had found a body in Mara's house decomposed beyond recognition and it seems the explosion had come from the house too but there were no signs of gas or anything."

"I see," remarked Father Declan, still trying to take in all that he had just heard. "That's a remarkable story."

"And you don't believe it, do you?"

"I didn't say that."

"You didn't have to, it's painted all over your face."

"Look, what's your name?"

"Phoebe."

"Phoebe, you've obviously been through a very traumatic time and you need some help." He held her hand. Phoebe wanted to pull it away, conscious that he didn't believe her.

"Look Father, it's all true. I'm not making this up. You can check out the hospital." Then she realised the nurses would not be too please as Michael and she had run away to try and find her dad. "Father, I just need some guidance. I've felt as though something strange has been following me and when I came in here it lifted, so I feel safe in here."

Father Declan, was further startled by this revelation. His mind began to race, wondering how best to help the girl. He suspected she was under a lot of mental stress and obviously hallucinating.

"I have some friends who might be able to help you, Phoebe. I can get their phone number for you. Will you wait for a moment or two?"

Phoebe nodded her head. Father Declan got up and went out to the vestry. Phoebe felt a sudden unease. She knew her story sounded crazy and was not certain the priest had really heard what she had been saying. She began to wonder whom he might have gone to call. A voice in her head told her to leave. She scanned the church. Only a couple of people were there but they were absorbed in prayer. Quickly Phoebe got up out of the pew and began to make her way towards the door. At the back of the church beside a collection of books and magazines was a collection of translucent plastic figurines of the Madonna. A sign indicated they were full of Holy Water. Phoebe felt compelled to lift a few. She dropped a couple of pound coins into a money box just as Father Declan caught sight of her and raced out of the vestry.

"Phoebe, wait. You need help!"

*The Fall*

No sooner had Phoebe left the church, the sensation of fear returned to her shoulders, weighing her down. She ran across the road, barely dodging two taxis that honked their horns at her. She nearly slid across the path of slowly melting ice and fumbled in her handbag for her car keys. The top of one of the Holy Water bottles came lose and the fluid spilt onto Phoebe's hands. Father Declan was calling from across the road. The car door opened and Phoebe wiped the perspiration from her brow. The Holy Water came into contact with her skin. There was a sudden release. Phoebe's mind became less clouded and she was focused. The priest was running across the road. Phoebe slipped the keys into the ignition, the car burst into life and she managed to accelerate out of the car park before the priest could note down her registration number.

Phoebe's car darted into the flow of traffic onto a roundabout and quickly took the second turning off. She noticed the holy water seeping away and with one hand, tightened the blue cap. Now she had to get home. Perhaps her dad would be there.

## CHAPTER THIRTY-THREE

A few streets away from where Phoebe had sped off in her car, Michael was walking towards a three storey building that was almost derelict. At the end of the street he could see busy traffic buzzing to and fro and pedestrians hurrying away lost in their own little worlds virtually oblivious to everyone else around them. Most of the buildings Michael passed were boarded up and demolition notices were pasted on the doors. However, one building remained intact and open for customers. A large Perspex illuminated sign informed him that he had reached the place where Peter Stoneywell's detective agency was located.

A security guard opened the main door and directed Michael up to the third floor. The lift was not working so he had to make his way up using the stairs. From what he could tell, there seemed to be other occupants in the building. Reaching the third landing, Michael pushed open a set of brown painted double doors. There was a damp smell to everything, a sense of decay or even death. The death one senses when a company has run it course and everything is being shut down, wrapped up and boxed for either destruction or, if lucky, relocation.

Through frosted glass windows, Michael could see the orange glow of tungsten lights. Stacked against the glass were piles of tan coloured files bursting with A4 sheets of paper. Michael knocked on the door.

"Come in."

Michael pushed open the office door marked with the detective's name and telephone number in gold. Inside Michael saw a young woman in her mid-twenties whom he assumed was working through one of the files at her desk. The place was just cluttered with files.

*The Fall*

There was a telephone on the desk but no other form of modern technology.

"Hi, I'm here to see… don't you have a computer?"

The young woman looked over her black-rimmed glasses like a schoolmistress.

"Pardon me, sir. There's no need to be impertinent."

"I'm sorry, it just struck me that you don't have a computer and it seemed odd in this day and age."

"But then we have records going back over the past 70 years that can be located in the traditional way within 30 minutes. Most of our rivals struggle to locate their computer files because they have backed them up on tape based systems that were replaced by digital discs which get scratched or on hard drives that after a few years don't work. Mr. Stoneywell believes it's all a fallacy. Technology is just a rouse to distract people from understanding the reality of the demise of western society and the conspiracy to control the populace. Now how can I help you?"

An ingenuous smile spread across the woman's face as she waited impatiently to know Michael's business. A nameplate on a triangular block indicated the woman's name was Emma Brooks. She pulled out an empty folder and lifted a pen.

"Name?"

"Oh, er, Michael Davies."

"That's good, for a moment I thought you had forgotten. Take a seat. Mr. Stoneywell will be with you in a few minutes."

Michael looked around to see where he could sit. Most chairs were piled high with files.

"Do you mind if I move some of these?" asked Michael pointing to a stack of folders on a chair.

"Not those. I need those there."

"Where can I sit then?"

"Just give me a second and I'll find you a place," came the irritated reply. Michael waited for a minute or so longer before Ms. Brooks finished what she was doing and came to his side of the desk to make a space for him to sit down.

*George John Kingsnorth*

"Thank you," Michael reluctantly responded to her gesture.

"Whatever." Ms. Brooks made her way back to her own seat and continued to work through a stack of papers, blocking Michael out of her mind.

Michael sat down and wondered how much more time it would take before he got to see Stoneywell. Through the frosted glass of another door, Michael could see two silhouetted figures. One was pacing back and forth while the other a taller figure remained static, so still in fact that Michael at first did not realise it was a person until the head moved slightly to follow the pacing figure. There was the muffled sound of a male voice speaking with annoyance and frustration but the words came to Michael as simple tones with no form or sense. He took a deep breath, lent on his elbows and looked down at his feet. Suddenly the door to Stoneywell's office opened.

"Mr. Davies, won't you come in?"

Michael looked up stunned. When did Ms. Brooks give Stoneywell his name? He saw no intercom. He saw no technology other than the phone. Michael got to his feet and passed Stoneywell who remained standing at the door to close it.

"Where did your other client go?"

"What other client?" replied Stoneywell a little bewildered.

"The one you were talking to a few moments ago."

"I wasn't talking to a client."

"I saw you pacing up and down and there was someone in there watching you."

"Na, you must have just seen my coat hanging over there." Stoneywell pointed to a large black coat hanging from a mahogany coat stand. Michael looked at where he had just come in and the position of the coat stand. It was not in the right position to have been what he saw from the chair. The stand was too far over to the left to have been visible from Michael's vantage point. He felt a sense of unease. When he turned back to Stoneywell, the man had a broad smile on his face.

"So how can I help you?"

"Are you sure you weren't talking to someone."

*The Fall*

"Dictating notes to Ms. Brooks when you came in. Bluetooth and mobiles."

"What?"

"Modern technology, wonderful stuff."

"But Ms. Brooks said you disliked technology."

"No, that's just Ms. Brooks. She's superstitious of computers. Thinks they are just magic boxes. Silly really. Anyway, back to why you're here?"

"Um," Michael still tried to puzzle over what he had seen and make sense of what Stoneywell had just said.

"Time is money, Mr. Davies. What can I do for you?"

"Sorry, uhm, a couple of friends have gone missing and I need help finding them."

"Lovers, eh? Happens all the time. He stole your girlfriend?"

"No."

"She stole your boyfriend? Messy business."

"No, it's nothing like that. They're just friends and they've vanished. I need to find them, I think they're in trouble."

"Why don't you go to the police?"

"I don't think they'd believe what I have to tell them."

"Why do you think I will?"

"Because I can pay you to find them."

"But can you pay enough?"

"Look," Michael stands up to go. "I'm sorry I've bothered you perhaps someone else can help?"

"No, don't be like that. Of course we're open for business. I'm just trying to find out how much you need to find them. Sit down, let's talk it over and see where to start."

Reluctantly, Michael sat down. He felt uneasy and did not know how far he could trust Stoneywell but time was running out and he needed to find the professor and see if Mara was okay.

"Do you believe in demons, Mr. Stoneywell?"

## CHAPTER THIRTY-FOUR

From where Mara stood, looking out of the grimy windows of the warehouse, she could see in the distance, planes rising in the sky from Birmingham International Airport. Each one cut across the brilliance of the sun, disappearing momentarily into the light before reappearing in silhouette leaving a vapour trail in their midst. There were no clouds, just the blinding sun and a pale blue sky nearly bleached of colour. The heat through the glass gently caressed her skin as she stood naked sipping a cup of coffee she had made in the makeshift kitchen.

Inside the fake house she did not care about how she appeared. She no longer cared that the fabrication took on forms of its own choice. Her home, an ex-boyfriend's flat, a stranger's house. As she bathed in the sunlight the pain in her limbs seemed to subside. The beauty she seemed to have had was fading, her skin sagged, her boobs drooped and her face was covered in zits, her hair was matted together and in desperate need of a wash but she had felt too tired to attend to any of these needs. Yet the sun on her skin seemed to revitalize her and she enjoyed the warmth and the way the light faded out the colours and eradicated the shadows.

A tear ran down her cheek and she wiped it away with the back of her hand. Then she heard a noise from behind her. She turned and looked at the inner shelter that had been built inside the warehouse. The rooms that had been at one point a replica of her home was now merely sheets of polythene hanging from a timber framework that made up the walls.

Again she heard the sound and her newly developed motherly instincts kicked in, driving her to want to check her newborn. Reluctantly Mara turned from basking in the sun and walked away

*The Fall*

from the windows to make her way back to the shelter. The shadow crept down from her head, across her back, over her buttocks, down the backs of her thighs, her lower legs, ankles and soles of her feet as they rose to take another step. She was sad to feel the heat of the sun leave her body but her new responsibilities took priority.

She pulled back the plastic sheets to create an entrance for herself. Inside, the room had taken on the form of a kitchen. She was drawn once more to sounds, the sounds of objects shattering and being munched. There was the debris of saucers, cups and plates on the floor.

Pieces of plates, dishes, cups and silverware were being tossed in her direction. She lifted one spoon to find teeth marks where a piece has been bitten out. Suddenly the sink unit collapsed and the baby crawled into the shadows. Two eyes stared back at Mara as she knelt down to see inside the darkness and smiled. The eyes appeared to smile too. Then there was a loud belch and a giggle from the dark. A movement to her side distracted Mara from looking at her baby. What ever it was had crept into another shadow on the far side of the room. A rage built up inside and Mara sprang across the floor picking up a metal splinter, she charged towards the dark shape. The adrenaline flushed through her veins and like an Olympic athlete she was on the threat before it could react.

Mara slashed the shard from side to side and the being was dismembered, totally shocked by what had just happened to it.

"You can't do this to me. You're human, it's not possible," cried out the demon as it fell to its knees and shattered into a million particles of black dust. From the shadow of the sink Mara's child giggled with glee and clapped his hands.

Mara grinned. "Don't worry, my son. Mummy is here to protect you. No nasty is going to get you I promise."

The child clapped his hands frantically with excitement and joy at the sport he saw.

"Do it again, mummy. Do it again."

Mara's smile slipped away. She shook her head. Her baby spoke. He can talk. How can this be? She had no time to ponder these

*George John Kingsnorth*

thoughts as she was suddenly snapped, thrown into the air and slammed against the fridge.

"Go get it, Mummy. Yeah," cheered the baby. "Go get it."

The demon was just as surprised by the infant. The distraction gave Mara an instance to get to her feet and pounce like a leopard onto her prey. She ripped the beast apart and scattered its limbs about the room in a fury she was shocked to find still harboured inside her when she stopped. Again the spectacle excited the child of his mother's prowess.

"There's another one coming, Mummy. Get ready to go again."

The lift doors slid open and Mara spun round to make ready to attack once more. A black shoe appeared followed by flannel trousers and a long coat. Mara tensed herself, ready to dash across the warehouse floor, some, 50 feet to the lift. She gritted her teeth.

"Mara, I'm back," shouted Professor Garrett.

Mara relaxed.

"No, mummy kill!" screamed the baby.

The professor stopped in his tracks, dismayed at hearing the little voice coming from within the makeshift rooms.

"Mara," he called cautiously. "Is it safe to come in? I've brought some provisions, a laptop and a mobile so we can see what's happening outside. We can see the news on the Internet."

"What's the Internet, mummy?" quizzed the baby. "I want to see. I want it. Let me see."

Mara turned to look at the baby as it crawled out from under the collapsed sink unit and stood up. Mara relaxed as she watched the child in disbelief. Then she wanted to share the experience with someone else.

"Professor, come quick. Look at this. Quick."

The professor rushed into the kitchen area, through the plastic sheets.

"Is everything alright, Mara?"

"Great, chipper, all hunky-dory."

The professor averted his eyes when he realised Mara was naked.

"Shouldn't you put some thing on?"

*The Fall*

"Why, have you never seen a woman naked before?"

"Its not appropriate Mara. I'd appreciate it if you could dress."

The child ran up to the professor and pulled the laptop away from him and the mobile. The shock hit the professor like being smacked by a juggernaut face on. He sank to his knees.

"How can this be possible?"

"It shouldn't be but it is," stated Mara as she watched the baby open the laptop and press the 'on' button. The child then began to fiddle with the mobile and search for a service.

"How does he know to do this," whispered the professor.

"I don't know, he doesn't get it from me. Perhaps it's because his father was…" She didn't finish.

"An angel," stated the professor. "No, that can't be. That's just theory, a myth, a made up story."

"It's real professor. Very real," stressed Mara.

"No, no, everyone said it wasn't true, that my hypothesis was way off mark. It can't be true, there must be another explanation. I've been fooling myself, I'm just dreaming, this isn't reality."

"Typical," scoffed Mara. "When the truth finally hits home, you can't face it and have to retreat into the falsehood of empirical studies. Well let me tell you, no scientific principles are going to save you now!"

Amidst the anger, Mara was also surprised to find how well she had been able to express herself. See, she thought, I'm not stupid.

"No, no, I'm sure I just got it all wrong. I'll surf the Internet and find some more up-to-date information," struggled the professor. But when he managed to focus on what was happening around him, the child had connected the laptop to broadband via the mobile and was scanning through page after page at such an incredible rate, soaking up all the data he could find. When the professor reached across to take the laptop the child turned round and growled at him.

"This is my computer, leave me alone. Go find another, old man."

The professor froze in his seat, stunned by the child's response.

"Professor," interrupted Mara. "There's no need to look on the Internet for information about what is happening here. You are living

*George John Kingsnorth*

the actual reality of his existence."

"If this is true and what I have been teaching to the students is true, then this is the most frightening thing that could possibly be happening." The professor momentarily took his eyes off the child and looked at Mara. "Do you want me to still believe this?"

Mara shook her head not knowing what to say at this point. The professor again turned his attention to the child.

"You have to believe this, professor," answered the child. "I exist. I am a reality. I am here and I won't go away. Now, I need to consume as much information as I can and you are disturbing me, so can you please be quiet? Mother, I'm hungry, feed me!"

No more was said. The child turned back to the screen, where each page was now just a blur of information that the professor and Mara could no longer see.

"Professor, this computer isn't fast enough. Get me another."

"I can't afford too. I don't have any more money."

"You can't afford not to professor. You'd better get one. Now!" The child's voice had deepened and the tones were sinister. The professor was suddenly gripped with fear and jumped to his feet.

"I'll go now and see what I can do," the professor stuttered.

"Don't be long," answered the child.

"Will you be okay, Mara."

"She'll be okay," replied the child.

The professor raced through the plastic sheeting and pumped away at the lift button in the hope that it would arrive quicker so that he could get out of this nightmare.

"Well, mother. What have you got for me to eat?"

*The Fall*

## CHAPTER THIRTY-FIVE

Phoebe fumbled with the keys to open the front door. Her hands would not stop shaking. It was as though a portal had opened in her mind to a whole new reality and nobody else seemed to be aware of it as they blissfully went about their lives.

Finally the door swung open and she had access to her home. Her sanctuary. She slammed the door behind her, pushed up the slide button to deadlock the mechanism and pulled across the secondary bolt-action lock lower down the door. Feeling a little more secure she rested against the back of the door and closed her eyes for a moment.

There was a silence in the hallway. She could hear the ticking of the mantel clock in the front room. In the kitchen the fridge began to hum. Outside she was aware of traffic passing at the top of the street. A bird whistled from its perch on top of the chimney. Floorboards upstairs began to creak as the sun passed from one side of the house to the other, heating the opposite side of the rooms. Rays of light spilt through the kitchen window full of dust particles. The pipes gurgled momentarily as the heating was automatically started. Everything seemed normal, quiet and peaceful. Phoebe felt safe.

From her handbag, Phoebe lifted the bottles of Holy Water. She opened one and splashed a few drops around the rooms on the ground floor. Then ran upstairs and did the same. Back downstairs she took off her coat and could feel the back of her shirt peel away from her perspiration drenched skin. Under her arms she felt sticky and was aware that her deodorant had failed leaving the smell of sweat a little too pungent for her liking.

Phoebe kicked off her shoes, tossed them beneath her father's old coat rack beside the front door and then raced upstairs to the bathroom. She pushed the button on the shower and swiftly moved her arm out of the way of the cold jet of water. In her bedroom, she stripped off and threw all her clothes into the laundry basket. Then made her way to the hot press on the landing, to pull out a couple of towels for her hair and body, and a third to soak up any moisture when she stepped out of the shower later.

When she returned to the bathroom there was condensation on the inner side of the glass shower doors. She placed the smallest towel on the floor and hung the other two on the radiator. As she stepped into the shower the initial sensation of the hot jets of water against her skin made her gasp, then she slid the glass panels together. She relaxed and closed her eyes, enjoying the spray pummeling against her skull. Through the long strands of her hair the droplets chased each other down her shoulders, spine and lower back. The aching of her muscles began to be soothed and she felt her legs begin to wobble. Perhaps a bath would have been better, she thought but then she would have had to wait for the water to heat up and she had been too impatient.

With the first thud, Phoebe felt all her muscles go taut once more. The echo reverberated around the whole house as the large iron knocker struck the base plate for a second and third time. Phoebe's skin tingled as energy spiked every nerve ending in her body. She jumped out of the shower leaving behind pools of water where she had missed the small towel. Grabbing the two towels from the radiator she wrapped one around her body and the other around her hair.

"Why don't I just ignore it," she thought but then the knocking became more insistent and she felt compelled to answer the door. She raced down the stairs leaving damp footprints of every step. At the door she pulled across the bolt-action lock, then stopped.

"Who's there?"

"It's me, Michael. I wanted to check you were alright."

"I'm busy now, can you call back later?"

"I've been to the private investigator and I want to look at your father's books. He was reading something I think might help. Can I come in? Please?"

*The Fall*

"Do you have to?"

"I must."

Phoebe was backing away from the door but then Michael began to wrap the knocker again continuously.

"Michael, stop it."

"Then let me in, I need to see the professor's library."

"Look wait. Give me a few moments."

She reached into her coat pockets and pulled out the bottles of Holy Water she had got from the church. She removed the top from one of them and carefully opened the door. As Michael impatiently began to push his way in, Phoebe soaked his face with the Holy Water.

"What did you do that for?"

"I don't know, Holy Water seems to burn monsters in Dracula movies, I thought it might work with you?" Her towel unraveled from her body and she quickly tried to retrieve it as Michael turned to face the other way. Phoebe blushed as Michael closed the door.

"Can you give me a few minutes to get dressed?" whispered Phoebe. Michael nodded still with his face averted.

"Promise you won't turn around until I'm up the stairs?"

"Okay, I promise."

Phoebe bolted up the stairs as quickly as she could, checking to see that Michael had not turned.

"Is it okay for me to go into the library?"

"Yes, I'll only be a few moments."

In her bedroom, Phoebe fumbled through her draws to find underwear and socks. She pulled on jogging pants and a T-shirt. Her hair was still wet and she was worried it would go all frizzy. Hastily she brushed through her hair and fanned a drier above her head to try and remove most of the dampness.

Her thoughts lingered on what had just happened and she was a little embarrassed to have been naked in front of Michael. She was pleased he had been a gentleman, then began to wonder if he had liked what he had seen? Was she pleasing to him? It then struck her that the dark thoughts she had previously had at Michael's apartment were no longer oppressing her. She felt happier, playful and at ease in his company. She could not explain it.

With her hair nearly dried she was keen to get downstairs to be with Michael. She laughed to herself recalling the memory of the blast when she peed herself and had to clean up before dragging Michael out of the house and now she had exposed herself to him but she felt comfortable about it. Not as embarrassed as she thought she should be. Michael made her feel content. Before going down stairs she sprayed herself with perfume and left her hair hanging over her shoulders.

She rushed into the library to discover Michael buried in a book on religious heresies.

"What you reading?" she asked.

"Uh? Oh. This is about the Origen Conspiracy."

"Oh."

She brushed up beside him under the premise of looking at what he was reading but primarily so he could smell her fragrance.

"What's it say?"

"Apparently, Origen was a theologian from the second to third century."

"Oh, that's interesting." Phoebe pushed herself in a little closer to Michael.

"Origen believed that angels when they sinned, their bodies gradually solidified in stages until they either had human bodies or even worse, turned into demons." Michael moved away from Phoebe and sat on a double seater sofa.

"But demons have spiritual bodies, don't they? They're not physical." Phoebe snuggled in beside Michael as he flicked through more pages of the book.

"Yes, I know, but this also seems to indicate that angels can change back and forth between spiritual and physical as part of their freewill. Origen also indicates that John the Baptist was a chosen messenger of God deliberately made into human form to serve Jesus."

Phoebe's attention was more focused on Michael than the pages of the book he was reading. Michael's sensed Phoebe's perfume and momentarily was distracted from the words on the page.

*The Fall*

"What are you doing?" he asked her.

"Nothing."

"I thought you didn't like me?"

Phoebe smiled searching his eyes, she was the centre of his attention. She leant forward, closed her eyes and waited for him to kiss her.

"Do you believe in devils?"

Shocked by his response, Phoebe opened her eyes again annoyed that he was not taking what she was offering.

"I might, I'm not sure."

Michael turned back to the pages of the book. "I want to see..."

"See what?" snapped Phoebe.

"I need to find out what's going on and I think the answers are in this room."

"Possibly sitting right in from of you?" replied Phoebe sarcastically.

"Precisely." Michael flicked through the book, his focus gone from Phoebe. Frustrated Phoebe grabbed the lapels of Michael coat and pulled him round ensuring both their lips met. As Phoebe wraps her arms around Michael's neck the front door burst open. Phoebe jumped back like a schoolgirl caught in the act. Professor Garrett passed by the library door and raced into the kitchen. Phoebe ran to the door leaving Michael still startled by what had just happened.

"Dad, where've you been?"

The professor had a whiskey glass in his hand that he had just emptied moments before.

"Dad, you okay?"

Still no comment, the professor did not even make eye contact with his daughter. Michael joined them.

"Professor, where's Mara?"

Finally, the professor looked at them both and laughed. "You're not going to believe me, either of you."

"Try us," encouraged Michael.

The professor poured another glass of whiskey and downed it in one gulp. He then left the glass in the sink and sat down at the kitchen table. Phoebe looks over to Michael and frowned. Michael shrugged his shoulders as the two of them pulled out chairs and sat.

"Well," requested Phoebe impatiently. "What's been going on?"

"Mara's had a baby."

"What," both Michael and Phoebe remarked.

"Are you kidding," added Michael. "She only told us she had been raped the night of the explosion."

"That's right, but you've seen it before, haven't you Michael?"

Phoebe again felt a certain dread rise within her. She had, for some reason, suspended her previous concerns, driven by her passions. Her father's presence once more instilled the fears she did not want to face.

"I have," replied Michael. "My wife on our wedding day."

"And the doctors convinced you that it was all in you mind."

"Yes."

"And you believed them?"

"Yes."

"And now?"

"I have my doubts."

"About what they said or about your actual experience?"

"I think it really happened."

"What really happened?" screamed Phoebe feeling left out by this almost cryptic conversation.

"Michael was a witness to an angel raping his wife on their wedding night."

"Is this true, Michael?"

"Yes, Phoebe. It's all true."

"Why didn't you tell me?"

"It was hard. I wasn't sure myself. It's only that the professor is putting it all into words now, that I'm able to accept it."

"So you never intended to hurt me?"

"Why would you think such a thing?"

"I..."

Michael glanced at Phoebe as she blushed.

"I misunderstood. I was confused."

*The Fall*

"Phoebe, I…"

"Listen," interrupted the professor. "It's not all over yet. Mara, has had her baby and there are things going on that I can't fathom."

"What?" asked Michael.

"I think the demons drew an angel to Mara, so she could conceive. The gestation lasted just three days not the normal 40 weeks."

"How's that possible?" quizzed Phoebe.

"I don't know," remarked the professor, "but the child can already speak and is soaking up all the information it can find on the Internet and it is growing rapidly. The child is an abomination."

"Oh, come on, dad. That's a bit strong."

"No, Phoebe, it isn't. Only humans are meant to procreate because they are mortal. They die so to keep mankind…"

"And womankind," added Phoebe.

"If you like. To keep the human race going we need to procreate and have babies."

"Obviously," commented Phoebe sarcastically.

"Go on, professor," said Michael eagerly.

"Angels have eternal life so there is no need for them to mate but they also have freewill. Some say there were beings higher than angels that, having grown tired of being in the presence of God, desired to be with the women on earth, seeing them to be comely."

"Isn't this getting a bit far fetched?" remarked Phoebe.

"It would be if it wasn't for the fact we were seeing it all happen here. The thing is that the child is therefore a Nephilim and in so being, its soul is not allowed to enter heaven. It is condemned like its father to the same fate as Satan and the rebellious angels."

"And why would you want to condemn yourself?" puzzled Phoebe.

"Well, I suppose," thought the professor. "If you want everyone to be separated from God then by getting them to commit suicide you've accomplished that end?"

"So how does that effect us now?" wondered Michael.

"In the Book of Enoch the Nephilim grew to enormous size and started to consume everything. When all ran out they started to eat humans."

"Err, gross," chimed Phoebe. "So you think Mara's baby is going to start killing?"

"Is Mara in danger?" asked Michael.

"We all could be."

"Where is she now?"

"She's in a warehouse near…"

At that moment the kitchen window smashed into the room. Shards of glass cascaded across the kitchen. The body of a crow lay lifeless on the tiles with it's blood seeping out. Phoebe ran out of the kitchen down the corridor while both Michael and the professor examined the body.

"Why do you think the bird did that?" questioned the professor.

"The birds have been congregating around Mara's house since this all started."

Phoebe re-entered the kitchen and dowsed the corpse with the Holy Water. Instantly the feathers on the bird began to sizzle and bubble up as though hit by acid.

"What's in that container?" demanded the professor.

"Holy Water, nothing else," Phoebe explained just as shocked as her father. "I didn't expect that to happen."

"Could the bird be a demon, professor?"

"If they are perhaps we've just found a weapon."

*The Fall*

## CHAPTER THIRTY-SIX

By afternoon the sky was overshadowed by dark clouds swept in by an easterly wind. Stoneywell pulled up his collar as he paced through the streets eager to get to his destination. The rain blurred his vision. A taxi crashed through a puddle of water from a blocked drain, sending a mucky spray over Stoneywell's legs. He swore at the driver but his oaths were in vain as a second vehicle sliced through the water, dousing him again.

Dodging the traffic, Stoneywell raced across the street to the city cathedral. Once inside he made his way toward the altar. There were only a few other sinners in sight. Some saying Rosaries, others lighting candles in front of the Madonna, a few were in deep thought considering how they would tell the priest their confession. None were aware that Stoneywell had joined them.

He sat in a pew. The sound of the pelting rain echoed around the interior of the cathedral, drowning out all other noise. The flickering candles cast high shadows across the limestone walls, exaggerating the movements of people blessing themselves before praying.

Then everything stopped. No sound, no movement, just quietness, peace. Stoneywell looked up as a winged shadow fell across the empty benches. The Archangel Raphael was gracefully descending. Stoneywell fell to his knees and closed his eyes.

"Fear not. What do you have to report?"

"My Lord, demons have snared another angel with a woman. She has given birth to an obscenity."

"We are aware of this grave sin. One has been chosen from the children of Adam to sever the life-force of the unholy one. Go and await your instructions."

Trembling, Stoneywell replied, "your servant obeys."

*George John Kingsnorth*

A brilliant light blinded him temporarily and as he regained his sight a few moments later the sound of beating rain flooded his ears so much he clapped his hands around them. Seeing the angel had gone, Stoneywell got to his feet to leave.

From the bell tower, Raphael watched Stoneywell trample through the rain, occasionally jostled by passersby.

"Hey, watch where you're going, mate," snapped Stoneywell to a young mother heavily laden with shopping trying to control her four year old son. Stoneywell marched on without another thought and jumped onto a bus just as it was moving off.

Across to the east of the city the rain had subsided and once more large shafts of light cut through the clouds. A patchwork of orange contrasted with the blue tinted areas of land overcast with cloud shadows. Further away towards Coventry and to the south the clouds had dissipated all together.

Raphael turned back to the interior of the belfry. To his surprise Grace lay on the wooden floor.

"Grace, what happened?"

Weak from battle, Grace attempted to rise. "The demons knew where we were going to install Mara and took the place. Sister Philomena was able to get in and help deliver the baby but there was no way I could stand my ground. They have legions there surrounding the place. The child is strong, he is able to hold them back by himself. He is growing physically, mentally and spiritually. The demons fear him."

"What about the professor and his daughter?"

"At the moment they are safe but I don't know for how long. When I fought with the demons one crashed through the Garrett's kitchen window. It's dead now."

"Good, the Garrett's are becoming aware. This will give them strength."

"What can I do?"

"Rest, there is another task soon for you but you'll need all of your strength. Soak up the prayer rays."

Below in the pews a new congregation had gathered and a Mass

*The Fall*

began. Grace felt the heat of the prayers cut through the wooden floor and her injuries melted away.

In the warehouse, Mara watched as the Nephilim boy absorbed all he could from the Internet. In minutes he had learned languages, absorbed encyclopedias and discovered how to hack into whatever system took his interest. Occasionally Mara saw her son get frustrated with leads that appeared to go nowhere and information that seemingly contradicted itself.

"I have been working this thing for hours and your kind still doesn't know what they are about. They're useless. They're like maggots. I'm hungry."

"There's nothing else left in the place, you've eaten everything. You're also spending too much time on the Internet. It'll do you no good."

"No, I need more information. I need to see how things work. I need food. Feed me."

Mara attempted to pull the child away from the computer but was flung across the room onto the bed.

"Stay away from me. You can't touch me. Knowledge is power. I need more."

"Do what you like, I'm going to get a bath. I feel dirty."

A pain dug into the boy's skull and he screamed out. Mara raced back into the room.

"What's wrong? Where do you hurt?"

"My head hurts."

"I told you, you're spending too much time in front of the computer."

"I thought you were getting a bath?"

"You can't speak to me that way, I'm your mother how…" As she went to slap the boy he stopped her arm and squeezed. Mara fell to her knees.

"You're hurting me. Let go."

"You are not to hurt me either. I can hurt you real bad."

He released Mara's arm and she fell to the ground. A red hand

## George John Kingsnorth

print seared her wrist. As the boy refocused on the computer and scrolled through numerous pages as soon as they appeared on screen, Mara got up and made her way into the bathroom. The immersion had been on so the water was piping hot.

Mara peeled off her clothes and noticed the bruises on her body and arms. Her face looked pale with dark rims around her eyes. Her hair lay like chords of rope and was very dull. The hot water seemed to sooth away the pain as she slipped into the back of the tub. She felt herself beginning to doze, to forget about the crazy things that had happened and to wonder what she had missed over the past nine months. Nine months, did not it fly by so quickly? Why did no-one come to see me? Why did Mr. Garrett from next door keep popping in then disappearing for so long and then pop up again as though he had not left. Crazy old hoot. They say academics are totally absent minded. He certainly is, Mara thought.

She slid down so her head was under the water and all the sound seemed muffled. Her limbs just floated and she began to feel more relaxed. Something fell into the water and struck her on the knee. Her face broke the surface and she wiped it with her hands. As the room came into focus she noticed the ceiling had gone.

"Baby, what you doing?"

She was suddenly startled to see the child had grown so big and was leaning over the wall of the bathroom, peering through the hole in the ceiling.

"I'm hungry, you didn't feed me."

"I won't be long I needed a bath. How come you've grown so big?" Mara scrabbled around for a towel to cover herself. "Listen love would you mind if I could have a little bit of privacy?" she asked nervously, not knowing what to expect next.

"How the hell did he grow so big in such a short period of time?" Mara wondered. "I've only been out of the room a few moments, surely?" She then noticed how cold the water seemed and her skin had wrinkled up like a prune. How long had she been in the bath? She lifted her watch the toilet seat. It read four 30 so she had been in the bath no longer than 20 minutes. What was happening in the room?

*The Fall*

No sooner was she out of the bath than the child's large hand, now spanning almost six feet, pulled up the tub and fed it into his mouth. Mara could hear the crunching of metal as the dirty bath water spilled over the lounge floor.

"Hey. I was just in there?"

"Were you? I'm hungry. The pain in my head is bad and the food helps it go away. What else can I eat?"

"I don't know you've eaten everything else. There's nothing left. Nothing at all."

"Nothing," pondered the Nephilim child. "Nothing. I need some meat."

"Well, I don't have any. There's none here."

The monster child frowned. "There is. I can smell it? Raw meat, it's here somewhere."

The child smelt the air and closed his eyes. Mara could see the steam from her moist skin being sucked into the child's nostrils and she began to realise what the meat was.

"You can't, I'm your mother."

The child's massive hand snapped around Mara's puny frame and squeezed. Mara sensed the air rush out of her lungs and her bones crunch but then everything went black.

Another growth spurt sprung through the child with the new protein injection from the meat of his mother's body. His frame stretched a further seven or eight inches along his limbs and torso. This time there was pain searing through his veins and arteries. The child's scream roared through the building, echoed down every corridor, like a foghorn. The Nephilim's mighty hand grabbed more plaster from the wall and stuffed it into his mouth but the taste was not the same as the flesh he had just consumed and he wanted more, more flesh, more meat and human meat tasted best.

It was time to leave the confines of this building, he had outgrown it and felt hemmed in. He wanted to explore the neighbourhood and see what else he could find. Besides, his fingers were now too large to operate the keyboard and he was becoming bored with not being able to soak up more knowledge.

With his fist he punched a hole in the ceiling and pulled himself out into the early evening sunshine.

## CHAPTER THIRTY-SEVEN

Phoebe followed Michael as he dashed out the front door. From the back of his van, Michael pulled out the catapult and began to gather pebbles from the gravel.

"What are you doing?"

"If the professor is right and the Holy Water can be of use, then I know I can kill the birds with these."

Unnoticed by them, two crows had taken positions on the telephone wires across the street.

"You'll be careful won't you?" quizzed Phoebe.

"Yeah." Michael stood and Phoebe suddenly wrapped her arms around his neck and kissed him. She didn't want to let go. She wanted to hold him forever. Initially she felt he was tense but as the kiss lingered his muscles relaxed and she felt he was enjoying the moment as much as she was.

The sudden jolt forcibly tore Michael away from Phoebe, causing her knees to buckle and she found herself falling on her backside. As she looked up she could see Michael was dazed by a black winged object, flapping about his head. Michael knocked the thing away as he stretched the rubber band and fired a pebble from his catapult. The black object jerked backwards with the impact but remained airborne.

Seeing Michael's weapon the second crow spread its wings and launched itself. In midair the bird transformed, grew larger and lost its feathers. A dark reptilian skin formed across its body and wings were shaped like bat's wings. Within moments it had joined its companion.

Before her eyes, Phoebe saw two demons flapping above Michael, who was struggling to raise his catapult to get another shot. There came a screaming roar from the front door. Startled, Phoebe looked across to see what other monster had arrived only to find her father brandishing a bottle of Holy Water. The liquid spewed through the air dousing the nearest beast and immediately blistering its reptilian skin as though it had been sprayed with acid.

Both creatures retreated, the second tending to the first, giving time for the professor to get to Michael.

"Professor the pebbles are having no effect."

"Pour some of this over them." The professor doused the pebbles in Michael's hand with Holy Water. Phoebe got to her feet just at the uninjured demon charged them once more. Phoebe was struck by one wing and sent flying onto the grass ten feet away. The second wing struck both the professor and Michael, launching them in the opposite direction. From the ground Michael loaded the leather pocket of the catapult with a doused pebble and fired. The stone ripped through the chest cavity, penetrating one of the beast's lungs and snapped through a rib close to its spine. The piercing scream made both Michael and the professor clamp their hands across their ears and fall to the ground in pain. Phoebe remained motionless on the grass. A trickle of blood rolled down her temple and dripped onto several blades of grass.

On hearing the screech of its companion the other demon became alert again and surveyed the scene. With both the professor and Michael rolling in pain they were unaware of Phoebe's vulnerability. The creature leapt to its feet, bounced 15 metres, grabbed Phoebe's by her arms and launched itself into the air. Initially, it miscalculated Phoebe's weight and was forced to make adjustments. Phoebe's legs were dragged across the gravel before the demon could get enough lift to sustain flight. A few more flaps of its wings and the beast made its escape.

Still with the pain in his ears, Michael caught sight of the first demon making off with Phoebe. Attempting to block out the pain, he lifted the catapult to fire but the second beast dashed his arm to the ground. The professor rolled away from both Michael and the creature and as the shrill stopped, grabbed a second bottle of Holy Water from his pocket.

*The Fall*

The beast dug its fanged teeth into Michael's arm. This time the shriek was human. The professor snapped off the top of the bottle and smashed it down onto the skull of the demon. Within seconds its entire head had melted into green oozing gunge. The rest of the body and limbs went limp and keeled onto the drive.

Michael's arm though cut and burning from the infectious bite had also been drenched in the Holy Water. To his surprise everything from the demon was dissolved.

"Let me take a look at that, Michael."

"It's okay, professor. I think the Holy Water has washed out the badness."

"We'll get you inside and dress the wound."

"Hadn't we better get after the other demon and Phoebe?"

"You'll be no good if you're bleeding all over the place."

The professor helped Michael towards the house. Away in the distance he caught sight of the silhouetted shapes of the demons wings with Phoebe's limp body hanging from its talons.

"Where's it taking her?"

"That's the direction Mara is, over by the old warehouses," replied the professor as the two of them raced through the hallway to the corridor.

"I've never really thought of this before but if Phoebe is still a virgin the demons will want to use her to produce more of their foul offspring." The professor pulled a roll of bandage and some gauze out of the drawer. Michael sat down beside the table and rolled up his sleeve. The professor found some cotton wool and disinfectant to clean out the wound. The first dabs stung. The professor worked in autopilot mode while his mind raced over what he thought was happening.

"This could mean the world is heading toward the Day of Judgment. The ranks of two opposing armies must be starting to swell, especially with the first born of the new Nephilim returning. Other angels must be rebelling."

With the end of the bandage, the professor got Michael to hold it in place while he found a safety pin. Locating one he fastened the

195

bandage.

"Okay, that's you sorted. We've got to get to Phoebe."

"Do we have any more Holy Water?" asked Michael.

"We'll have to stop off at a chapel and get some. You can find a couple of empty plastic milk cartons under the sink in a bag. Grab a couple and we'll go."

## CHAPTER THIRTY-EIGHT

The staleness of the air within the warehouse had been replaced by the fresh evening scent. There was a slight chill in the breeze even though the Nephilim could feel the warmth of the last embers of sunlight as the orb drifted towards the horizon. A few yellow, orange, gray and red clouds clustered around the Earth's falling star. The breeze ruffled the Nephilim's straggly hair. He closed his eyes and drew in breath through his nostrils. The initial freshness of air gradually mixed with the carbon dioxide fumes, cooking bacon, sausages, the fat of a deep pan fryer, vinegar and pepper. The Nephilim swished the excretions of saliva around with his tongue.

His stomach gurgled and he felt the gas in his stomach building. He needed more nourishment, something to fill him up. Then another scent caught his nostrils. A rosy perfume at first stung his nose but stirred his curiosity. He was drawn to the edge of the warehouse but saw nothing. The building opposite was about 30 feet away. He took a few steps back and then propelled himself from one roof to the other. Still no joy. A lorry sped passed in the street below, filling the air with burnt diesel. A disgusting taste which annoyed the Nephilim as he felt deprived of the sweetness of the fragrance he was pursuing. He jumped to street level, saw the headlamps of a second lorry, smashed the cab with his hands and ripped the driver from his seat. The damaged vehicle careered into the side of a redbrick warehouse, spraying the pavement with broken bricks. The Nephilim crunched the top half of the driver in his mouth leaving the lower body and legs dangling in his fist. Like a large gorilla he sat gnawing at the morsel of human flesh but still it was not enough. Again the Nephilim's body stretched causing him great pain. He could feel his bones like an arthritic. It took several minutes for the pain to subside.

Then the beast got to his feet and once more began sniffing the air for a fresh scent of the rosy perfume but it was not there. As he listened he could hear the sound of evening rush hour traffic roaring in the distance. Following the sound he eventually found the M6. Stepping out into the flow of traffic the first set of cars and lorries attempted to avoid the obstruction by ploughing into the concrete walls at the side of the carriageway. Subsequent vehicles careered straight through and piled into the Nephilim's feet and lower legs. The speed of the small number of lorries and cars sent him onto his back crushing several other vehicles. The Nephilim smashed his fist onto the roofs of others that had been fortunate to stop in time but not soon enough to get out of their cars.

Further down the motorway, people were braking and as quickly as possible leaving their vehicles to run back in the direction of the city centre.

The Nephilim felt the pangs in his stomach once more and seeing the stream of people racing away, pounced on the nearest group, scooped them up in his hand and crunched on their bones two at a time, while those waiting for their fate screamed.

Again another spate of pain tore through the Nephilim's body as it grew, now reaching almost 50 feet in height, 27 feet round his stomach and chest; 10 feet diameter biceps and 17 feet around the thighs. Hair covered most of his head and body like a lost feral child. His head was constantly throbbing with a headache that roamed around his skull like a migraine. But still he felt hungry.

The light from the city centre had grown stronger with the sun slipping beneath the horizon and the Nephilim's attention was drawn there until he suddenly saw a dark shape flying across the orange sky. The creature had wings and something hanging beneath its body. The Nephilim's curiosity was spiked. He clambered off the motorway down to the roads that passed underneath and raced towards the gas storage containers, clambering on top to get a better view.

Further towards the city centre, the demon carrying Phoebe detected the movement of the large biped and altered course in the

*The Fall*

hope that it could out fly the Nephilim with the weight of the virgin held in its talons. It would not be long before it reached its destination and could then be instructed on what to do.

Jumping off the gasworks, the Nephilim began to give chase, leaping from one building to another leaving in his wake a trail of destruction as roofs gave way and car became crushed.

The demon landed on the roof of Stoneywell's office, broke through the skylight and clambered through, dragging Phoebe with it. Inside it began to search through the office. Stoneywell worked through a selection of papers and was all alone when he heard the sound of doors being bust open outside in the corridor. He got up from his seat and timidly opened the reception area door. A shadow stretched across the translucent windows. Suddenly the glass shattered and Stoneywell shielded his face from the flying shards.

The demon swooped through the shattered window and slid Phoebe across the floor to Stoneywell's feet.

"What the hell do you think you're doing?" screamed Stoneywell.

"I have another virgin," stated the demon slightly confused, thinking it had only done what had been requested.

"You fool. My identity will be compromised by your presence here."

"I have this virgin and was told you would set up another angel. Where is he?"

Stoneywell leant over Phoebe and checked her pulse and breathing.

"You're lucky she's not damaged," Stoneywell chastised the demon. "She's getting a bit old. Couldn't you find anyone younger?"

The demon didn't answer. Stoneywell scribbled on a sheet of paper.

"Here's an address, take her there."

The demon looked at the scrap of paper and shrugged its shoulders.

"Can't you read," demanded Stoneywell.

"Why should I, that's for humans!"

"Can you understand a picture of a map?"

"Might. I understand patterns."

*George John Kingsnorth*

Stoneywell pulled out a map of the city from his draw and pointed to an area close to the railway storage yard. The demon picked Phoebe up once more and made its way to the roof. After it had left, Stoneywell rapidly began to gather papers and books into a cardboard box, realising it was time to relocate the business.

## CHAPTER THIRTY-NINE

The flames in the lorry cab were still flickering away as Michael drove himself and the professor towards the warehouse.

"It doesn't look good, Michael."

"What could have done this, professor?"

"Let's just get to the warehouse." The professor fell silent and Michael could tell from the expression on his companion's face that he intended not to say another word until they arrived at their destination.

A light breeze had whipped up newspapers, tossing them from one side of the street to the other. Many of the street lamps were out, seemingly smashed, leaving only the headlamps from Michael's van sending out cones of light. None of the buildings were illuminated. Michael felt a tingle ripple down his spine.

A few more corners and Michael pulled up outside the warehouse the professor had left Mara in.

"We may be too late, Michael."

"Shouldn't we look, just to make sure?"

"Okay but be warned, you may not like what you find."

Cautiously the two of them got out of the car and made their way up the three steps at the entrance. The professor pulled out a key to unlock the door but realised there was no need as the door swung in with a gentle push.

The click of a switch sent the fluorescent tubes pinging on in random order along the long corridor.

"Sorry, professor. Didn't mean to startle you."

"That's okay, lets take the stairs. I don't want to alarm anything of our arrival."

"Bit late with all these lights going on?"

The two of them clambered up the stairs. The professor took a little longer than Michael as he needed to catch his breath every now and then.

Finally they reached the landing where Mara had given birth in the makeshift shelter.

"Listen, Michael. I'm not sure what to expect in here. The last time, the shelter that was provided for Mara was different to what you would expect."

"How do you mean?"

"Hmm, well. It's hard to explain but you'll see."

The professor pushed open the door and went inside the vast floor expanse. Michael flipped the switch to light the place up. In the middle was the makeshift shelter. The only sound was that of the flapping translucent polythene sheets on the exterior. The professor pulled back the flaps and went inside. There was only plastic sheeting and cardboard boxes, no furniture, no set. There was a wooden stairway leading to a makeshift second floor. The kitchen area had just a microwave attached to a long extension cable that plugged into the floor. A gapping hole had been torn through the lower and upper ceiling and then on through the roof of the warehouse. The draft was causing the sheeting to rustle around.

"There's no sign of Mara," stated Michael.

"We're too late."

"This place is a mess. What could have done this?"

"In the Book of Enoch, chapter seven, verse 11 to 14 it talks about the human wives of the fallen conceiving giants that were 300 cubits tall." The professor could see Michael was having a hard time taking it in. He moved to where a load of boxes had been over turned. A pool of blood had been caught in the polythene.

The professor continued. "These giants consumed all people could produce and when there was nothing else left, the Nephilim turned on humanity, eating their flesh and drinking their blood."

"What?"

"We're too late to help Mara. She's dead."

The professor could see the tears in Michael's eyes. "It's

*The Fall*

happened again. The demons got to Mara the same way they got to my wife."

"You were married?"

"Many years ago. On our wedding night they came. I was helpless then too. Couldn't do a thing. Everything was hazy with dark shapes and bright lights. When it was over, I found myself with Melissa's lifeless body. Her stomach had been torn open. They said she had been pregnant but I don't now how. She had never been with anyone. I knew something was wrong with Mara when I saw all the crows, Just like the day of the wedding and I thought I could do something."

The professor laid his hand on Michael's shoulder. "Don't beat yourself up. It's not your fault. You couldn't prevent this. As soon as the angel fell and the union was consummated, Mara was lost. This sin is unforgivable."

"I can't accept that. If what you say is true then Melissa is also lost. You're wrong, you have to be wrong?"

"The text indicates this leads to the death of the body, soul and spirit."

"But surely, it's just like someone being raped, surely the sin is that of the rapist not the victim?"

"I don't know, I'm just telling you what it says," stated the professor. "It depends on whether each party has been allowed their own free will. If they haven't chosen…… look I don't really know. Until a few days ago I just taught this subject at the university. It was all about research and backing up evidence in an empirical manner, now all that has changed. Now we are seeing it for real and the consequences are unimaginable."

"So what do we do now?"

"Phoebe isn't a willing candidate, perhaps there is still time to save her?"

"But you said.."

"I know but she's my daughter, I have to believe there is hope for her."

"How?"

"I don't know but there is nothing we can do here. If the Nephilim has left a trail of destruction perhaps we can follow it?"

"But it wasn't the Nephilim that took Phoebe, it was a demon."

A light beam lit up the professor's face, momentarily blinding him. Michael turned round to see what was causing it.

"Freeze," a voice commanded. "Get on the ground face down. Put you hands behind the heads."

"What?"

"Do it now," demanded the voice.

Both the professor and Michael followed the order. The flaps were pulled back and three Specialist Firearms officers armed with Heckler & Koch MP5 German designed nine millimetre submachine guns aimed their weapons directly at each of the detainees' head. Both were handcuffed then pulled to their feet and marched out onto the landing and down the stairs.

## CHAPTER FORTY

The moonlit sky allowed the Nephilim to see the outline of each building. His great hulk could also be clearly seen by those who were both scared of him and who wished his demise for invading their city. He continued to bound across the flat roof tops and shopping malls toward the industrial and business sectors where he deduced the winged creature had flown. Some roofs were less able to take his weight and an odd time one of his feet would pierce through fragile ceilings and he would have to wrench himself out. The hunger pains still gripped his stomach and each time he ate his body expanded another few inches. Occasionally cuts appeared in his skin causing pain to skitter through his nervous system. But gradually, he learned that, by using his willpower, he could force the atoms to cling together and reseal the wounds. He found that he could prevent the pain signals stabbing into his brain and the whole experience was becoming less traumatic for him. He began to analyse the substance he was eating and learned to distinguish the proteins and nutrients that his body required.

The debris the Nephilim ejected crashed through windows in buildings and cars. Though reasonably small, about the size of a potato, when compressed and ground down, the material could be deadly, especially for humans. Unfortunately, several experienced the effects. An old woman making her way to a bus stop, oblivious to the commotion was sprayed causing her skull to collapse into her brain. A taxi driver rushing to get away and taking a short cut down a side alley had his cab peppered with the compressed masonry. Both his legs were shattered and his stomach punctured. A young man managed to push his fiancée through a doorway just as another downpour of rubble extinguished his life. But the Nephilim was unaware of the threat he posed to these puny creatures. Like an infant he followed his curiosity and explored his surroundings, intent on discovering the identity of winged thing he had seen.

Finally, the Nephilim, now almost a hundred feet tall, found the three storey building location of Stoneywell's office. Briefly he examined the broken skylight, which was too small for him to reach inside with his hand. He punched his fist down creating three more holes. The blood oozed out of his knuckles but he was quickly able to seal the injuries. In fact he was now able to predict the effect of his actions on his body and could harden his skin to cope with the impact. With his forth punch through the roof his skin held and no wounds were sustained.

Inside the offices the Nephilim used his fingers to search out each crevice but found nothing of interest. There were no other creatures, humans, or flying beast that came within reach. The rage built up inside the Nephilim and he released his fury using both arms and fists like battering rams, demolishing the building layer by layer, floor by floor until there was nothing but a pile of rubble.

A series of blue flashing lights, followed by the blaring warble of sirens, drew the Nephilim's attention toward the open end of the street leading to a main thoroughfare. Being so alert the Nephilim found the colour range of his eyes change to a different spectrum. He could now detect infrared and the heat signatures of the men inside the vehicles racing along the road toward the street he was in.

Again the Nephilim's curiosity got the better of him and he began to make his way toward the sounds and lights. Three armoured vehicles sped round the corner into the street. Being confronted with the now huge creature before them, each driver swerved his van and pulled to the side. The back doors swung open and a troop of specialist firearm officers leapt out and aimed their rifles. The infrared spots targeted the Nephilim's chest and head. As a volley of bullets struck their target, the impact triggered the giant's defences. His skin grew thicker and the penetrating bullets only managed to drive in five millimetres before they were expelled, landing on the ground like two pence coins, totally flattened out.

*The Fall*

The marksmen intensified their fire but the thickness of the Nephilim's skin had adjusted to this threat and the bullets just bounced off.

"Inspector Andrews, we need more fire power. Our hand weapons are ineffectual. We'll have to withdraw," screamed a police sergeant into the radio handset in the lead vehicle. Before he could say another word the Nephilim had sprinted to the three vehicles and began to launch them across the streets burying them deep into the second and third floors of adjacent buildings.

As scared officers raced for their lives, the Nephilim scooped them up and chewed the top halves of the bodies off to quench the gurgling hunger of his stomach. It seemed no matter how much he fed the hunger quickly returned.

In the main street a second force began to approach, this time supported by army vehicles, a light tank, rocket launcher and armoured troop carrier. The Nephilim entered the main street and with a full view of him the tank began to fire its 25 millimetre rounds, while the rocket launcher released six missiles. The force of each blow toppled the Nephilim over, rolling him away from his attackers. Each blow scorched his skin, requiring massive amounts of energy to repair the skin and muscle. This process slowed the Nephilim's reactions and forced him to retreat momentarily. The soldiers cheered tasting a morsel of victory but the elation was short lived as the Nephilim ground down masonry with his teeth, regurgitated acid from his stomach and coated the rubble stones, then flung them at the troops. The tank seemed like it was made of tin foil offering no resistance as the acid coated stones cut through the armoured plating. A shell inside was struck and the vehicle exploded. The blast knocked over the rocket launcher and as the men attempted to scramble out the Nephilim jumped on them bursting their bodies like grapes in a wine press.

A few streets away a driver of another police van received an urgent message.

"Help, we need immediate reinforcements in High Street Deritend. We are retreating into High Street Bordesley. Hurry."

"This is Foxtrot Bravo Three Seven Five, traveling down Watery Lane. Time of arrival 60 seconds. We'll call for airborne assistance."

Another officer switched on the siren and flashing lights. In the back of the vehicle, Michael and the Professor were flung to the left side of the vehicle as it overtook traffic at high speed up Coventry Road. Pulling sharply to the right it then sped up into High Street Bordesley. The brakes were applied sharply, burning rubber as the van pulled up nearly skidding. Two officers seated in front, leapt out and began to open fire with their MP5s but to no effect. Each was scooped up and felt their ribs crushed and the air in their lungs squeezed out before the light was extinguished from their eyes.

The pain ripped through the Nephilim once more and he roared in agony, lashing out with his fists. One struck the police van launching it across the road and smashing into a mainstream cloths shop demolishing rows of the latest fashions. The blue light continued to flash from inside the building.

With the doors punched open, Professor Garrett attempted to pull his handcuffs off the rail they were attached to. It took a few moments and soon were free.

"Quick, Michael, lets get out of here. Michael?"

The professor noticed Michael was not moving. A cut to his forehead showed he had smashed it against the side of the van and was now unconscious. Frantically the professor slapped him around the face to try and rouse him.

"Michael, wake up, come on. We have to go."

The Nephilim raced to the side of the building and began to search around with his fingers. He managed to hook the tip of his index into the open back doors of the van and flicked the van back out into the open. The vehicle slid across the road and crashed into a furniture store. This time the dazed professor realised the rail had dislodged and he was able to crawl out. With Michael still unconscious the professor managed to pull his companion clear of the wreckage. As the Professor stood he noticed a large shadow pass over him and stopped. Slowly he turned round to receive a rush of carbon dioxide gushing out of the Nephilim's nostrils.

*The Fall*

Within a split second the giant had grasped the professor in his hand and had tossed up into the air so he could drop into the creatures mouth. Everything seemed to pass in slow motion. The professor felt the Nephilim's grip grow loose, he began to fly up then fall.

Two large explosions propelled the Nephilim across the street as the professor fell to the road. A large elbow slammed into the van and the jolt snapped Michael back into consciousness. A Lynx mark nine, multi-role helicopter released two more Hellfire missiles just as the Nephilim was about to stand up. The force of the two blasts knocked him some 50 to 75 feet away from the damaged vehicle. Unable to take the pain of all these beatings, the Nephilim jumped to his feet and began to sprint up North Street Deritend into Digbeth, leapt onto the roofs of the buildings at Moat Lane and sprang across to Upper Dean Street to make his escape. The Lynx followed but the pilot and co-pilot lost sight of him. The Lynx circled for a few moments but were unable to track him down. They flew lower to get a closer look but as they did a red Peugeot 406 came rushing up from the ground, tore through the rotor blades and struck the fuel line. The explosion rained debris and flames across the surrounding streets and the bulk of the bird plummeted onto a transit van, forcing a second explosion.

As Michael climbed to his feet and began to search around for the professor he heard the sound of running feet.

"Get down on your front, hands behind your head. Now" barked a SF officer as three others pointed the HP5s directly at Michael's head. He complied, trying to scan to see any signs of the professor. There was nothing and Michael began to fear the worse, that the professor had also become a meal for the Nephilim.

From the interior of the furniture store, tears streamed down the professor's face as he bit into the side of a sofa to stop himself from screaming. Outside the SF officers threw Michael into the back of an armoured vehicle. The static from a radio alerted the patrol and they all jumped into their vehicles and sped off.

The professor was now safe to release the sofa.

"Aaaaaaaarrrrrggggghhhh, Jesus, it hurts!"

He rolled onto his left side and fainted.

*The Fall*

CHAPTER FORTY-ONE

In a derelict building, with water dripping all around, Phoebe woke to find herself strung up by her wrists. Large lamps lit the place almost blinding her. A small generator hummed in a darkened corner away from any pools of water. The walls had thick yellow paint peeling away from the plaster, which was crumbling into a pinkish powder in places. The wire frames within the pillars were revealed where the strain of age had cracked the concrete.

A gapping hole above Phoebe revealed the floor above her. The ropes around her wrists ran up through the ceiling and she was unable to see where they were suspended. Water from burst pipes flowed over the edge soaking her hair and clothing. Goose bumps had risen all over her body as the cold bit into her skin.

Under a boot came the crunching sound of debris being crushed into dust. Phoebe spun round in an attempt to locate the movement.

"Who's there?"

A dark shadow stopped just as Phoebe thought she had seen a figure.

"Who are you? Show yourself."

Phoebe struggled to define where she thought she had seen the figure and the shadows of the room. She pulled on the rope to see if she could get closer to make out the shapes but it is no good.

Through a large gap in a wall to Phoebe's right, she heard voices growing closer, their footsteps splashing through puddles and clapping on the concrete floor.

"This is getting way out of hand. We've never had a Nephilim grow to this size. The physical body has always been destroyed by this time to release the demon. Why's this not happened now?"

"Stoneywell, your impatience is a tiresome agitation," snapped a

## George John Kingsnorth

guttural voice that was a shock to Phoebe's ears. She screamed and began to tug away at the ropes hoping to find a release but her wrists were held fast.

"The girl is awake. No more talk," demanded a human voice.

Stoneywell peered through the hole in the wall but Phoebe was still unable to see the man, he had been talking too. Stoneywell stepped back into the darkness of the other room.

The water still dripped onto Phoebe and her saturated clothes made her cold. She still could not get her hands free and finally, exhausted from her struggle found her knees begin to sag. She closed her eyes and began to whisper.

"Our Father, who art in heaven…"

A hissing sound came from the corner, like disturbed snakes. Phoebe stopped her prayer and listened. The noise stopped.

"Hallowed be thy name! Thy kingdom come!"

The roar of hissing began again and Phoebe noticed the darker shadows attempting to move away from her. Some seemed to be near panic. A sense of hope swam through Phoebe's body and her spirit was lifted.

"Thy will be done," she spoke louder. The reaction was a clambering of dark shapes scurrying through the holes in the walls into other rooms, frantic to escape.

"On earth as it is in heaven!"

"Look I think I should go, there is nothing more for me to do here," came Stoneywell's voice.

Phoebe screamed at the top of her voice, "On earth as it is in heaven! Give us this day our daily bread and forgive us our sins as we forgive those who sin against us."

Footsteps moved away into a distant room. There was no longer movement in the shadows. Phoebe kicked water in every direction but nothing stirred. A door clanged shut.

"Lead us not into temptation but deliver us from evil."

Only the sound of dripping water broke the silence all around Phoebe. Again she spun around to see if there was any presence that might pose a danger to her. Then she noticed one light appeared

*The Fall*

brighter than the rest. She tried to shield her eyes.

"Who's there?"

Movement, brilliant white against tungsten light.

"Who are you?"

"A friend," said the soft voice, who's tones sent a wave of ecstasy through Phoebe's body. She had not expected this but something in the back of her mind warned her that this was a danger as deadly as the ones she had perceived from the darkness.

There was a great temptation and desire to give in but Phoebe fought her inner feelings and told herself they were wrong.

"There is no point in resisting me."

"There is every point," snapped Phoebe. "I have no desire to be here. This is not my choice. You are abusing your power, angel."

"And what would you know, little girl? I, Ezekiel, angel of death and transformation, I have been on Earth for millenniums, guiding men and women away from their follies. I have seen the way a man has longed for a woman and the intimacy they have had. I have waited a long time and you are my chosen one. I have watched you grow. I've seen the men chase after you but I have turned them away. You are mine."

"Then you are no better than a demon," scolded Phoebe. "My father talked about how the Bible tells of what happened when the Angels fell. It was a great sin because they rejected God and put their own needs before everything else, like you are doing now."

Ezekiel laughed at her. "You have plenty of spirit for a mere mortal. I've always loved that in you, it's such a challenge."

"My Lord Jesus will protect me."

"Aren't you forgetting, I'm an angel," scoffed Ezekiel. "It's just me and a few of the boys from the other side. That's all. No-one else is here to save you."

"How can you say that when you've seen what there is?" Phoebe was stunned. "Haven't you just become blinded by your own lust for me? You've spent too much time here you've become contaminated."

"I love you, Phoebe," Ezekiel smiled.

"But you haven't won my heart. It doesn't belong to you. You have had to take me by force, which makes it all meaningless."

"I know more about love than you could possibly imagine."

"Yet you choose to abandon love for your lust?"

"Your tongue, woman, is like a venomous viper. No wonder you drove Adam from Eden."

"I thought you said you liked a challenge?"

"So you think you can teach an angel?"

"If you want a woman you have to play by the same rules as men, especially if you want me to want you!"

"And how do I do this?"

"Well, to start with perhaps you could let me down and feed me?"

For a few moments Ezekiel stood and thought. He splashed the water beneath his foot and pondered some more, then reached over to unshackle her.

"I hope you don't take me to be a fool? If you try to escape it will be a short lived excursion," he threatened.

"And isn't a relationship supposed to be built on trust?"

"You are certainly a puzzle, even for an angel? No wonder men have difficulty understanding how a woman works?"

"Isn't that the challenge?" teased Phoebe. "Isn't that why developing a relationship is exciting? You can force yourself on my body but if the spirit is not willing then it is an empty act, a simple desecration."

"You try my patience," snapped Ezekiel. Phoebe became a little scared by the angel's roar.

"To build a relationship each person involved has to be prepared to make sacrifices for the other. To do so of their own freewill not through intimidation," warned Phoebe. "I am fragile and weak and you can easily squash me but to win me you have to nurture me, strengthen me. Are you prepared to do that?"

With great courage Phoebe took a chance to look the angel directly into his eyes to see what kind of reaction her words were having. The sight of looking into the blackness of his pupils made her tremble and she feared what she might discover. Would she be consumed or would she live?

*The Fall*

## CHAPTER FORTY-TWO

A light came on in a small windowless room with one mirrored wall. Michael was pushed inside and thrown into one of four seats. He caught sight of his own reflection. Blood ran from his mouth down his chin and there was a graze on his forehead. Two uniformed officers took up positions either side of him. A non-uniformed officer stepped into the room and set up a small compact flash recorder and pressed the record button.

"Twenty-three thirty-one hours, interview starts with suspect Michael Davies. Detective Sergeant Morris interviewing officer. Okay, let's start at the beginning Mr. Davies, why were you and Professor Garrett at the warehouse?"

"Shouldn't I have a solicitor present?"

"What's your involvement with Ms. Mara Sanford?

"Can I have a solicitor?"

"Are you going to cooperate? Can I remind you that by not saying anything you will also hinder your case. Do I make myself clear?"

"Yes!"

"So what was your involvement with Mara Sanford?"

"She lived next door to where I've been working for Professor Garrett. I also saw her band."

"You're a bit old for that kind of stuff aren't you?"

"I thought she was in danger."

"What kind of danger?" asked DS Morris.

"There were demons around her. I could sense them."

"Mr. Davies, we are aware you spent around ten odd years in a mental institute having been found guilty of the murder of your wife. We believe you pursued Ms. Sanford to commit the same kind of sick perversion on her as you did your wife?"

"And what about the monster that's just destroyed half of Birmingham? How do you explain that? Where do you think he came from?"

"A monster roaming around Birmingham? What are you talking about that was a tornado or something. Not a monster?"

"Who told you that?"

"Don't you listen to the news?"

"How could I? Either I've been in here or chased by the thing outside? So have your men? Don't any of you remember?"

The two uniformed officers restrained Michael as he jumped to his feet and forced him back into his chair. Morris got out of his chair and headed for the door.

"This guy is still insane. He should never have been let out. Take him to the cells until we can get a psychiatrist in here. Get him out of here."

Michael was pulled out of his seat and dragged out of the interview room.

"None of you believe what's happened do you?"

"Shut it," barked a uniformed officer.

As Michael was taken through the corridors of the police station he noticed how calm everyone seemed to be. There was no urgency or fear, no concern about the threat that had attacked the city. They all seemed totally oblivious to the Nephilim. Michael could not understand what was going on. How could they all be deceived?

A cell door swung open and Michael was thrown to the floor. The door was slammed behind him and locked. He crawled to the side of the bed and pulled himself up onto his knees. Inside his head he saw Melissa smiling.

"Do you remember the prayer I used to say?" she asked.

"How did it start?" replied Michael.

"Oh angel of God, my guardian dear," whispered the vision of Melissa.

"...to whom God loves commits me here... I remember."

"Go on."

"...ever this night be at my side to light, to guard, to rule and

*The Fall*

guide. Amen!" finished Michael.

"You're not alone, Michael."

Another cell door slammed shut and the echo reverberated around the corridor driving the image of Melissa from Michael's mind.

"I'm not alone."

Michael pulled the blanket up around his body, then clamped his hands across his ears to dull the sound of an old man snoring in an adjacent cell. Elsewhere another prisoner coughed continually and another was crying. The moonlight cast blue streaks across the room from the securing grid over the window. The glow allowed Michael to see most of his white walled cell and solid bed with a simple mattress.

Again he closed his eyes with the hope that sleep would capture him and take him away from this dreaded place. He wondered if Phoebe was still alive and thought about the professor and how the Nephilim had killed him. There was too much to take in. Michael's body gave am impulsive shudder.

"Put on your shoes, Michael."

The shock of hearing the voice snapped Michael upright and his eyes were wide open. Before him was Grace.

"How did you get in here?"

"I've no time to explain but we have to go."

Then it suddenly struck Michael that the whimpering, snoring and coughing had stopped. "What's going on, Grace?"

"Come on we have to go."

Michael slipped on his shoes. There was no time to undo the laces. The heels were crushed but he managed to pull them up so the shoes were not uncomfortable. He pulled his coat from the end of the bed and slipped it on.

"Quick, Michael. Let's go."

"I'm coming, give me a second."

"We don't have that. Let's go."

The door was already open. "Hey, how did you get in here?"

"No more questions, let's go," Grace demanded.

Through the corridor, passed all the other cells, Michael noted that there was not a single movement. No rolling, tossing or turning in their bunk, not a sound. They passed an open door. Inside Michael saw a policewoman out cold with her head resting on the table. A policeman had collapsed onto the floor.

"What happened to them?"

"Ssshh."

"Are they dead?"

"No, just asleep."

"Are you sure?"

"Yes, now come on, before you wake them."

The two of them progressed through to the reception area of the police station. More men and women were sprawled across decks or lying on the floor totally unconscious. Grace led Michael through the main entrance into the street. In the distance, Michael could hear the sound of rockets being launched, small arms fire, small canons and explosions. Grace turned round and faced Michael.

"You'll be safe now but you'll have to be quick because those inside the station will be waking soon. You need to find a Sister Philomena. She's at the church in Chapel Street."

"Why is this all happening, Grace? Who are you."

"Michael, Phoebe needs you…"

"She's still alive?"

"At the moment but you don't have long and you need some help from Sister Philomena. Now go."

Michael looked in the direction Grace had pointed then turned back to say something and she had gone. From inside the police station, Michael heard the sound of a chair scrape across the floor and realised everyone was waking. He took in a deep breath and began to sprint down the street as he had been directed and hoped he would be in time to save Phoebe.

About 20 minutes later, Michael found himself near Digbeth. He was reluctant to go down High Street Deritend, scared he might come across the professor's mangled body. He didn't want to see the sight of the van they had been in but just wanted to blot everything

*The Fall*

out except reaching Phoebe.

The whole city was deserted. No taxis, no cars, no lorries or buses. No pedestrians but in the distance came the booms of destruction as the weapons of man raged against the Nephilim.

In a doorway, Michael could see a man's leg stretched out into the path. He stepped closer to the road to by pass the homeless man.

"Hey, you. Please help me?"

Michael stopped in his tracks and spun round.

"Professor? You're alive."

He raced over to the professor's side.

"Michael, how did you get away?"

"I was taken back to a police station and Grace let me out. Can you stand?"

"My arm's broken."

"Can I lift you to you feet?"

"Yes."

Michael put his arm around the professor back and tried to lift him. The professor screamed in agony but after a few moments he was up, tears streaming down his face.

"Where were you going," asked the professor, trying to think of something to take his mind of the pain.

"Grace told me Phoebe was still alive and that I had to get to Sister Philomena for help."

"Grace, how is she involved?"

"I don't know quite what happened but all the people in the station were out cold and Grace had all the doors open."

"Grace took me to where Mara was and then disappeared. I'm not quite sure what she is but she's involving Sister Philomena again. Take me with you, she can sort me out."

"Shouldn't we get you to a hospital?"

"Your priority is Phoebe, I'll be alright."

The two of them struggled on. It took a further 15 minutes for them to struggle up Moor Street Ringway towards Chapel Street. Michael could see the professor's distress but the older man insisted they push on.

Michael burst open the church doors. The sound echoed around the interior startling two nuns who were at prayer.

"Who are you? What do you want?" demanded the elder nun.

"Please, I'm looking for Sister Philomena. My name is Michael and this is Professor Garrett?"

"Professor Garrett. Is he hurt?"

"He's broken an arm. We were attacked by the giant and were lucky to get away alive," explained Michael.

Sister Philomena rushed over with the other nun to help Michael with the professor.

"Sister Teresa, the professor needs to be in a hospital. Call an ambulance," requested the nun. She then turned back to Michael. "I'm Sister Philomena."

"Sister, there's no time. We have to save Phoebe, my daughter?"

"What happened?" asked Sister Philomena as she began to peel away the professor's jacket and shirt to look at his injuries.

"I'm not sure if you'll believe this but a demon flew off with her," stated Michael.

Sister Philomena sighed. "Well, hard as it is for me to say this, I do believe you. And I believe you too, professor. You were right about the Nephilim."

"It's okay, sister. I was doubtful myself."

"What can we do?" asked Sister Philomena.

"Grace sent me to you, I was hoping you could tell us?" Michael sighed.

"Well, there's no broken skin, just the bone. We'll get you to a hospital, professor," stated Sister Philomena. "We'll just make you comfortable for the time being."

The professor's mind was elsewhere. "The Nephilim is the same as Goliath from the Bible story. David stopped him with a stone to the forehead."

"He must be delirious," commented Sister Philomena.

"No, sister. He's right," realised Michael. "We were able to kill a demon with a stone soaked in Holy Water fired from my catapult. And maybe that's why bullets and rockets don't work."

*The Fall*

"According to Enoch, the spirit of a Nephilim is a demon. It could work."

"That's why Grace sent me here."

"Who's Grace?" puzzled Sister Philomena. "The professor mentioned her before."

"Grace is......" started Michael.

"She could be an angel or a demon but I'm not sure," whispered the professor. The pain was getting the better of him and he slipped into unconsciousness.

"You had better go, Michael," instructed Sister Philomena. "We'll take care of the professor. Take some of the bottles of Holy Water from the side of the main door. We'll be praying for you."

Sister Teresa returned. "Sister, an ambulance is on it's way. There were delays as most of the hospitals are filling up with casualties."

The sound of explosion seemed closer shaking the church, dislodging small pieces of masonry and dust.

"The Nephilim must be close," commented Michael.

"You should go now and see what you can do to stop him." Sister Philomena put her hand on Michael's shoulder. "We'll pray for your success."

"Thanks."

Michael turned and made his way to the back of the church. As Phoebe had done previously, Michael gathered together as many bottles shaped as the Holy Virgin Mary and stuffed them into his coat pockets. The inner layer also had pockets so he slipped a bottle into both. He turned to look back into the church and saw the two nuns watching him. He smiled then waved, both nuns replied with the same gesture and then he left. The door closed behind him, the sound reverberated around the walls and ceiling. The two nuns first checked on the professor and then knelt and began to recite the Rosary, beginning with the Lord's Prayer and five decades of the Hail Mary.

## CHAPTER FORTY-THREE

In the old derelict warehouse, Phoebe was seated at a large wooden table set out with a full set of silver cutlery for two. Phoebe's wet jeans and shirt were gone and she was wearing a silk gown but her ankles were still shackled with the end bolted to the concrete floor. Ezekiel made his way to the table through several shafts of light cast from the lamps in an upper floor. He pulled out a chair and sat at the opposite end to Phoebe. Phoebe did not look him in the face but cast her eyes around the room. She found that if she did dare glance in Ezekiel's direction a sharp migraine type pain stabbed her across the right side of her head. The sensation made it hard for her to open her right eye.

"You should put some makeup on and make yourself all beautiful."

"At this point a box of pink migraine tablets would be handy?"

"I'll see what I can do, but you should at least attempt to do yourself up."

"I don't need to cake my face up. I'm happy with the beauty God has given me."

Ezekiel rose from the table and stepped into a shadowed area. He slid a panel across the floor which screeched on the concrete further sending a pain across the interior of Phoebe's head. She gripped her head with her hand as the pain grated through the Eustachian tube toward the middle of her right ear. Ezekiel stopped the mirror beside Phoebe.

"But you have blemishes, Phoebe. Surely you want to hide them?" He pointed out some spots and black heads on her face. Phoebe looked at herself in the mirror. She could see the girlish complexion had long gone and the pores in her face seemed dry and

*The Fall*

mottled. Her hair was uncombed and greasy and she felt ashamed of her appearance. She looked aware from her reflection.

"Surely, it's okay to clean yourself up?"

"I'm happy the way I am, thank you," she replied still with the conviction to resist. Ezekiel pushed the mirror away, it toppled and smashed.

"Oh dear, seven years bad luck," commented Phoebe.

"Ah, so you are superstitious? It's just a piece of glass with silver foil. Nothing else."

Behind the angel there was a scurry of activity in the shadows. Phoebe could not see what but Ezekiel suddenly turned away from her. She struggled with the shackle on her legs but Ezekiel had returned with a plate of hot food.

"There you go. Some roast beef, potatoes, runner beans, cauliflower, gravy and horseradish."

The smell made the juices in her mouth run.

"No thanks, I'm a vegetarian. I won't eat meat," she lied.

"I can provide you with all your needs," boasted Ezekiel. "You know I can, if you worship me."

"I'm a slave to no-one," Phoebe insisted stubbornly.

"Not even Michael?"

Phoebe blushed and again tried to hide her face. While her gaze was away from Ezekiel he transformed his appearance into that of Michael's.

"I can give you everything he can and much more."

Hearing Michael's voice, Phoebe turned back to face Ezekiel.

"You may look like him, but inside you're something else. You could never take his place. Never." Tears formed in her eyes. "Why do you torment me?"

"To break your spirit. To control you and make you mine."

"That will never happen."

"We'll see."

"My love for Michael is too strong."

"You are a mere human. You have no strength as you are weak. I can do as I please with you."

"But you will have shown that you are no better than a mere man through your actions."

"I will have you submit to me and only me. I will be your god."

"At what cost?"

"To whom?"

"You'll condemn yourself."

Ezekiel cast away the illusion of Michael and reformed his previous shape.

"I've had enough of your insolence."

The table was flung through air, crashed into a wall and splintered. Phoebe covered her face but nothing hit her. As she lowered her arms, Ezekiel grabbed her by the throat.

"You are mine," he roared and pulled her off her seat like a rag doll and forced his lips against hers. Static sparked from their lips. Ezekiel shook his head surprised by the pain of the electric shock then pressed his lips once more against hers. To Phoebe's amazement, Ezekiel dropped her to the floor. She felt intoxicated as the angel stumbled around trying to regain his balance. Phoebe felt weak, unable to raise herself onto her elbows, she lay on her back in a daze. She wanted to escape but the angel's kiss was like a narcotic. For a moment Ezekiel watched as Phoebe, sprawled on the ground, her chest heaving to gain breath, and attempting to push her legs back and forth in the hope that her feet would take grip but without success or co-ordination. Ezekiel knelt beside her and ran his hand across her left knee and up her thigh. Phoebe fumbled with her hands to restrain his advances but was too weak. She wanted to scream yet her vocal chords let her down. She was helpless and his fingers drew closer.

A door burst open at the other end of the warehouse.

"Ezekiel, Ezekiel, quick…" shouted Stoneywell who then had to stop to catch his breath.

"What?" Ezekiel's voice rumbled through the building, like a shockwave shattering several walls.

"The Nephilim is…"

A massive fist punched through the ceiling crushing Stoneywell

*The Fall*

to pulp. The Nephilim wrenched up the upper floor and cast it across the way onto another warehouse. Ezekiel grabbed Phoebe but as the Nephilim reached in once more he knocked the angel to the ground. Phoebe, still groggy, slid across the floor, coming to rest near one of the two remaining walls.

Ezekiel regained his footing and drew his sword. Several times he struck the limbs of the Nephilim, causing him to withdraw his arm in pain. Troops began to surround the warehouse, firing every available weapon they had but still their attempts were futile. Ezekiel lashed out again and again with his sword. Each swipe the angel felt his strength grow weaker. The Nephilim flicked him with his index finger shooting him across the floor crashing beside Phoebe.

"Surprise, Angel boy?" whispered Phoebe. "Ever heard of the kiss of death?"

"What?" snapped Ezekiel.

"You kissed me," taunted Phoebe as she found the energy to get to her feet. "I felt something happen in my spirit. I told you it was wrong. You can't court a woman. It's not allowed."

Phoebe attempted to distance herself from the angel but he wrestled her to the ground, flipped her over and sat on top of her.

"You can't get away. I won't let you." He smiled down at her. Behind him Phoebe saw the Nephilim's large hand being lowered through the hole in the roof. She smiled back at the angel just as a large finger and thumb pinched Ezekiel, splattering his body into the air like a can of paint hurled upwards. The lower part of the angel's body saturated Phoebe as she pushed herself downward against the floor with every muscle in her body. Her eyes tightly closed, she held back a scream not knowing what to expect next.

Outside, Michael raced through the line of soldiers to find a way into the warehouse.

"Stay back, sir. You'll get hurt," screamed an officer.

"I know someone in there. I can help."

"Stay back."

Michael dodged them and raced through a side door with several soldiers giving chase. Inside, Michael found the Nephilim groping around with his hands. Then Michael saw Phoebe lying on the ground covered in blood.

"Phoebe?"

To his surprise Phoebe looked across and shouted back.

"He's killed the angel and doesn't know what's happened. He squished him."

"Are you alright?"

"Yes. Nothing's damaged."

The Nephilim spotted Phoebe and reached down to grab her. Michael pulled out some pebbles, his catapult and a bottle of Holy Water. As quickly as he could he doused the stones and loaded the catapult, then took aim just as a large hand reached in for Phoebe. The pebble was propelled through the air, struck into the giant's fleshy forearm, scored past the bone and zipped through into the air on the other side. The shock stopped the Nephilim in his tracks. This was the first time anything had had such an impact on his body. He turned to face Michael in a rage.

Michael nervously sprinkled more Holy Water across six more stones and made ready to fire as the Nephilim's face drew closer to see what had attacked him. His nostrils were Michael's target. He fired three pebbles at once. Each zipped up the Nephilim's nasal passage, piercing the skull and finally embedding in the giant's brain. Instantly, the giant stood back as though a stick of dynamite had exploded in his head. He sneezed, soaking Michael with a gush of blood. Then the Nephilim's eyes rolled upwards and for a brief moment he stood motionless before toppling backwards into an adjacent building and several army vehicles.

Phoebe jumped to her feet and raced over to Michael. She found him unconscious. The force of the sneeze had knocked him back against the floor, bashing his head. He was dazed and bleeding. Phoebe ripped the bottom of her dress and padded the back of his head to stop any further bleeding.

Four soldiers raced in around Phoebe aiming their rifles at Michael. As Phoebe turned round to see what was going on, a dark mist rose from where the Nephilim had fallen. The demon escaped

*The Fall*

the corporal body and swiped the four soldiers with it's talons. It loomed over Phoebe and she used her body to shield Michael. Squeezing her eyes tight she began to pray.

"Holy Michael, Archangel, defend us in the hour of battle. Be our safeguard against the wickedness and snares of the devil."

The dark spirit grew, lashing out at every soldier, policeman and civilian, draining them of their life.

"May God, restrain him we humbly pray and do thou, O Prince of the Heavenly Host, by the power of God, thrust down into hell Satan and with him all the wicked spirits who wonder the world for the ruin of souls! Amen."

A blinding light cut through the darkness of night. All humans shielded their eyes and the Nephilim's spirit recoiled in horror, lashing out at the light source. Then the demon started to convulse as it insides began to flare up as though set alight by an inner torch. From within its darkened shell, Phoebe could see strands of fire lick through the demon's torso from its heart, into every limb and then expand to the outer skin. The demon began to glow brightly and the creature roared in agony before exploding. A ring built up, expanding across the city from the force of the exploding demon yet no-one was injured, no buildings fell, no cars were raised from the roads, everything remained in place.

On the horizon, embers of light pushed back night as dawn returned. Troops rushed into the warehouse and paramedics were called to attend Michael's injuries. Phoebe cradled his head on her lap keeping the bundle of skirt tight against the back of his skull until help arrived. Michael rolled his eyes open in an attempt to keep conscious, fighting the darkness that threatened to engulf him. In a low whisper he spoke to Phoebe.

"Is it over?"

"Yes, you did it. The Nephilim is dead and something destroyed the demon."

"What was it?"

"I don't know how to describe it?"

"Do you believe what happened?" whispered Michael.

"I do, but I don't know who will listen if I try to tell anyone."

"Will they ever?"

"Probably not."

Michael briefly managed to hold his eyes open and focus on Phoebe.

"Will you listen to me?" asked Phoebe.

He smiled, "probably not."

He stroked the side of Phoebe's face as she smiled and combed his fingers through her hair. Gently, he pulled her closer to him and kissed her. Then she pulled back.

"You'd better, I can be a little demon when I want to be."

"You have to have the last word, don't you."

"You bet!"

Printed in the United Kingdom
by Lightning Source UK Ltd.
132975UK00001BA/10-54/P